Ingrid Alexandra is based in Sydney. Her work has previously been long-listed for The Ampersand Prize and while living in London, Ingrid had the privilege of being mentored by the Guardian First Novel Award shortlisted and Nestle Prize winning author Daren King. THE NEW GIRL was her first psychological thriller novel, followed by ACROSS THE WATER.

@ingridwrites
ingridwrites
www.ingridalexandrabooks.com

Also by Ingrid Alexandra

The New Girl
Across The Water

Across The Water

Ingrid Alexandra

One More Chapter
a division of HarperCollins*Publishers*
The News Building
1 London Bridge Street
London SE1 9GF

www.harpercollins.co.uk

This paperback edition 2020

First published in Great Britain in ebook format by
HarperCollins*Publishers* 2020

A catalogue record for this book
is available from the British Library

AU, NZ Ebook ISBN: 9780008363253
ROW Ebook ISBN: 9780008355494
B Format Paperback ISBN: 9780008355487
Trade Paperback ISBN: 9780008358990

Set in Birka by Palimpsest Book Production Limited,
Falkirk, Stirlingshire

Printed by CPI Group (UK) Ltd, Croydon CR0 4YY

For Mum

Chapter 1

Liz

June, 2017
Saturday, 7:17pm

We're wet to the bone, teetering on tipsy feet and laughing as we reach the front door. Adam scoops me up and takes a wobbly step forward.

'You don't have to do this!' I protest, though I'm secretly thrilled. 'We don't even live here!'

Adam grunts and digs determined fingers into his pocket until I hear his keys jangle. He fumbles with the lock and kicks the door open. 'Well, it's ours for the time being. And I want to. I want to do this right.' He flashes me a dazzling smile as he carries me over the threshold. 'Welcome home, Mrs Dawson.'

My heart feels so full it might explode. 'You're a sap,' I tease, but I love that he's doing this.

Inside, we trip about peeling off sopping clothes before

tumbling into bed. His hot mouth on mine, those determined fingers finding all my spots, I'm devouring him while being devoured. It will never be enough.

Afterwards, still catching my breath, I murmur, 'Shit. I hope the neighbours didn't hear.'

I know Adam's smiling, though at some point during our frantic coupling the room had grown dark. 'I hope they did.'

'Adam!' I shove his shoulder. 'What if there are kids next door?'

There's a merry *plink!* as Adam turns on the bedside lamp. He stretches out his long, broad torso, still tanned from San Sebastian, and yawns. 'I was kidding. No one would have heard. Nobody lives on this side of the creek.'

'Oh?' I pull the blankets up around my neck against the evening chill. 'Nobody lives in any of them? But there's, what, eight?'

Adam shrugs. 'They've all been abandoned.'

'But could people be on the other side?'

'Not sure who's there now. I think Rob and his wife still live in the middle house; they're a bit older than you, I think. And I used to know the couple who live in the end house. Erica and Samir. Bit older than me, been there since the old days.'

'Ah, yes. The golden summers when you and the lads gallivanted around town, breaking hearts.'

A smirk steals over Adam's lips. 'Long before you were born, of course.'

I smile. It's silly, I'm only eight years younger than him, but it gives me a thrill to think of myself as the younger woman. I think Adam likes it, too.

I kiss him and snuggle against his chest, breathing in the smell of my new husband. *My husband!* His arms close around me and he presses his lips to my forehead with a tenderness that steals my breath. It's impossible, this kind of bliss.

Adam's breathing slows and evens and I feel myself slipping with him, down into oblivion.

***

2:07am

I wake with a start. For a moment, I don't know where I am. My head is fuzzy with jetlag and the remnants of too many drinks. What exactly were we celebrating this time? And then I remember. All those months of dreading it and now we're here. We're actually here.

I glance at my phone and smother a groan. We must have fallen asleep just after dark and now it's only, what ... around 5pm, UK time? It would take a miracle for me to fall back to sleep. Just as well I'm prepared.

Glancing at Adam's hazy silhouette, noting the slow rise and fall of his chest, I slip out of bed. I'm still naked, so I throw on my fluffy winter robe and some slippers and tiptoe out the door. It's cold in this house, draughty. The wind blowing in from the water is like ice. As if it weren't bad enough that we had to come here, we're doing things the wrong way around. Sacrificing summer for winter.

Padding across the uneven floorboards, I approach the staircase that leads to the loft. Our honeymoon luggage sits at the foot of the stairs; unpacking seems too much like giving in and I can't fathom it yet. The thought of the next couple of months makes my jaw clench, but it will be okay soon – at least for now – because my sleeping pills are somewhere in that luggage and when I take one, I'll be out like a light. The luggage can be tomorrow's problem.

I unzip the front pocket of my carry-on and slip my hand in until I hear the tell-tale crinkle of foil. As I pull my hand back, something comes with it: a crumpled pack of the Camel cigarettes we bought in Champagne. I smile and slip the cigarettes into the pocket of my robe, pop two pills from the foil pack and swallow them dry.

It's still raining, but only lightly now. I can hear the pitter-patter on the roof beyond the loft. An eerie light bathes the stairs in a pale glow; I don't know this house yet, but I imagine it's the moon shining through the loft's bay window. It should be safe up there. Adam won't smell the smoke.

I lift my foot to ascend the staircase when I hear it – a sharp, high-pitched keening. My foot pauses on the stair. I don't need to wonder at it; it's the most universal sound in the world. The sound of a baby crying.

I must be imagining it. Adam said that no one lived on

this side of the creek. I tiptoe up the stairs and on to the creaky wooden floor of the landing. It smells of mould and dust. The wailing continues, louder up here. I get a shiver, as I always do at the sound of a crying infant. A flash of porcelain skin, a halo of soft, downy hair and blue eyes flash through my mind and I squeeze my eyes shut, willing the image away.

I'm either going mad or there is undoubtedly a baby crying nearby. Where is the sound coming from?

Pulling my robe tighter around my body, I approach the window. Moonlight touches the windowsill with its icy fingers and when I look up, sure enough, the moon is full and low in the night sky.

The cries have reached fever pitch; I'm tempted to cover my ears. Leaning close to the glass, my breath mists its dusty surface and my eyes are drawn to another light across the water.

A wide, oblong window marks the top floor of a house, the middle of the three identical houses visible from this side of the creek. The creek must be at least ten metres wide, but sound travels across water, especially at night. The flanking houses are dark, but in this dimly lit window a shadow flickers and a figure appears. It's a woman; I can see her quite clearly, swaying to and fro like a branch in the breeze. Thick hair, dark red or auburn – it's hard to tell from here – tumbles over pale, rounded shoulders. She's nude, Botticelli-esque in the soft lamplight, cradling a child to her chest.

The wails ascend like a siren. The woman rocks and sways and the infant squirms as she presses its tiny face to a large, white breast. Her hair falls over the child, her gaze on its face, and there's a stab of something, sharp and deep, in my chest.

The woman stills, straightens. She turns to the window. It's as if she's seen me; she's looking right this way. I'm paralysed for a moment, unable to breathe. She stands, motionless, as the child's cries ring through the night.

The sound reaches an abrupt end, as if a switch has been flicked. And then the woman moves swiftly, and the light goes out. The window reveals nothing but blackness.

Chapter 2

Dee

December, 2016
Thursday, 7:59pm

I can see the lights flickering on in the house across the water. It's that time of year, high summer, so I'm guessing the Dawsons have arrived. The father, at least, and maybe the son, although I hear he's moved abroad. I used to wonder about the mother. I saw her once, all shiny silver bob and powder-blue cashmere, carrying boxes. Now she visits once, maybe twice, a year. Town gossip is she ran off with some Frenchman when the son was only six.

Running both hands over my swollen belly, I wonder if I'd be capable of the same. The afternoon light is dying, the sky growing dark, and since I've been still a while, the baby is starting to stir. I can feel her above my pubic bone and under my ribs. She's small, they tell me, and I suspect I know why, but you wouldn't know it, the way I feel. Tense and achy, I'm unable to relax. It could be any day now. I think of what's to come and panic blooms.

Rob will be back soon. I'm counting the minutes, listening to the sounds from the neighbouring houses that signal the day's end. The Spanish couple in the short-stay apartment on the top floor of the McCallister place are squabbling good-naturedly; there's the clang of pots and pans from the kitchenette, glasses clinking, the aroma of something rich and spicy on the evening breeze. They're the nicest of the parade of couples and families who've come through this season. The McCallisters like to keep the bottom floor free so they can come and go as they please, but they're rarely there, so it falls to Rob and me to crisis-manage when things go awry. I'm getting bloody sick of it.

I hear the rumble of Samir's voice from the balcony on the other side of the house followed by Erica's nasal response. If I listen carefully, I can hear every word. I try not to, of course. There's nothing worse than overhearing things you wish you hadn't.

Erica's the only one I've had to talk to, what with Rob gone so often and her home on stress leave. She's told me she'll help when the baby comes and I know she means it. But I'm not like most women. This is not like most pregnancies. And Erica, well-meaning as she is, is the last person who'd be able to understand.

The abandoned houses across the creek, left of the Dawson place, stand in shadow, ghosts of their former selves. I wonder about the people in those houses, what brought them here, why they chose to leave. Did they have children? Were they happy? I never imagined the two could be synonymous. Soon I will know for sure.

There's the rumble of a car engine and I stick my head out of the window as a car pulls up beside the McCallister place. I recognise the embattled pale blue station wagon. He's back. The Spanish couple are due to depart; he must be coming to collect the keys and resume his old job as caretaker in exchange for cheap rent. Slacker.

As he steps out, I'm reminded of why he gets away with it. Young, toned, healthy. He looks up and our eyes meet. He gives me that slow smile of his, as if we're both in on a secret. And my thoughts stray, despite myself, and I fantasise that if I weren't so pregnant ...

I'm the first to look away and at that moment the front door slams. I flinch. Rob's home. There's a sharp stab in my lower abdomen, the vibrations of tiny feet kicking, and for the thousandth time I wonder at the repercussions of what I've done.

***

3am

I'm edgy, anxious, as though insects are crawling over my skin. I really need him right now. But somehow, on the other side of the bed, Rob seems too far away to reach.

I slip out from between the sheets and creep silently

along the hall. Out on the balcony, under a veil of barely visible stars, I squeeze my eyes shut against a thrust of guilt. I take a half cigarette from the pack hidden behind a pot plant and light it, inhaling deeply once, twice, but the smoke comes spluttering back out again. It tastes acrid and wrong. Like failure. Yet, still, I crave it.

Something catches my eye and when I look up I see a faint red glow in the window of the Dawson house across the water. I squint, heart racing, but it disappears.

I stub the cigarette out hastily, lungs burning, tears spilling from my eyes. A single sob escapes, echoing through the silent night.

As I slide into bed, Rob murmurs in his sleep and rolls towards me. *Shit*. I clap a hand over my mouth, but it's too late. I know it. Even though I've washed my hands and scrubbed my teeth, it was all in vain. Rob is still. Silent. And I can feel the disappointment radiating from him like waves.

***

Sunday, 4pm

I can't go through with it.

I pace the house, stopping at the fridge to take out one of Rob's beers, stare at it, then put it back. I do this four times before relenting and throwing back a long, hard swig.

I can't go through with it.

The thought won't go away, no matter what I do, no

matter where I go. And I can't go anywhere much, not in my condition. I'm sick of being trapped here like a beached whale, a ticking time bomb, alone, even though Rob promised – he *promised!* – he'd be here for the final week. Three days until my due date and I know in my heart, in my bones, I cannot go through with this.

I call the hospital, wait impatiently while it connects, and ask to be put through to the prenatal ward. I'm told everyone is busy, as per usual, and I nearly scream as I end the call and throw the phone in to the piled-high laundry basket.

Leah, bloody Leah Jones, who's never taken my concerns seriously, calls back sounding polite, distant, harassed. 'Delilah Waters, that you again? You doing okay?' she says, a sigh in her voice, and I want to shout at her, tell her no I'm not fucking *okay*, I have never been this *not okay!* But my voice sticks in my throat. I'm suddenly mute.

'Miss Waters?'

Help me. My brain screams. *Please help me.* But it's useless. Because what can they do? What can *anyone* do? What's done is done. It's far too late to change anything now.

'I'm sorry. It's nothing. Just Braxton Hicks, I think,' I murmur. 'All good now.'

'Oh, yes, that. Well. Glad you're okay, love. Not long to go now!' her voice rings with false cheer, her words more threat than promise.

I hang up. I can already see Leah mentally checking me

off a list, moving on to other things. I'm just a number. I don't matter. Nothing matters.

***

2:09am

I wake to blinding pain. Reaching across the sheets, my fingers find Rob's arm and grip, vice-like, as the pain rolls through me with the force of a tidal wave.

'Dee?' his voice is thick with sleep. 'What is it?'

I double over on my side, listening as a low, animal moan, a primal sound unlike anything I've ever heard, fills the room. It takes a moment before I realise it's me.

Rob bolts upright, flicks on the lamp and I screw my eyes shut against the glare. 'Dee? It's happening, isn't it? Is this it?'

I nod, then shake my head. *I don't know. I don't know. Something feels wrong.*

'Dee? Talk to me! What's happening?'

My chest expands and my lungs fill with air as the pain dulls to a throb. I can breathe again. 'I ... I don't know. I think ... I think she's coming.'

'Oh, God,' he whispers. He clasps my hands. 'Dee. Dee! We're going to have a baby!'

His voice is too loud. It's too bright in here. '*Rob*,' I pant. 'Please. *Please*.' I don't know what I'm asking for, but he's nodding, kissing my forehead, tripping out of bed and into the clothes he's had laid out for weeks. He's beaming at me, delirious and terrified, bringing me my warm robe and slippers I've set aside for this occasion, fetching my overnight bag and the things for the baby. All I can think is, this is it. *This is it this is it this is it.*

Another wave rolls through me, so powerful I can't even scream.

'It's fine; it will be fine,' Rob's saying as his face fades in and out of focus.

But I know he's wrong. And I feel like I'm drowning. Like no matter what happens from here, my life as I know it is slipping away. As another life flutters frantically within me, mine is coming to an end.

Rob's eyes hold mine and I grip his collar in two fists, pulling his face close to mine. I try to capture it, this beautiful thing we share – the essence of what we are, what we *were* – one more time, before it's gone.

'Don't leave me,' I beg him.

Rob's eyes, familiar and foreign at once, are full of warmth and fear and something new I can't identify.

'Never.'

Chapter 3

Liz

June, 2017
Sunday, 8:49am

The smell of bacon tugs me from a fractured dream. I haven't had this one before: a blue-eyed child stares at me with pleading eyes, reaching out as if asking to be held. It's innocuous enough out of context, but I jerk awake, heart pounding, and reach out to find Adam's side of the bed empty. I panic. Is it Monday already? Has he left without saying goodbye? But then I register the smell – bacon! – and remember – it's Sunday! – and my heart sings.

I sit up and smooth down my hair just as Adam appears in the doorway wearing nothing but the cheesy love-heart boxers I bought him for Valentine's day. His smile steals my breath.

'Beautiful,' he says when his eyes catch mine, with that

breathless awe that makes me giddy. Grinning, he crawls across the bed and cups my face, then kisses my lips. 'You're so fucking beautiful.'

'Shut up,' I shove his shoulder, beaming beneath his attention. I marvel at how different he is to all the men I've known before – openly loving, saying whatever's on his mind. He reminds me of an exuberant child. 'Aren't you cold?'

'How can I be cold when I'm close to you?'

'Ha.' I roll my eyes, laughing despite myself.

'Actually, I am a bit.' Adam mock-shivers as he slips under the covers and wraps me in his arms. His skin is like ice. 'Kitchen's a bit draughty.'

'The whole house is draughty,' I mutter, then bite my lip because I know I've done nothing but complain since we got here.

My husband frowns.

'Sorry,' I say, feeling bad for spoiling the mood.

'Stop it.' He lifts my chin with his finger. 'You know what? If this is too much, maybe you should come with me.'

'What do you mean? Where?'

'To Sydney. If things go well, I'll only be up and down the next few weeks. I could do without the commute, and if you hate it here so much, we can find a short-stay apartment ...'

I stop him with a finger to his lips. 'Adam. We can't afford it.'

My husband's face clouds, the way it always does when we talk of money these days.

'I'm sorry, baby,' I keep my voice light. 'It's a lovely idea. I know it won't be easy for you either, driving all that way. And I'll hate being apart for so long. But it's a short time in the scheme of things, and it will be worth it, when you get the deal.'

Adam exhales through his nose. 'It's not just that. I'm worried about leaving you here all alone. Especially after what you've been through.' He looks up, his eyes so full of concern I have to look away.

'I know. But I've been getting better.'

As a case worker for a counselling and respite centre for women in crisis, I can encounter some pretty distressing situations. But one case in particular involving a young, single woman and her baby really stayed with me. Post-Traumatic Stress Disorder was the diagnosis. I saw a counsellor, was put on medication and it seems to be helping. But sometimes, still, I wake in a cold sweat.

Adam doesn't say anything, so I add, 'And we don't have a choice. This is just what needs to be done. And it will be worth it, in the end.'

'You're right,' he says with a sigh. 'And when the settlement date for the sale of this old place is finally here, and we get the rest of the money. *Then*. Then we'll be out of debt and we can finally relax.'

I smile and rub his arm reassuringly. 'They've seen the house, paid the deposit ... they're keen. It will happen.'

Adam nods, but his sunny mood has evaporated. I can't blame him. As if losing his father wasn't bad enough, Tim's left behind one hell of a mess to clean up. And until it's sorted, until the sale of this house is final and the money from selling his dad's business is in the bank, we're neck-deep in debt.

Last year ended terribly for Adam. One thing after another went disastrously wrong for him and it was so hard to watch. My upbeat, generous husband – then, my fiancé after only a month's courtship – was screwed over by the business partner who had not only stolen his girlfriend (he caught them in bed together a couple of months before he met me) but had cleared out the company's joint bank account, leaving him penniless. And this year hasn't been the easiest so far either. He says more often than I'm comfortable hearing from someone so dear to me, that I'm the only thing that's keeping him holding on.

Adam has felt the loss of his father more than he's let on, and I suspect that, in part, it might be that he's mourning the relationship he wished he'd had with his father. They were never close and, according to Adam, visits between them were brief and strained.

I think part of Adam blames his father for his mother walking out on them when he was little. We have that in common, Adam and I. Absent mothers, both of whom shirked the role of motherhood and chose to lead lives separate from their families. I sometimes wonder if this has anything to do with us not wanting children, or whether some people just prefer their independence to willing slavery. Personally, I'd prefer to regret not having children than to regret having them. And there's no way of knowing which way it will turn out until it's too late.

Whenever Adam speaks of his father, which isn't often, I get the sense that he's never really respected him. 'He was weak,' he's said more than once. 'He should have tried harder – with both of us. I can hardly blame her for getting bored.' And then he'll get a faraway look in his eyes and, as I often do when I think of my own mother, I wonder whether he's wondering why she didn't take him with her. Perhaps it's easier for him to blame his father than accept the terrible truth: his mother simply didn't love him enough.

Adam's father, Tim, only became successful after his wife, Diane, left and moved to France with a wealthy banker. Perhaps he thought he was showing her, in her absence, that she'd made a mistake. That he could succeed in business and provide the sort of life she wanted, after all. But with the exception of a brief phone call when Tim died, Adam hasn't spoken to his mother in years.

In the end, I suppose we should be grateful to Tim because, for all his quirks and flaws, he raised Adam single-handedly, and he's the reason Adam gets a second chance. And now – fingers crossed – we'll have enough money to buy a house back in London and to rebuild the business. I want Adam to achieve his dream so badly it hurts. And I want him to make peace with the memory of his father.

***

I roll onto my side and drape an arm over Adam's waist, kissing the patch of skin at his neck. 'The woman across the creek has a baby,' I say conversationally, determined to change the subject and coax back Adam's good mood. 'A new one, five, six months old maybe. Lucky we're on this side of the creek, hey?'

'Erica?' Adam's brow furrows.

'No, not her. The younger one, the one in the middle house.'

Adam shakes his head. 'No, that can't be right.'

I laugh. 'What, you think I've imagined it? I saw her! She was holding a new baby. It was crying, I could hear it from here.'

'What did she look like?'

'Long, red hair. Quite beautiful, actually.'

Adam taps a finger to his lips. 'I don't think I actually ever met Rob's wife, but I've seen photos on Facebook and I'm fairly sure she had red hair. Hmm. Maybe she was babysitting or something.'

'Ah. I didn't know breastfeeding was part of babysitting services these days.' I blush at what I've accidentally confessed. 'Er, not that I was looking. I couldn't help but see. She was standing right in the window.'

Adam looks strangely pensive.

'What's wrong?'

'Nothing.' He shrugs. 'It's just I'd heard they ... you,

know. *Couldn't*. But maybe I've got that wrong. What did Rob say her name was …? Oh, I have it. Delilah! Like the song.'

I stare at him blankly and he laughs. "Hey there, Delilah'. No?'

'Must be before my time,' I quip and Adam grins. He leans in and kisses me on the lips.

'Dee, Rob calls her. He's been a local since Dad bought this place. Decent guy. I had a few pints with him at the pub once or twice and he got quite pissed one night … I'm pretty sure I remember him saying he was keen for kids, but …' He looks thoughtful, then breaks into a warm smile. 'Well, that's great news! Good for them.'

I think of the woman, the jaybird cries of the flailing infant. 'Is it?' I say with a snort.

Adam tugs me to his chest, his stubble grazing my cheek. 'I said it's good for *them*,' he repeats. And we both laugh.

Chapter 4

Dee

December, 2016
Monday, 9:45pm
Recovery Unit, Brave Cove Hospital

'That's not how you do it, little one,' the midwife, Lisa, is cooing while another midwife I've never seen before hovers at my bedside. 'You need to open your mouth, darling.'

Lisa's been here since 7:30 this morning, and until recently I've been glad to have her around, but right now I just want her to fuck off.

I'm exhausted, numb with shock and disbelief, and the tiny creature she's trying to coax to suckle at my breast looks bizarre and alien to me. She's too skinny and doesn't look right. Her features are unfamiliar; nothing about her is anything close to what I expected.

Lisa's persisting with the breastfeeding, even though

nothing's happening. The baby doesn't even seem to realise I'm it's mother. I'm feeling more than faintly irritated. I don't give a shit about breastfeeding right now. I don't give a shit about anything. I just want to sleep. The lights are too bright in here, and I'm so groggy I feel half dead. I want everyone to go away and leave me alone instead of expecting me to pass some fucking breastfeeding exam when I've been in labour all day and was just drugged to the eyeballs after my emergency C-section went wrong. It's all I can do not to shout at them all; except of course I haven't the energy for that.

When the epidural wore off during the operation, the pain was so excruciating I screamed. I begged the anaesthetist for some relief (I swear to God he was the only person in the hospital who actually listened to what *I* wanted) and he was very obliging. He'd been there when they first started cutting me open; I asked him whether it was happening yet, as I was feeling a faint pulling around my abdomen. He told me yes, it had begun, and I remember lying there looking up at Rob, both of us paralysed by the enormity of what was happening.

I can't remember what drug I was given, but it knocked me out so much I could barely process anything. Once it – Ruby – was out, they allowed Rob to cut the cord before taking him away. I couldn't believe it. Why had they taken Rob away? Where was the baby? It seemed appalling that after what I'd just endured, my husband got to see our baby before I did. When I'd done all the work, made all the sacrifices, and was still lying on an operating table with my abdomen sliced open.

'Come on, sweetie, you can do it,' Lisa's coaxing me again, and I can't take it anymore. Where is Rob? Does he know where I am? That the baby and I are okay? It seems ridiculous that family aren't allowed to be in the recovery room.

I try to speak but I can only croak. The midwives are oblivious to me anyway; the focus is all on Ruby. Is this the way it will be, now? Am I to be invisible forever?

How long do I have to lie here and let them do this to me? I just want them to take it away – for everyone to just leave me alone and let me rest.

Finally, finally, they accept defeat and they tell me Ruby needs to go to the special care unit. I'm not sure why and I don't have the strength to ask. I know in some deep part of my brain that I shouldn't want her to go, I should be wanting to hold her, to bond with her. But I feel none of that. I only want to close my eyes and have everything disappear. When they take her, all I feel is relief.

In the furthest corners of my consciousness, I'm aware that this isn't right. My baby shouldn't be an 'it' – it should be a she, *Ruby*. The name we chose for her the moment she came out with flame red hair. And I should be wanting to hold her. But the pain is creeping back in, even though the drugs are clearly still in my system, as my head feels like it's full of concrete and I can barely keep my eyes open.

***

10:30pm

The next thing I know, I'm in a hospital bed in a tiny space with half-drawn curtains all around me. I'm in agony, the whole lower half of my torso feels like it's on fire, but I can't seem to move; I can barely lift my pinkie finger. Has something gone wrong? I can't even call for help. I can barely breathe, let alone speak.

Every part of me yearns for sleep, but the pain keeps me conscious. It's dark in here; the only visible light is a soft orange glow coming from behind the curtain next to me, and the one in front. What time is it? I don't remember being brought here, and I don't know where Rob and Ruby are. Why have I been left here alone? I want to die. The pain is too much; I simply can't bear it.

I don't know how long I've been lying here when Rob appears. His eyes widen when he sees me. 'Are you okay?'

I try to speak but the pain is too much and I can only whisper. He leans in and puts his ear near my mouth. 'Please. Help.'

'What is it? What do you need?' Rob looks panicked.

'Pain. I'm ... in ... pain.'

Rob nods and springs into action. He disappears for a minute then reappears with a nurse who tells me they'll contact the pain team, but it might be a while as they're in the operating theatre.

I don't know if I can survive that long. Every breath is agony.

'Hold on, baby,' Rob says, kissing my forehead, his eyes bright with tears. 'It's going to be okay.'

But I can't imagine it's ever going to be okay again.

***

Tuesday, 7:12am
Post Natal Ward, Brave Cove Hospital

Monday's child is fair of face, Tuesday's child is full of grace.

I can't remember the rest, but that's what's going around in my head as I gaze at Ruby's funny, squashed face. She is a Monday child, but so far the poem is proving to be inaccurate. At this moment she kind of reminds me of an old man. I don't think she's going to be very pretty, but I'm sure I'll love her anyway. I can't work out who she looks like just yet. But her colouring is all mine.

It's bizarre to be holding this creature. I'm not one of those people who think all newborns are beautiful, and it seems my own child is no exception. But she *is* pretty miraculous, even if the very sight of her fills me with a panic so intense I almost can't breathe.

Rob is in love. It's almost worth it, seeing his face. He got to feed her her first meal while I was in recovery, after they couldn't get any colostrum from me. It's all fine, now, though, as she's breastfeeding like a champion. I didn't get to see her until this morning, however, because the pain team didn't make it to me until three fucking thirty in the morning and once the morphine finally kicked in I passed out cold from sheer exhaustion.

The social workers have been in, as apparently the entire medical team who witnessed the birth, and learned of what happened afterwards, was worried that I might experience some post-traumatic stress. But seriously. I'm not worried about what happened before, that bit's over. I'm worried about what on earth I'm going to do next, how we're going to work out how this tiny creature fits in to our lives. Everything feels different now. And all I feel is a distant sort of terror.

Ruby makes a face and a different feeling takes over. I go cold. The expression that passed across her face in that moment was so familiar that I *knew*. I knew with cold-blooded certainty that the very thing I hoped wasn't true, is. I glance worriedly at Rob. He meets my gaze and there's the tiniest of frowns between his eyebrows, as if he is carefully considering something.

It's then I feel the stab of an entirely different sort of terror.

Chapter 5

Liz

June, 2017
Monday, 6:45am

It's the first time we've been separated for any significant length of time. Well, aside from Adam's brief trip to Australia when his dad was first diagnosed with cancer. But at that time, I was still so consumed by what had happened at work I scarcely noticed.

This is different. I get the distinct feeling that the honeymoon is over – and, I suppose, technically it is. Adam kisses me on the nose and smooths my bed hair down behind my ears and though I put on a brave face, I can already feel the empty day stretching ahead of me. Bleak, pointless hours. I can't think of it, I have to focus on something, so I pull my husband closer and kiss him on the mouth. I draw him in, gratified by the immediate hardness against my hip and the surprised, slightly annoyed look he gives me.

'You can't do that, Lizzie. It's not fair,' he says, slightly breathless.

'I miss you already. We've barely even had time to speak this morning.'

'I know. And I'll miss you like crazy. It's not ideal, I know.' He pins me with that intense gaze of his that makes me feel both treasured and unsettled. 'God knows this is the last thing I want to do.'

'I know. I'm sorry.'

Adam's gaze softens. 'Don't be. I understand.' He presses his lips to my forehead. 'Take the chance to relax. Remember what the doctor said about exercising and keeping up the meds.'

I nod, once.

'And now I really have to go.' He kisses me, too briefly, and lifts his satchel over his shoulder. 'Bye, darling.'

And just like that, I'm alone.

***

8:30am

Back in London, I'd be on my way to work by now. Hell, I'd probably have already made my way from Liverpool Street to Euston, stealing sips from my precariously balanced refillable coffee cup, having inserted myself into a crammed tube carriage and lugged that cumbersome old briefcase I keep meaning to replace the two and a half blocks to my office building. I can almost smell the petrol fumes, the summer air, the aroma of freshly ground coffee beans and bacon grease.

As a case worker for a counselling and respite centre for woman in crisis, my job could get pretty intense. You'd think I'd be grateful for the break from it all, but in truth it was a matter of necessity. After my client, Christy and her six-month-old baby Bella were found murdered, I didn't take it too well. I felt guilty, started having nightmares. Night terrors more like. I felt I'd failed her as her case worker. I should have seen the signs, listened to her fears. This had never happened to me before, and I simply couldn't process it.

And then it was politely suggested by my boss that I might want to take some compassionate leave. They provide free counselling for employees, he said. You've been through a trauma; it's the best thing for you.

I took the hint.

I saw a counsellor, was put on some meds and over the last few months I've been improving. But I know Adam worries, and he wishes we didn't have to go through all this business with selling the house when I'm still recovering. I stare out of the grimy kitchen window as I pour the cold remains of my coffee down the sink. I find myself longing to be with Adam in Sydney, but if we're to get out of here as soon as is humanly possible – and God knows that's what I want – someone is going to have to sort through and get rid of all of Tim's things of which, thankfully, there are few. I thought Adam might want to do it, but he's said he doesn't care what happens to any of it. I suppose I'll see if there's anything of value to sell and then throw away the rest.

Pinpricks of light sparkle like stars on the surface of the creek and the houses over the other side, shadowed by night when I saw them last, stand gleaming white in their grand, colonial-style glory. Large bay windows look out like lidded eyes and lush green lawns slope down towards the shimmering water.

London feels a world away from here.

I look for the woman from last night, but her curtains are drawn. The house to the right appears empty, but on the left, in the least grand of the three houses, the one with the peeling paint and shabby awnings, the curtains are open on the top floor. There's movement in the window. A man – no, a boy? I can't tell as his back is to me – stands shirtless, lifting weights. I watch him for a moment, mesmerised by his rhythmic movements. Then I shake my head and look away.

Someone's in the backyard of the house on the right. It's surrounded by a beautiful garden, full of brightly coloured flowers and lush with shrubs and trees. A woman stands beneath a row of trees that descend in size from left to right. What did Adam say her name was? Erica. Erica and Samir. She's on her knees on the grass, her face in her hands.

It's hard to tell from here, but it looks like she might be crying. Short, pale hair fluttering in the breeze, Erica stands and pulls something from her pocket and runs it across her face. A tissue, most likely. She reaches up towards one of the four trees and runs a hand over the leaves and then – wait, is it my imagination or did she just plant a kiss on one of the branches? I rub my eyes. Ridiculous. I must be seeing things.

I make another coffee, hoping to muster the energy for a jog. It's the least I can do to occupy myself since I've sworn I won't look at or touch anything work-related (doctor's orders, literally) and the thought of starting on the piles of junk makes me want to gouge my eyes out with a rusty spoon. Besides, it might be nice to see the town, take in the scenery, 'let myself relax', as Adam says. Pearl Bay is 'a little slice of paradise', they tell me. Might as well make the most of it.

***

1:15pm

I wasn't hungry – I rarely am, these days – but I forced down some soggy, left-over salad and managed to locate my running shoes at the bottom of a suitcase, and now I'm looking for a way across this God-forsaken creek. Adam's taken the motorboat, of course, and I'm not keen on trying out the rickety-looking thing with oars. I'm sure he said there was a footbridge not far along the way, but I've been walking for at least five minutes now and all I've encountered is sludgy, marshy earth and dense bush.

I hadn't known I'd be so isolated here. Adam painted this stop gap as if we'd be on an extended honeymoon. It's a house by the water in sunny Australia, after all! But the reality is entirely the contrary. It's creepy, if I'm honest. I'm trying not to get lost down a rabbit's hole of negativity, but I really am starting to think we could have organised things a bit more sensibly. That I could have had some forewarning of what staying in this place, if only for a few weeks or months, would really be like.

The sun is so hot here, even at this time of year, and despite the wet season being over and winter creeping in, Adam's warned me it can still get humid during the day. I wipe the beads of perspiration from the back of my neck, remembering how I hate the heat.

Something crunches loudly under my foot and I rear back in fright. I look down to see the long, curled up body of a snake.

'Fuck!' I stumble backwards, my heart pumping, before realising that it's not a live snake, merely its discarded skin.

A whimper of relief escapes before I feel a surge of anger. For fuck's sake, let's admit it, this place is a nightmare. I'm either going to be killed be some horrible Australian creature or go mad imagining I might. How could anyone choose to live in a place like this?

Gathering myself, I trudge along, determined to find the footbridge and, in turn, civilisation. After a minute or two, the rhythmic thud of my shoes on the pebbly shore sounds suddenly amplified. Confused, I stop for a moment, listening. *Crunch, crunch, crunch.* Silence. I whirl around, straining to see through the dense trees, but I can't see anyone. My pulse leaps in my throat. No one lives over this side of the creek. Adam said the other two houses are abandoned. Why would anyone be here?

It's then that I notice it. In a small clearing just a metre ahead, something dangles from a tree. Squinting, I see it's a plastic baby doll. Something has been placed on its head, vaguely representing hair – dark green tendrils of seaweed, still glistening with moisture, and its painted eyes stare vacantly ahead.

An unpleasant tingle travels down my spine. There's what looks to be the remains of a campfire, some empty beer cans and a pair of tattered and muddied trainers strewn about beneath the doll. Has someone been camping over here?

There's the crunch of leaves behind me, and instinctively I break into a run, feeling foolish after a time when no one materialises. I tell myself the campsite could have been there for a number of days – weeks, even. *Except the seaweed was still wet ...*

I'm out of breath when I finally reach the bridge. It's made of wood that looks partially rotted and is covered in moss. I sigh in disappointment, unsure I can trust it to carry my weight. Vines dangle from two large, moss-covered trees flanking its entrance, and the other side seems very far away. The river has widened here and when I look into its murky depths I can no longer see the bottom. From the direction of the water flow, it seems the tide is coming in.

I shiver, suddenly cold despite the humidity. It seems everything is damp here – the air, the earth, the plants. No wonder the house is full of mould.

I hesitate, pressing the ball of my foot down onto the first mossy plank. To my surprise, it doesn't give an inch. Tentatively placing one foot after the other, I make my way across, breathing a sigh of relief when I reach the other side. I'm safe.

Chapter 6

Liz

June, 2017
Monday, 4:15pm

I've made it across the three-mile beach that runs along the other side of town, parallel to the creek, and now my lungs ache with each breath. I'm out of practice. Adam and I spent our three-week honeymoon over-indulging on everything imaginable (not to mention sending us knee-deep into debt) and now I'm paying for it in more ways than one.

The sun has passed over the mountain and a fog has descended. The air is thick with moisture and beads of perspiration cling to my forehead. I hadn't realised how long I'd been gone, how early it would grow dark.

I reach Cockle Street on my way back to the house and stop to admire the three matching houses all in a row. They're vastly different street-side; less decorative than the grand facades facing the creek. I'm staring at the house on the left with it's perfectly trimmed hedge when a heinous screeching fills the air. I stop and cover my ears, looking up towards the sound. A flock of large white birds with yellow crests fill a tall, gnarly tree, one of several lining the street. They're making an awful sound, like harpies squawking, and then another sound chimes in, battling to be heard over the din. The baby crying again, I think, but it isn't that.

I turn to see the red-haired woman, Dee, standing in her driveway, the blue door slightly ajar. A fair-haired woman – Erica, I assume – is blocking her exit, waving her arms, screaming something incomprehensible, too hard to hear from where I stand, beneath the raucous birds. Dee's cowering, shoulders hunched, head down. She's shaking her head, the baby clutched to her chest, its chubby legs flexing at her hips.

I feel suddenly too visible, exposed. Should I go over there, check everything's okay? Wrapping my arms across my chest against the sudden gust of cold air, I hesitate. Dee looks defeated. She stands, jiggling the baby mechanically, and lets Erica's tirade crash over her, and I feel a rush of protectiveness. Leave her alone! She's holding a baby, for fuck's sake.

It's then I realise who Dee reminds me of. My stomach clenches just as I feel the familiar pang of guilt. And when the baby begins to wail, I clap my hand over my mouth, closing my eyes against an unwanted image.

The urge to intervene has vanished. I walk fast, pulling my hood up around my face, hurrying along the narrow end of Cockle Street which tapers to the creek's entrance. I'm not looking forward to crossing that bridge again, to the trek through the bush, but I do want to get warm and pour myself a glass of wine. As I pass the final house there's a rustling in the bushes to my left. I lose my footing, tripping over a crack in the path as a tall shadow enters my peripheral vision.

My breath catches as I take in the tangled beard, tattered beanie and fierce eyes. The irises are piercing, electric blue against deeply tanned skin. The man makes a sound like a growl and I give an involuntary yelp, side-step him and run like hell.

***

8:48pm

Adam's still not back. I spoke to him earlier; he was sorry I'd had a shock but explained there are plenty of fishermen about town. 'He was most likely heading over to collect oysters,' he told me. 'There are oyster beds along our side of the creek. I'm so sorry, darling, I should have warned you.'

'Yes, you should have,' I grumbled, feeling foolish. I allow the familiar sound of his voice to soothe away my fears at being left alone in this house, especially after the campsite I spotted earlier. But since ending the call they've crept back in, whispering that 'someone's out there', even though I know I'm just shaken from my earlier scare. Was the man I saw the one who's been camping over here? Or was he just a local fisherman, like Adam said?

I check the lock on the bathroom door twice before I shower, startling at every sound as I stand beneath the spray.

I knew Adam would be late, but it's disappointing all the same. It's a two-hour commute one-way to Sydney and that's excluding the short boat ride across the creek. I don't know how anyone could live here permanently. And they don't, really. Not on this side of the water. People eventually figured out that a nice view wasn't adequate compensation for the damp and the mould, the proximity to tangled bushland and marshy swamp, the boat-only access. Everyone except Tim Dawson, who apparently thought there was nowhere better on earth.

I was trying to be positive for Adam when I told him the buyers that have paid the deposit will come through with the settlement, but the possibility they won't does worry me. I won't be able to rest until it's finalised; the thought of living here indefinitely terrifies me. I think I'd go mad.

But no matter how I feel, I have to try to be strong for Adam. He's been through enough, and I know he worries about me as it is. This is a partnership, the first real one I've had in truth. Men used to be just for fun, for distraction, but Adam's changed all that. I'm married now. I have to be prepared to pull my weight.

I pull the musty blanket up to my chin, glass of red in hand, watching through the loft window as the lights flicker on across the water. People arriving home after a day's work, no doubt exhausted after the long commute, happy to be home. Since there isn't even a bloody television here, it seems they're all I have for company.

Adam says the houses on this side of the creek are old fisherman's cottages, and that back in the thirties when this town was established the wealthy lived on the main land and the fishermen lived over here, in the boat-access only part of town. Now Oyster Creek is more of a suburban commuter town, and all but this house across the water have been abandoned. There are still fishermen, apparently, but every sensible one has chosen to live on the 'good side' of town. The man on the left – it's definitely a young man, not a boy – appears, passing across the upstairs window and through a door, emerging a minute later with a towel around his waist. He's attractive in a generic, athletic sort of way. Probably an Aussie, born and raised with a surf-board under one arm.

It appears that the top floor of the house is self-contained: kitchenette, bathroom, lounge chair, wardrobe. I don't see a bed, but perhaps there's one on the left, out of sight. Is he travelling? Renting? Living alone? He looks like someone who'd park himself, if temporarily, in a generic seaside town somewhere on the Australian coast. The towel begins to slip from his hips and I quickly look away.

The couple on the right, Erica and Samir, are in the

kitchen, sitting at an island, bathed in red-gold light from an overhead lamp. Erica stands and runs fingers through her short, light-coloured hair. There's something about her stance, her movements, that makes her seem tense. What was she shouting at Dee for earlier? She picks up a wine glass and tips her head back to drink. The man sits with his head in his hands. I wonder if they're fighting, and if so, what about?

I kneel on the window seat and press my nose to the glass. I've left the light on downstairs but up here it's dark, rendering me invisible. I feel like a voyeur – and I suppose I am in this moment – and it gives me a guilty thrill. As I lean forward, my fingers touch something cold and hard. I pick up the thing, half buried in dusty cushions, and it's heavy and black. Binoculars.

I snort and put them aside. Tim Dawson and his bird-watching. I always thought it was such a strange, isolating hobby. But then, as Adam says, he was a fairly isolated man. Just like this house.

Erica has put down her glass and is stirring something on the stove now. The man stands behind her, puts his arms around her but she tenses and pulls away. She turns to face him and points an accusing finger to her left. A light blinks on in that direction, as if her pointing triggered it.

It's the upstairs light in the middle house. There she is, the Botticelli woman with long hair. Dee. She opens the sliding door to the balcony and walks slowly outside, as if trying to be silent. She looks from side to side then squats in the darkest corner. A small flame appears, lighting her face briefly, and then there's the unmistakeable small, red glow of a cigarette.

I take a long sip of wine, an unpleasant tightness in my chest. I can't help it; even as I pity her, I wonder about the baby. Where is it? Has she left it alone? Or is Rob there somewhere?

As if on cue, the wailing begins. It's fever-pitched, loud even from here. My heartbeat speeds up. That sound can still get to me.

The woman doesn't move. It's a good minute before the red glow disappears and then she rises, slowly as if it's a great effort, and half limps inside. Is she injured? Recovering from something? There's something familiar about her gait, but I can't put my finger on it. Despite the chill, she's in a thin slip of a nightgown, her cascade of hair spilling everywhere, her engorged breasts low-hung and stark white as she bends, lifts her child from its cot and slides the straps from her shoulders.

Silence. The infant suckles, little legs kicking, and my heart thumps. There's something world-weary, defeated, about the woman as she stands, motionless against the incessant wriggling of the baby, and turns to stare out of the window.

There's something different about her face – a darkness surrounding one of her eyes. Without thinking what I'm doing I grab the binoculars and aim them at the window.

I have a clear shot of her face, and there's no doubting what I'm seeing. Dee is sporting a black eye: purple and blue and tinged with yellow. I feel a twinge of empathy and something else. Something deep in my muscle memory triggers a sense of panic. Did she have this when I saw her last, or is it new?

As if in slow motion, Dee bends and places the baby down, out of sight. Then she swings wildly to the right, grasps the stem of a floor lamp and throws it, like a javelin, to the floor. There's the distant sound of splintering glass, and the scene goes black.

Chapter 7

Liz

June, 2017
Tuesday, 7pm

Adam will be late again tonight, so instead of being miserable and hiding in the attic like a crazy voyeur, I've taken his advice and crossed the creek to have a meal at the pub. Never mind about the money, he said, your sanity's far more important. I didn't miss the jibe, albeit well-intended, so just to prove him wrong, here I am, having made sure I crossed the creek in daylight. At least Adam will be here soon to escort me home, and we can take the boat.

It seems I've inadvertently arrived on locals' night. There are at least fifty people here, unlike when Adam and I were last here and there were maybe two or three people at the bar. There are specials on the chalkboard, half-price drinks, and I'm fairly sure I recognise most of the faces from my walks about town.

I order a glass of white wine and stand by the fireplace, warming my hands over the flames. It really is a lovely old pub – or what counts for old in this country. Roughly cut stone walls, polished wooden counter tops, a fireplace taking up almost an entire wall. I smile as the wine starts to take effect, pleased I took Adam's advice to come. Beats sitting alone in that draughty old house.

A woman is standing by the window, looking out into the darkness. She stands out not only because of her petite stature and pale gold hair but for the simple fact that she's one of the very few women here. Then a tall, broad-shouldered man with dark skin and hair appears at her side holding a beer and a glass of red wine. She turns and gives him a small smile and I realise who they are – Erica and Samir.

I'm about to raise my hand to wave before catching myself. How ridiculous! Just because I've got nothing better to do than spy on my neighbours doesn't mean they've been doing the same. I shake my head at my own stupidity and head to the bar for another drink. It's a funny sort of feeling, seeing people in the flesh you've only watched from a distance. Almost like spotting a celebrity in the wild. I wonder whether the young man from the house on the left will come too, whether Dee will be here with Rob and their baby.

As if on cue, a woman with long red hair bustles through the door with a baby on her hip, bringing with her a gust of icy wind. I recognise her immediately, but she is so much more striking close-up. Her deep, dark auburn hair, while a bit wild and unruly, gleams in the low light, her vivid dress hugs her generous curves and contrasts sharply with her pale, almost translucent skin. She smiles at someone behind me, revealing straight, ever so slightly too large, white teeth.

Dee spots Erica and Samir and makes her way over to their table, bending to kiss Erica on the cheek and then handing her the baby.

I frown, thinking of the row I witnessed between them yesterday. Has it all been forgiven and forgotten then? As soon as the baby is in Erica's arms, Dee turns and strides towards the bar until she is standing right beside me, so close I can detect the scent of perfume; it's sharp and citrusy.

The barman appears in an instant, all smiles, filling a wine glass almost to the brim with white wine when Dee asks for 'the usual'.

The breath I hadn't realised I was holding comes out in a rush. I must make a sound because Dee turns towards me, and all of a sudden that dazzling smile is directed at me.

'Bless you,' she says, and I don't correct her. Instead, I smile back and tell the barman, 'I'll have the same, thank you.'

'Good choice,' Dee nods in approval, taking a sip from her glass. There's only the faintest hint of blue beneath her eye now; she must have covered the bruise with make-up. 'It's the only thing I'll drink in this place. They mainly cater for the beer drinkers around here.' She rolls her eyes.

'Thanks for the tip. The one I was drinking earlier wasn't particularly nice.'

'What did you have?'

'Erm ... the sauvignon blanc?'

Dee makes a face. 'Ugh. No, that one's no good. This one's the pinot grigio. Notice the use of the word *the*. As in they only serve one of each type here. Ha!'

Not knowing how to respond, I smile and take a sip of my own wine. My cheeks have grown warm and my pulse has quickened. Am I nervous? Embarrassed? I've been watching this woman without her knowledge, have witnessed vulnerable moments when she thought she was alone, when until now we hadn't exchanged a single word.

'You're not local, are you?' Dee squints at me, not bothering to hide her curiosity. 'I'd have noticed you if you were. Not many young women in this town.' She guffaws. 'Not many women, period!'

'I'm not local, no. We're just passing through.'

'Right. So is that a British accent?'

I can't help but smile at her directness. Distinctly un-British. 'You got it in one.'

Unable to help being nosy, and with Dee seeming so open, I nod in Erica's direction and ask, 'Is your friend okay? She looks a bit upset.' I refrain from mentioning that I've seen her crying through the window on one occasion, and raging at Dee on another. There is definitely something a little odd about Erica.

Dee follows my gaze and gives a little shrug. 'Yeah, she's as fine as she can be, I guess. She's just like that – a bit up and down. I guess you could say she's been a bit ... unwell lately. Which is understandable. She's been through a lot.'

'Oh, I'm sorry to hear that.'

Across the room the baby starts wailing and Dee groans. She catches my eye and rolls hers as she tips back the last of her wine and gestures for another. 'Sorry, I'd better go see to her. My Ruby's due a feed.' She shrugs apologetically and takes her new drink with her. 'Nice meeting you.'

'Yes, you too.' I smile and wave as she leaves. It's a shame, I think, to have the conversation end when it was just beginning. I'm about to order a glass of mineral water when a pair of arms slide around my waist and a warm, wet kiss greets my neck.

'Do you come here often?' Adam whispers in my ear before he appears beside me, grinning.

I roll my eyes and slap at his shoulder. 'God, you are so cheesy. How did I end up with such an old man?'

Adam gasps, mock-offended. 'Can this old man buy you a drink?'

I tap a finger to my lips, pretending to consider his offer. 'I suppose so. If he's paying.'

As Adam buys drinks I let my gaze wander to the table in the far corner. It seems Ruby has had her feed and is now sleeping peacefully in Dee's arms. She catches my eye and winks and I feel myself smile. Maybe Adam's right and there's a chance I could enjoy myself in this place. It's not for long, but maybe Dee could be someone fun to spend time with while we're here.

Samir bends and murmurs something to Erica, who still seems intent on staring out of the window, and heads towards the bathroom. Dee taps Erica on the shoulder and holds Ruby towards her. Erica's face lights up as she accepts the tiny bundle and holds the baby close to her chest.

Dee makes her way to the other side of the bar, closest to the bathrooms, and I feel a pang of disappointment. She's served straight away, and as she stands sipping her drink, Samir comes out of the bathrooms and with a glance in the direction of the corner table, approaches Dee. She turns her body to face him so that her back is to me, and even as Adam returns with the drinks, I find I'm craning my neck to see.

There's a familiarity in the way Dee greets Samir, her hand on his shoulder as she leans in to kiss his cheek. She lingers – is she whispering something in his ear? Samir nods, his expression stern, and then Dee heads back to the table and Samir orders more drinks for him and his wife.

As Dee approaches the table, I see Erica looking at her, baby Ruby clutched to her chest. And for a second I could swear I see a flash of emotion cross her face before she's quick enough to hide it.

Anger.

Chapter 8

Erica

May, 2017
Monday, 2pm

She's calm now, nestled to my chest, her tiny body comforted by the warmth of mine, the gentle rocking motion of my arms. Her skin is as soft as the petals of the roses I tend to in my garden, her fine hair barely covering the pink skin of her small, perfectly round head. She smells so sweet and new; a scent I will never tire of.

'Your silly mother is sleeping when she should be feeding you,' I whisper to her, watching as she suckles greedily. I stroke her cheek, encouraging her, but nothing is coming. She's starting to grow frustrated; she grizzles and beats her tiny hands against my chest, searching with her infant instincts for the sustenance she craves.

There's a shriek from down the hall, and I look up to see the silly girl in her dressing gown, hair in an unwashed cloud, milk stains on the front of her night-dress. So she's finally woken up then, I think, turning my back to the girl as she rushes at me at such a speed you'd think I was murdering the baby.

'What are you doing!' she shouts, her mouth agape, eyes blazing. She looks down at the infant sucking at my breast. 'What the hell are you doing to my baby?'

Chapter 9

Dee

February, 2017
Tuesday, 5:09pm

Ruby's dark lashes rest against her soft, round cheeks as she sleeps. She's so fragile. Not as delicate as she was at birth – she was such a scrawny, twitchy thing, all skin and bone, a side effect of the placenta depleting early due to my gestational diabetes. But she is soft in all the ways a person can be soft. Her duckling-down fuzz of ginger hair, her tender ivory skin, her dewy eyes like a blue galaxy.

Despite it all, she's healthy. I've fed her well, my supply plentiful in spite of my vices, and she's filling out in all the right places. She's a round, wriggly pudding, the picture of health when things could have – should have – gone so wrong. I've tempted fate, yet Ruby wasn't punished. I couldn't have forgiven myself if she was. It's me who must pay the price.

You hear these names – gestational diabetes, mastitis, colic, croup – but no one can ever prepare you for what they actually are, the fact that they are not just innocuous words floating around in the ether but actual and, frankly, bloody horrible things that humans are occasionally forced to endure. I have new respect for people who have diabetes (it is relentless, and I can't tell you how many times I nearly passed out from a hypo) and am pretty impressed whenever someone whose child has colic hasn't killed them – or themselves – yet.

I can't stop thinking of all the roads that led to here, which path I could have chosen to end up somewhere different. Somewhere far from here, an alternate reality where Rob and Ruby and I could be happy. How far back does it go? Which moment in time would I have to go back to in order to change things, make things right?

I'm worried, restless. I've got myself into a mess bigger than anyone else knows – well, anyone other than Samir – and now I have this beautiful creature I'm responsible for and she's going to be dragged into it too.

Nobody listened when I told them I didn't want a baby. Nobody believed me when I said I'd be a bad mother. And now it's too late. There's no going back.

'Don't you worry,' they told me. 'You'll want kids by the time you're thirty.' And they'd laugh as though the thought of anything different was impossible. But thirty came and went and my biological clock seemed to have missed the memo.

They told me when I found the right man I'd start craving a family. But Robert came along, showed me the right kind of love, the sort that's supposed to change you, and still ...

They didn't believe me – didn't *hear* me – when I suggested that motherhood might just not be for me. 'When will you be making a little friend for Johnny?' my friends would ask, as though it was as simple as that, no question of it. As though I were a machine designed to produce playmates for their bratty kids.

Rob thinks the reason I didn't want children is because of what happened with Mum's boyfriend when I was younger. He wants to talk about it even though I beg him to leave it alone. He thinks it's the source of all my problems, that everything will miraculously resolve itself if I can make my peace with it. What's to make peace with? It happened. Talking about it isn't going to change that.

Besides, does there have to be something wrong with me? Why does not wanting children require justification, whereas wanting them is natural ... even admirable? It didn't seem enough that I simply would have preferred to do other things than to take care of a screaming infant who would quickly become a tantrum-throwing toddler, who would all too soon become a sullen teenager. No, my decision had to *mean* something. Something bad.

They meant well, I know that. But they just didn't get

it. It's not that I looked down on mothers – though, honestly, there was some of that. The whole idea of instantly becoming this sort of *slave* has just never appealed to me. I simply couldn't understand the desire for children. It seemed I was a biological anomaly – a woman who didn't have the urge to push out kids. It was lonely, shameful. I was tired of fighting what the world seemed to think was my duty.

When I fell pregnant, I cried for a week. I knew that the deep, burning terror wouldn't go away until I did something about it. So I called a clinic and made an appointment, my cheeks hot with shame. But when it came to the day, I couldn't go through with it. The look on Rob's face when I'd told him he was going to be a father ... How could I bear to take that away from him?

That was the second of many stupid decisions I made. I doomed myself to learn the hard way that you shouldn't have a child for any reason other than the desire to do so.

And yet, biology took over, the pregnancy progressed, and I lived in denial of what was coming. People were full of helpful advice, shamelessly lying about how brilliant it was all going to be. How much *love* and *joy* motherhood would bring. And yes, it does, but that's not fucking all it brings, is it? When I couldn't generate the appropriate amount of enthusiasm, they were so *helpful* and *positive*. The first ultrasound will change things, they said. You'll 'feel it' then. And when I couldn't connect to the fuzzy black and white image on the screen, those twitching, wriggling parts they told me were arms and legs, those black holes where the eyes were meant to be, it was, 'Oh, it will happen when you feel the baby moving.'

But I felt those tiny flutters like butterfly wings, the 'quickening' as they call it, and was sickened. There was this *thing* inside me, stretching my womb, nudging at my organs, sucking the blood and nourishment from my body like a parasite. A being who would come out screaming and needy, utterly dependent, wanting things from me I didn't want – or know how – to give.

It was like watching it happen to someone else; it never quite felt real. And because it never felt real, I suppose I never truly thought anything would come of it. Totally stupid, I know. I'm not sure what I thought would happen – an accident, a miscarriage, *something*. Everyone knows plenty can go wrong during pregnancy. But somehow it all spiralled away from me until it was too late. Even when I thought something was wrong during the labour, and there was – the cord was wrapped around her little neck and I needed an emergency C-section to get her out safely – it still all turned out 'just fine'.

But nothing is 'just fine' any longer. I can't imagine it ever being fine again. I'd thought – hoped – once upon a time that Rob had frightened the darkness away. Perhaps not for good – I wasn't that naïve – but for long enough that we might stand a chance at happiness. I'd hoped I'd managed to cut all ties with my previous life in Sydney. With my ex.

I was an idiot to think I'd escaped. My ex is a shitty character. He was involved with all the wrong sorts of people, in debt more than he wasn't, and he's managed to track me down and make my problems his once again. It's the threats that concern me most. They've only just begun – I thought I had more time. But these blokes he's indebted to are never the patient sort, and he'll be sweating bullets by now.

I'd hoped I'd found security in Rob. In his warmth, his simplicity. I could press my face to the crook of his neck, breathe his scent and imagine I was absorbing his goodness. If I could be more like him, could be as hardworking, as simple-minded, life would be different. Easier. But I'm not simple. I never have been. It's fantasy to think Rob could protect me from myself.

It's all come to a head since Ruby came along. It's like any problem we have ever had has been amplified. I know having a baby isn't meant to be easy. 'The first six months are the hardest.' That's what they say. But they don't know my story. They don't know how the darkness changes things, warps things, makes me different from other people. This isn't the baby blues. This isn't postnatal depression. I never wanted this – *never wanted this* – and now there's no way out, no one I can tell, nobody who will understand and nothing that can make this go away.

If they knew the truth, I would be despised. Shunned. So now I'm trapped. A prisoner in my own house. And it makes me restless, edgy. Eager for distraction – any distraction. Eager for escape.

My phone pings and it's Erica, asking if I need help with Ruby. I sigh. I'm not sure I can face anyone right now. With Erica it's all shallow, surface stuff. Despite being the closest thing I have to a friend here, she isn't someone I can be honest with.

There's only one person who knows the whole truth, and it seems even he can't help me.

Suddenly not wanting to be alone in this house, I text Erica a quick reply, suggesting I go over there for coffee. She'll get distracted by Ruby – besotted, more like – and maybe I can sneak in a quick nap.

My hand trembles as I trace my finger along the silken curve of Ruby's cheek. She's a vortex, drawing me in, even though I want to turn away, to run. It's too much, this tight band constricting my chest, the ache that fills me when she smiles and coos. The love tinged with guilt.

***

3:04am

I stare at the shadows on the ceiling, waiting. It can't be long now; she only sleeps two, sometimes three hours straight at a time. No sense trying to get back to sleep. Rob snores beside me and I feel a surge of anger. How can he just fucking sleep through it all?

Everything has changed. Rob's changed. I can sense it in his body when I flop, exhausted, into bed beside him. Can sense it in the way he touches me – still the perfunctory goodbye and hello kiss. The Saturday morning fuck before Ruby screams for her morning feed is robotic, lacking the tenderness I'd grown to expect. The tenderness I took for granted.

Am I imagining it? Is it possible I'm so jetlagged from this stop-start sleep routine, the constant feeling of drowning, the not knowing which way is up, that I can no longer see what's real? Maybe things *are* as they were. Maybe it's me who's changed. Ruby who's changed me.

But then I see him watching me. Standing at the kitchen sink, dressed in his suit, hair slicked back, coffee mug pressed to his lips. I can feel his eyes. And, when I look up, they're narrowed, suspicious, fixed on me. I'll smile and jiggle Ruby on my hip and sing 'Say goodbye to Daddy!' and she'll stretch out her chubby fingers and grin at him and he'll dissolve. He'll smile at her, tears in his eyes, and kiss her cherubic face. But it's too late. I've seen. And it's like being touched on the inside with cold fingers.

A wail pierces the air and my skin zings with adrenalin the way it always does, even when I'm expecting it. I rush to her room, lift her warm little body from the cot and cradle her in my arms. Her seeking mouth finds my nipple and she latches on.

There's no point pretending. The darkness, it's back. As I stare at the electronic swirl of blue stars on the ceiling above Ruby's cot, her squirming body – always squirming, never still – in my arms, the tinny, stylised rendition of 'Twinkle, Twinkle' filling the room, I can feel it. Unfurling within, scratching at the inside of my ribs. An anxious awakening. A bad omen.

Chapter 10

Erica

June, 2017
Saturday, 5pm

The garden is lovely at this time of year – a sea of pinks and purples, baby blues and daffodil yellows. Winter is beautiful here, most of the time at least. In summer it's far too hot on this side of the house, and my babies tend to suffer in the heat. Still, I've managed to keep them alive all these years. More than twenty years and counting and I haven't lost a single one. Letting them down a second time simply isn't an option.

David is always the first I tend to, then Lucy, then Amanda, then You. It's silly, perhaps, but I find comfort in keeping to a routine. That's the order in which they were created, and that is how I always think of them. David, Lucy, Amanda and You. The family I'd have had if everything had gone the way it was supposed to.

Sometimes I lie on my back amongst them and close my eyes, letting the sunshine warm me and the gentle wind soothe me. I do this now, the freshly mown grass soft against my back and fragrant in the air, and in my mind they're all here. David, the larrikin – he was always so active! Lucy, my gentle girl, Amanda my little livewire. And You. The angel I held in my arms.

In my mind I'm reading a book on the patio and David's haring around after a ball – to think he's now a young man! How time has flown. And Lucy and Amanda are squabbling over who's the mother and who's the baby in the make-believe game they always play. You're in my lap, nearly ten years old but still loving to cuddle. The baby of the family, Mummy's little shadow, my precious angel.

Samir's upstairs making dinner – he's a fabulous cook, much better than I am, try as I might – and the smell of something rich and savoury makes my mouth water. He's the most wonderful father, as I always knew he would be, and the children just adore him. How jealous my silly sister was when I met him! How she envies me even now, because her two-year-old twins are giving her grief, unlike my angels, and Gary isn't half as supportive as Samir. Nor half as wealthy. Fortune truly smiled on me on that fateful day, so many years ago now.

A sharp wailing shatters the illusion and reality rushes back with such force it leaves me breathless. I squeeze my eyes shut as the baby's cries pierce through me like broken glass.

Chapter 11

Liz

June, 2017
Wednesday, 6:15am

My head aches as if I drank a bottle of red last night. The sleeping pills have left me groggy, dehydrated, and still I lay awake most of the night, worrying.

I gaze out of the window through aching eyes just as the side gate to the left of the Haddads's house opens and someone enters the yard. It's Erica, her back to me as she reaches up to touch the leaves of the tallest of four green, leafy trees. It's hard to see clearly from here, but when I squint it almost looks like she's *caressing* them. She does the same with the tree beside it, which is slightly smaller, and the one beside that, which is smaller still, moving along the row to give each plant the same attention. I shake my head. Some people really believe that stroking and speaking to their plants helps them thrive. But who am I to judge? For all I know, they could be right.

'You're already up,' Adam says with surprise as he enters the kitchen, his eyes running over me. I'm huddled at the counter by the window nursing a strong cup of coffee, and I know I look like death warmed up.

'Couldn't sleep,' I murmur, rubbing my eyes.

Adam's brow creases. 'Is it the cold? I know it's a bit draughty ...'

I shake my head. 'It isn't that. You're like a furnace.'

Adam grins and I manage a weak smile.

'It's ...' I trail off, suddenly reluctant to finish my thought.

Adam comes up beside me and places a hand over mine. He smells of the cologne I bought him for Christmas and there's a faint whiff of toothpaste when he speaks.

'Have you been having nightmares again?'

I pull my hand away and immediately regret it.

'It's not that,' I say stiffly. 'It's ... that woman. Across the creek. You said her name is Dee?'

Adam frowns. 'What about her?'

I hesitate. 'The other night I saw her in the middle house, through the window.'

Adam looks confused. 'Well, that's where she lives, Lizzie.'

I sigh, annoyed that my foggy brain isn't sorting the words right. 'I know that. It's just, she ... she had a black eye. It looked pretty bad.'

'How do you ...?' Adam trails off then grins, amused.

'Have you been watching? Found Dad's binoculars, did you?'

'I wasn't—' I feel my face heat up. 'Look, it isn't the point. This isn't *funny*. What do you know about her husband? I haven't seen him around.'

Adam shrugs. 'I didn't know him *that* well, but we did share a few pints now and then. And like I said, he seemed like a pretty good guy.'

'Ugh, I hate that phrase. What does it even mean? A lot of guys can *seem* pretty good and then turn out not to be. I should know, shouldn't I? Christy and her baby were killed by that bastard because ...' I choke up and Adam puts an arm around my shoulder.

I take a deep breath and swallow the lump in my throat. 'My instincts are playing up, and you know I should have listened to them last time. Don't you think it's strange we haven't seen Rob?'

'I know how you must be feeling, sweetie. But I honestly don't think it's that strange. Rob was always away a lot. He's a pilot, I think. Rolling in money.'

There's a trace of resentment in his tone, but I can hardly blame him, given our circumstances.

Adam pours cereal into a bowl and drowns it in milk. He chews thoughtfully. 'I don't want you to get too excited, but I have some news that might cheer you up. I think we'll have closed the deal within the fortnight.'

My face breaks out in a smile. 'Really? That's brilliant!'

Adam grins. 'Fingers crossed. I just need to bring the

buyer up to speed on Dad's business model, which will take a while, as you know, as I'll basically have to decipher it myself first, but then apart from that we're good to go!'

'That's amazing news,' I clasp my hands together. 'And the house ...?'

'Still working on a settlement date, but we're looking at about a month's time at this stage.'

My face falls. 'Another month here?'

'We might not have to be around for that, but I'll have to make sure. I don't want to be overseas and have them say something's gone wrong and we need to sort it out in person. Although there are usually ways around these things these days, with most things being digital. The good news is that once the company buyers have signed on the dotted line, they'll be transferring a deposit into my account. We'll finally have a bit of money until the rest comes through.'

I brighten slightly at that, but I'm desperate not to be stuck here for an entire month longer. Hopefully, as Adam says, it's not something we have to be around for.

My gaze drifts to the window. Dee's blinds are drawn and there's no sign of life. A pair of birds land on the stretch of lawn in front of her house, screeching and squawking – I can hear them from here. Plovers, according to Tim's bird book. (Yes, I've been *that* bored). Ugly things with big yellow wattle under their sharp little beaks. This particular breed is native to this coastal region and rarely found anywhere else. Lucky us. They're so bloody noisy I can hardly hear myself think.

Following my line of vision, Adam places a hand on my arm. 'Look, I wouldn't worry. Dee's got a new baby, so she's probably sleep-deprived. Maybe she walked into a door or something.'

I raise an eyebrow.

That earns me a chuckle. 'I know, I know. Sorry. But I just can't believe Rob would do something like that,' he says, shaking his head. 'He's the softest bloke. Wouldn't hurt a fly.'

I furrow my brow. 'I didn't think you knew him that well.'

Adam stares out of the kitchen window toward the trio of houses. 'I didn't. I don't. It's just ... you get a sense about a person, don't you? He spoke so fondly of her. Dee, I mean. And the way he was so keen for children ...'

'That doesn't mean he can't get angry, can't, you know ... lose his temper.'

'I know, darling,' Adam sighs. 'And you never know what goes on behind closed doors. God knows the people I've thought I've known, have trusted, who've turned out to ...' He trails off and I'm sure we're both thinking about what happened with his business partner and his ex. 'It's just such a shame, isn't it? I remember how chuffed Rob was when he met Dee. Never thought a woman like that would look at him twice!' he chuckles. 'I can't help but wonder ...'

'What?'

Adam looks sheepish. 'Well, she had a bit of a reputation.'

'Oh, so she was asking for it, is that what you mean? Because of course, if a man does something bad to you, it *must* be your fault.'

Adam chuckles and kisses my cheek. 'You know that's not what I meant.'

'What did you mean, then?' I fold my arms and turn my head. I know it's childish of me, know I've got the wrong end of the stick, and yet I continue the show. Sometimes I wonder if I'm testing Adam.

'Almost the opposite. I'm just wondering if maybe his insecurities finally got the better of him. Maybe he's taking it out on her. You know what jealous types can be like.'

'Oh.' My shoulders lower from beneath my ears. I forget, in moments, that Adam isn't like the others. I expect him to act in certain ways and then he surprises me. It's a reminder that things are different, now.

'It was a shock, that's all.' I clasp his hand – my way of apologising. 'What if I see something again? Should I ... I don't know, should I report it or something?'

Adam looks at his watch and curses under his breath. He gets to his feet and takes his empty bowl to the sink. 'Yes, I suppose if you see something actually happen. But I don't want you ... *stressing* about this, Liz. It's the last thing you need.' He gives me a meaningful look. 'You're taking the medication? Exercising?'

'Yes, thank you, *Dad*.'

'Good. Keep it up.' He gives me a swift kiss on the forehead, looking apologetic. 'I wish I could stay. But it won't be long now.'

'I know. Go.'

My husband kisses me deeply before he walks out of the door, and I think of poor Dee, left alone, and how sinfully, unfairly lucky I am.

***

1:17pm

The child's doll with seaweed for hair has gone, but the number of empty beer bottles has doubled. I quicken my pace, unable to shake the sense of unease I feel as I pass the campsite.

I approach the row of houses on Cockle street, looking up instinctively when I reach the middle one. All the windows are open, plantation shutters flung wide as if to air the place of an unwanted smell. It's a different house to the one I passed the other morning. Airy, inviting. Sheer white curtains billow in the breeze and I can see straight through the floor-to-ceiling windows to the other side, to a patch of blue sky. Dee and the baby are nowhere to be seen. But as I near the house I see a figure standing on the other side of the road. It's a man wearing a faded blue baseball cap, a grubby grey jacket and tracksuit bottoms. He's staring up at the house, hands buried in his pockets, unmoving.

For some reason I think of the discarded trainers and empty beer bottles. Could this man be homeless and squatting in the bush? It seems a strange, cold place to park yourself if you've nowhere to live.

I'm so busy staring that I nearly collide with a woman pushing a pram.

'I'm sorry!' I say, side-stepping to let her past. It's then that I recognise her. 'Oh, Erica. Hi!'

Erica looks confused.

'I'm sorry ... I'm, uh ... I'm Adam's wife, Liz. Adam is Tim Dawson's son? I'm sorry if I gave you a start!'

Erica hesitates before offering a cautious smile. 'Oh. Hello.'

'We're staying at Tim's place until it's sold. He passed away recently, as you've probably heard.'

'Oh dear, I am sorry,' she says slowly, as if choosing each word carefully. Her eyes flick towards the direction of the creek. 'I hadn't actually heard. He hardly ever seemed to be there. Worked down in Sydney much of the time, apparently.'

'Yes, he did.'

There's an awkward silence. I smile down at the baby as two big blue eyes, framed with long, dark lashes, blink up at me from beneath a crochet beanie. A halo of gorgeous red curls peeks out from the hem of the beanie.

'Oh, isn't she lovely,' I say, smiling up at Erica. 'She looks like her mother.'

Erica's brow furrows. 'Do you know Dee?'

'Not really, but I met her the other night at the pub. She seems nice.'

Erica seems distracted and I can't help but feel she'd rather be elsewhere.

'Right,' she says absently, glancing down the street in the direction of the park.

'She's a cutie. Is Dee at work or something?'

'Dee's a kept woman. She doesn't work,' Erica snaps. Her eyes widen as if she's as surprised by her words as I am. Regret flits across her face, and she bends quickly and coos at the baby.

So the husband *is* around. Maybe, as Adam says, he's just away for work at the moment. And the black eye was just an accident.

But there's definitely something funny going on between Erica and Dee.

The baby gurgles and grins up at Erica and my chest swells. I've never had any desire to be a mother. It seems I inherited Mum's absent maternal gene. But there's something innate, instinctive, that makes me want to pick her up.

'Oh,' I say, swallowing the lump in my throat at an unwanted memory. 'Well, it's awfully nice of you to babysit and give Dee a break. Is she with friends or family ...?' I'm aware that I'm prying but I can't seem to help it.

Erica looks up from the pram and her face is the picture of adoration. I suppose babies have that effect on people. 'She doesn't really have either. Well, apart from me. I'm her friend.'

Didn't look like it the other day, I think, wondering why Dee would leave her baby with Erica if they were at odds about something. And why things seemed so civil between them at the pub.

'Oh dear, how hard it must be for her raising a baby with no family. Lucky she has you!'

Erica nods slowly. 'Yes. Lucky.'

I supress the urge to sigh. Trying to get conversation out of Erica is like drawing blood from a stone.

'So, are your children at school today, or ...?'

The smile vanishes from Erica's face. 'I don't have any children,' she says brusquely.

'Oh! I'm sorry, I—'

'Just assumed? Yes, I suppose you would.' She eyes me with an expression resembling disdain. 'Don't you know it's ignorant to assume all women of a certain age are mothers?'

'Yes, of course, you're right. I'm sorry, it was a silly thing for me to have said.'

'Well, never mind. It's done now, isn't it?'

'I really am sorry,' I say, desperate to resolve this uncomfortable exchange. 'It was a thoughtless thing to say.' Erica's eyes narrow, but some of the anger leaves her expression. 'Well,' she says, looking suddenly weary. 'That's okay I suppose.' She gazes down at the child and fusses with her beanie as if she'd rather look anywhere but at me. 'Just think twice before making assumptions next time.'

***

2pm

I'm not in the mood for a jog today after my run-in with Erica so I walk into town instead. What a strange woman. So defensive. As if I needed any other reason to want to leave this place.

But I suppose, if it's the case for her – and I suspect it might be – wanting children but being unable, for whatever reason, to have them, is something that might never wholly leave you. I should really be more sympathetic.

As I reach the town centre I notice an acrid smell in the air. There are people milling at the foot of the stairs that lead to the pub, and beyond the old building with its exposed brick, bullnose veranda and old-world charm, the sky is thick with smoke. It appears to be coming from the mountain separating Oyster Creek from the rest of civilisation. At the sight of smoke, I feel a pang of panic. Earlier, when scrolling through my newsfeed, I'd noticed there were fires burning in a couple of nearby suburbs.

I elbow my way through the cluster of locals, who all give me lingering, curious looks, and into the main bar that fronts the pub. The television is on, a technicolour glow in the corner of the room, and a newsreader is talking about fires sweeping the coast.

'Ugh,' I groan when the announcement is over. Apparently, there's only one road in and out of town and it's blocked. I text Adam.

Heard about the fires? The road to town has been blocked, might still be blocked tonight. I hope not!!!

'What are you after?' A voice startles me, making me remember where I am.

I look up, flustered, and into a pair of vivid blue eyes. 'Oh, I wasn't going to ...' I pause. The young guy behind the bar watches me expectantly, something familiar about his stance, those eyes. He looks like he's smirking.

'Let me guess. A sauv blanc? Or, wait. Maybe a pinot?' His voice is more gravely than I'd expect from someone of his age, inflected with a broad Australian accent. He reminds me of an Australian actor I can't recall the name of in a film I saw on the plane trip over.

'I, uh ...' I shake my head. Wine. Yes, I could definitely do with a glass. I check my watch. It's after midday; that's okay, isn't it? 'Pinot grigio, thanks,' I say, remembering Dee's tip.

He's still smirking. What secret am I not in on?

'Sorry I scared you,' he says as he pours my glass just a touch fuller than it needs to be.

'I'm sorry?'

'The other day, by the creek. I think I gave you a bit of a fright.'

I stare and he smirks and then it dawns on me. I feel my cheeks grow warm. 'That was *you*? You ... you're, uh ...' My brain screams 'much better looking than I thought' but thankfully it doesn't slip out. 'You've shaved.'

'It's been known to happen, on occasion. Six fifty, thanks.'

I wrinkle my nose and hand him my card, but he shakes his head.

'Sorry. Card reader's buggered. Cash only I'm afraid.'

'God, this place,' I mutter, scrounging for change in the rarely-used side pocket of my handbag and finding a couple of unexpected twenty-dollar notes and some loose change. I must have withdrawn money on our first night when we visited the pub and forgotten about it.

He chuckles. 'Not all people take to it. You're not from around here, are you?' He hands me the glass and I sip gratefully, relishing the cool liquid as it slips down my throat.

I laugh. 'No. God, no.' Then, feeling bad, I add lamely, 'It is quite lovely, though.'

His eyes meet mine and his eyebrows twitch. 'Right.'

A customer gestures for his attention, and I pretend to take an interest in the flickering television until he returns, as I somehow knew he would, to my side of the bar.

'You shouldn't go that way, you know.'

'What way?'

He grins and I find myself irritated. 'Are you deliberately talking in riddles?'

He laughs easily, unfazed. And I realise that's what he wants – to rile me up. It occurs to me then that I'm being flirted with. I glance down at my ring, place my hand on my glass so the diamond shows.

Pub Guy's eyes catch mine, flick to the diamond and back, and his grin widens.

'You shouldn't go over the creek that way. Over that bridge, the way you go.'

I purse my lips. 'And why not? There's no other way across.'

'Untrue. You can take the boat. The one you've got sitting there, waiting to be used.'

Unsettled, I take a deep swallow of wine and pull my coat close to my chest.

'I haven't been spying on you,' he says in a gentler voice. 'It's hard to miss when someone's over there, what with the other houses abandoned and not much else going on. I'm on Cockle Street, the house on the north end.'

'Oh! You're—' I bite my lip, embarrassed. Funny, I never noticed he had a beard when I'd watched him lifting weights, although I suppose it's the furthest house from where we are, and he's mainly been faced away from me. 'Yes, well. I suppose you're right. Hard to miss,' I allow. Knowing where he lives, I can hardly fault him for noticing me. It's not like I haven't noticed him.

He catches me inspecting his tanned arms and smirks. 'Been here a while. Came on holiday from Melbourne once and just never went back. I come and go – caught the travelling bug a while back – but I always end up right back here.'

'Right,' I say, unable to imagine wanting to swap metropolitan Melbourne for this place.

His expression turns serious. 'Just be careful crossing the creek, especially coming home at night after a few.'

'Oh?'

'The bridge isn't exactly new, as you've probably noticed. And if the tide's in the wrong place, it can get deep.'

'How deep?'

Pub Guy stretches his arm over his head. 'Pretty deep. And when the tide goes out, the pull's pretty strong. Could end up dragged from your place to the open sea in ten minutes flat. Had a couple of tourists drown after getting swept off that bridge last year.'

I shiver. 'Gosh, that's horrible. Thanks for the warning.'

'Another thing, we've got a king tide coming in tonight.'

'King tide?'

'Yep. The water can come right up to the fence at my place. One year it was so high the Haddads's downstairs flooded.'

'Oh, gosh. Is ... is it safe to cross by boat? When there's a king tide, I mean?'

Pub Guy eyes me over the rim of the glass he's polishing. 'If you've got a strong motor.'

I take out my phone and text Adam.

Maybe you shouldn't come back tonight, even if the road is reopened. There's going to be something called a king tide and it might be dangerous to cross the creek.

My phone pings almost immediately.

Oh no!! First fires and now this! That bloody place!!!

And even though my heart aches at the thought of a night apart, I smile because it echoes my earlier thoughts exactly. I love the way our minds sync; it reminds me of how effortless it was from the start.

I finish my drink and glance involuntarily at the rows of bottles in the bar fridge.

'Another?' Pub Guy asks.

'Please.'

'All right. But after that, you'd better head off.'

I frown. 'Excuse me?'

He gives me a slow, lazy smile. 'Tide's coming in.'

Chapter 12

Dee

March, 2017
Thursday, 5:16pm

There's blood on my baby's mouth.

A whimper sputters out as I lift her from the cot and cradle her in my arms. What have I done? I've left her to cry and now she's hurt. How could I be so selfish, so reckless? She's only three weeks old. I can't leave her on her own. Not even for a minute.

I grab a baby wipe and press it to her tiny mouth. A smear of blood comes away and beneath it is a small scratch. I sob with relief. I know straight away that it was made by her tiny, too-long nails that I can never cut because she screams and clenches her fists.

I kiss her sweet brow and stroke her hair and murmur softly to her. 'I'm sorry, baby, I'm so sorry.' I know it's only a scratch, and she's fine, but every minor injury to her perfect little body breaks my heart. How is it possible to love someone with all your body and soul and yet for part of you to wish they didn't exist at the same time?

I'm feeling a bit wild at the moment, if I'm honest. I feel like I'm doing everything wrong; I can't even cut the child's nails. Rob isn't as involved as I thought he'd be. It's not his fault; two weeks paternity leave is a shitty, near-useless amount of time. You've barely absorbed the fact that you *have* a baby and then the father is forced to leave his family, and the mother's one source of support is taken away for most of the day. The nights are the worst. Even though I haven't slept, when I see daylight creeping through the curtains I'm filled with relief. I survived another night.

She has colic, so screams almost constantly unless she's asleep. Today I just needed a minute – one minute! – to breathe because I was so worked up I was afraid of what I might do. I've joined a support forum on Facebook – I couldn't think what else to do, I'd never even heard of colic before – and it's supposed to last twelve weeks. Three fucking months! I don't know if I'll survive another month of this. And then what if it doesn't stop? Some of the mothers on this forum are saying they have twelve-month-olds who still scream day in and day out and don't sleep. A few of the women in the forum are suicidal. I would be too if I'd had to put up with this shit for a year.

I get up with Ruby in the night because she's breast-feeding and I don't want Rob to drive when he's had no sleep but I can't seem to express enough milk in time before she needs another feed so Rob isn't bottle feeding that often. It feels like that's all I do. Feed Ruby and milk myself and sleep when she sleeps. It's simultaneously the most stressful and the most boring thing I've ever had to do.

I should call the postpartum depression hotline. That's what Rob says. But what's the point? There's nothing anyone can do. Can they change the past, rewrite history? I have Ruby now; that's it, there's no way out. Well, there is one.

But I can't choose the coward's way. Because I deserve this. I did everything wrong, right from the beginning, and I deserve to face the consequences. I should have been honest, should have come clean while I had the chance. He might have forgiven me. I might not have had to live in constant fear of being found out.

***

6:03pm

Ruby is finally starting to show signs of falling asleep, so I fetch a blanket from the pile of clean laundry and place it over her, rocking her gently as I head to the kitchen. I put the kettle on for some chamomile and anise tea, which is good for lactation, apparently. The kettle is starting to bubble when I check the time. After six.

Fuck it, I think, and pour a dash of red into a wine glass. I throw it back. Pour another. I return to the living room and sit on the edge of the sofa and stare out of the window at the starlight reflected on the water.

If I'd been more like Rob – less complicated, more open – things might have been different. But it's like there's something missing inside me, and I'm always looking for the next thing to fill it. The next high, the next distraction. Why can't I just be satisfied, sit still and feel content for once?

There's a saying I can't seem to get out of my head; you can live your life two ways: as if nothing is a miracle, or as if *everything* is a miracle. Rob's the second category, for sure – a firm believer that everything is magical, has a meaning, was 'meant to be'. I fall more into the former category. And perhaps that's been my downfall. I don't want to be the one to shatter Rob's shiny world view, but I fear it might already be too late.

Rob was wonderful during my pregnancy. He truly saw it as miraculous. I was the centre of attention at all times and I didn't even have to do anything. I just had to *exist*. If I could forget for a moment, I could revel in it. The very fact that I was carrying his child (a concept that was surreal to me at all times, without exception), the fact that his seed had been planted in my womb, I could see it in his eyes, the pride that my body was changing because there was something of him inside me.

People are funny like that. We get this biological ego boost when all our bits work, a confirmation of our cohesion with the Way of All Things. And similarly, when our bits don't work, we feel we've failed somehow. As if we ever had any control over it, any say at all.

Sometimes, despite myself, I saw it Rob's way. It wasn't just that he gazed at me like I was the goddess of fertility, that he marvelled at my burgeoning belly and blue-veined breasts. I was beautiful pregnant. Everyone said so and I could see it myself. It had never occurred to me there would be beauty in it at all, let alone that I could feel so beautiful, so womanly, with a tiny human growing inside me. I'd only ever thought of the pain, the discomfort, the 'ickiness' of it all. So I, too, marvelled at the changes in me with a distant fascination.

But it wasn't just that. It was when I was alone with her – the *her* she became when we found out the sex at the twenty-week ultrasound – and I felt her move, when there was silence. It was just her and me and one night, when I was emotional, when I'd been screaming and crying and throwing things and was calm again, exhausted, and I felt her – I spoke to her. I'll take care of you, I told her. And while the feeling was fleeting, I meant it. And I could feel her reaching out – an arm or a leg I wasn't sure – this entity, this creature that had been created out of his cells merging with my cells and, of their own accord, morphing into a third being. And I could see. I could see how Rob would think it was a miracle.

That I could share those feelings with him, that sense of magic and wonder, felt like a betrayal. Not the worst of my transgressions against him, but a betrayal nonetheless.

Another thing I'd robbed him of, something that – with another woman, in other circumstances – would have been a natural, beautiful, shared thing. But knowing the risk, of what might be coming at the other end of it all, I could never quite relax.

Maybe Rob's right about more than I've given him credit for. Maybe I do tend to self-sabotage. Maybe it is – maybe it always has been – about my mother's boyfriend *interfering* with me when I was young. I've never spoken to anyone about it, apart from him. It had happened to so many others, the other girls and women I worked with at the strip club, and I figured it was normal. I knew there was this *thing* inside me – this pain, this self-*hate* almost, like I was worthless, unclean – but they all had it too. They all told their stories in their dismissive ways, cigarettes held aloft, wine glasses in hand. Snorting lines. Drinking themselves senseless. Numbing. Pretending. Play acting at being powerful when they were just lost little girls.

My drug of choice came in human form. Older ones, of course, with a little grey in their beard, a fan of lines around their eyes. Rough hands. Hard eyes. But, really, I was an equal rights offender. Any man, any time.

It was just the once. Only the once. We'd been 'trying' – or Rob thought we had. I thought he'd lay off the idea if we found out we couldn't. I was *sure* we couldn't, somehow.

It was during that time – the invasive tests, the jabs and probes – that I realised there was more than one way for a woman to be objectified. In my experience, it came in the most obvious form. There were those who sought a fuck and those who sought a wife, someone to bear his children, someone to give him the title of *loving* husband, *doting* father. Either way, her worth was in her pussy.

When we went for tests, I felt like a sow being inspected for the quality of my meat. 'You're young and healthy,' they'd say. 'A prime specimen for breeding' was what I heard. And it made me sick. I didn't feel that differently from when I was up on stage, my leg around a pole. Somehow, I felt worse. I can't explain why, but I did.

So I looked for escape. Fell into old habits. Rob was away on business. And *he* was back from his travels – he was always traveling; the men in this town never stand still – deeply tanned from Vietnam or Bali or Samoa or wherever. And in a moment of weakness, I was tempted.

And now, here I am, standing barefoot in my living room with unwashed hair, three-day-old clothes, a glass of wine in one hand and a baby in my arms.

***

Mercifully, she's asleep now. I stroke the little hand that's curled up beside her soft cheek and can't help but smile. It helps that she's so beautiful. I know everyone thinks their babies are beautiful, and I'm starting to agree. I see babies differently now, I can admit that. But Ruby really is gorgeous, unlike the strange, skinny creature she was when she came out. Her eyelashes are long and dark, her eyes huge and the deepest blue. She has a little button nose and perfect, cupid's bow lips. She's perfect.

And I know that, whatever comes, it isn't just about me anymore. I have to try to do what's right. For her.

Chapter 13

Liz

June 2017
Wednesday, 5:45pm

They didn't clear the road in time. I come away from my conversation with Adam feeling discombobulated, unsettled. We agreed earlier that it was best he stayed in town. No sense traveling back to find some hotel up this way only to drive back to Sydney in the morning.

Still. Not ideal, really. Particularly considering the price of Sydney hotels.

Adam sounded out of breath on the phone and my mind went to default, picturing another woman in the hotel room with him, and then the old mantra – *he's not like the others, this is not the same*. But the things I've seen, and muscle memory, make me respond as I once would have (though – gradually – that's changing) and that old, heavy brick lodges itself in my gut. On the phone, my voice shook and it was made worse by the plovers squawking in the background, so loudly I could barely hear him.

'Sorry, darling. These damn birds,' he'd laughed as he reassured me he'd be back tomorrow, he'd get an early start and leave in the afternoon so he could be home before dark. And I had a sudden stab of nostalgia for the life we'd left behind, so acute it hurt my chest.

It won't be long now, I tell myself as I wonder how I'll survive the night.

***

9:59pm

The power is off. It's been off since just after I microwaved a lonely bowl of leftover chicken korma. That's lucky, I suppose. The sky has since erupted, at one point sending sheets of rain past the windows so thick I couldn't see out, and while the fires must almost certainly be out as a result, the power still hasn't returned. We're probably not much of a priority, being way out here in the middle of nowhere.

It's cold, dark. Using the light from my phone, I found an unopened box of tea candles in the cupboard above the refrigerator, lit seven of them and arranged them around the kitchen. They've cast their eerie, dancing light on the walls and ceiling and it gives me the feeling of being surrounded by ghosts. I can't see anything across the water – obviously, with the power out – and my imagination runs wild, picturing all the horrors that could be just outside the window in the pitch blackness, so the curtains have been drawn, sealing me in.

My phone isn't working – no internet, and I can't send messages out – my texts to Adam bounce back with: *ERROR! MESSAGE NOT SENT*. For fuck's sake. There's not even reliable phone signal around here.

I can't help it. It's foolish, but I'm frightened. Or *is* it foolish? I'm in a run-down old house, alone, in the dark in the middle of the bush. Access – or escape – is boat-only, or a trek into the wilderness followed by a treacherous bridge-walk over the creek (which I now know should not be attempted at high tide) and the only other people for miles live across a deep body of water. Horror-movie material, if you think about it. Maybe it's perfectly natural to be frightened.

I feel a surge of anger towards Adam. How could he leave me here? How could he possibly have thought this was a good idea? And then I remember his offer of the short-stay in Sydney, and I remember why that's impossible, and I'm so frustrated I almost burst in to tears.

***

10:02pm

I can hear the roar of the ocean from all the way across town, and the distant whistle of a train. Sound travels at night, I suppose, and it's eerily quiet on this side of the water.

None of the across-the-creek residents have appeared

tonight; the three houses stand in darkness. There are squares of flickering light beyond them, in the windows of the houses further into town – families acting out their evening routines in candlelight, making dinner, tucking children into bed. It's a small comfort, seeing people going about their normal lives.

I think of Dee, of Erica and sweet little Ruby and wonder where everyone is. I feel terrible for the social faux pas I made and how my conversation with Erica ended. Perhaps she was in her rights to be cross. Maybe if more women felt able to speak their minds as she had, we'd have a better understanding of one another.

Having children isn't everything. Doing what I do for a living, I see how much harder it is for them with children, particularly for those in domestic-violence situations. Children complicate things. Complicate everything. Freedom as it was known prior is non-existent. That's why Mum left, I imagine. In a way I don't blame her.

I didn't really know my mum. She left when I was a baby, and my gentle dad raised me all on his own. I'm happy to see him settled down with Ruth now; she's a kind woman and he deserves to be taken care of after all he's sacrificed. I do wonder at times whether my aversion to having children stems not only from not having had a maternal influence, but from fear. What if I take after my mother? What if it's something innate? I couldn't live with myself if I abandoned my child. It would haunt me forever. Best just to avoid the possibility altogether.

An image of a child's face, not dissimilar to Ruby's appears in my mind and I shake my head against the guilt. I take another sip of wine. And then there's a spark in the darkness. My heart skips. It's Dee, lighting a candle. Her face is lit from beneath, her tangle of dark curls dangerously close to the flame.

I blow out the candle next to me and fumble for the binoculars. The smell of melted wax and smoke fills my nostrils as I press the cold metal to my eye sockets. I don't know why I'm doing this and I don't stop to think.

She's walking across the top floor, past the cot – it must be where she sleeps – *they* sleep. Is he there, the husband, Rob? Sleeping, perhaps? She disappears to the left. There's a staircase there, I think. The dancing light disappears for a few seconds and reappears on the bottom floor. I can see so much more through the binoculars, even in the feeble candlelight. It's a living area, bookshelves crammed with ornaments and books, a coffee table, an enormous wide-screen television. There's a vase of wilted flowers – roses, it looks like – on the coffee table.

Dee's crossing the room and I realise with a jolt that she's naked. Up close, I can see the contrast of her fair skin and dark hair. A straight, sharp nose. Almond eyes, full mouth. The image is so clear it's like I'm watching her under a microscope and, with a rush of shame, I yank the binoculars from my eyes.

What am I doing? This is sick. Sitting here in the dark spying on some poor woman. I take two large swallows of wine. I hunt in my dressing gown pocket for my pills and swallow one with another slug of wine. Stop. Shit. I've already taken one tonight, haven't I? I screw my eyes shut, trying to think, but I can't remember.

This place is sending me loopy. How did I end up in a loft watching the neighbours through a pair of my husband's dead father's binoculars? Sure, in our London flat we saw people through their windows all the time, but you didn't go looking for it. They were just *there*, airing laundry, cooking, fucking, arguing, watching television with their backs to the window. That was high-density living. That was east London.

This is different. Shaking my head, I retrieve the soft, crushed pack from between the cushions and light a cigarette. I'm practically a smoker again, what with Adam gone most of the day and nothing better to fill my time. I could read, of course. Candlelight would allow that. I could try to sleep, although the pills have yet to induce even a twinge of tiredness.

But I can't stop the memories coming, can't quell the restlessness in my bones, can't find a position that feels comfortable. So I finish my wine and smoke my cigarette, ignoring the flickering light in my peripheral vision.

And then I see it. Movement, just out of my line of sight. I turn my head to see a dark figure standing in Dee's doorway.

My breath catches. Who is that? Rob? There's something strange about the way he's standing. Something that makes my skin go cold. He – I know from the build it's a he – is standing perfectly still, a shadow in the open doorway. Dee's left a candle on the coffee table but there's not enough light and I'm too far away to see details.

My mind snags on a memory – earlier, the man watching her house. The beer bottles and campfire behind in the woods. Are the two connected?

Dee is nowhere to be seen. She must have gone to take a shower; I'm pretty sure the bathroom is on the top floor, on the right, and she was headed that way.

The figure stands, unmoving. I hesitate before grabbing the binoculars, searching blindly in the new close-up perspective for a moment before landing on the doorway. But there's no one there. I swing the binoculars sideways but the living room is empty. I swing upward but there's nothing else to see. The upstairs is pitch black.

There's a soft *thunk* and a *plink!* and suddenly the lights come back on. Momentarily blinded, I blink rapidly until my vision returns, lunge for the lamp switch and turn it off.

I peer through the binoculars again but there's no one in Dee's doorway. The house, from this perspective, appears to be empty. But if anyone is out there, there's no doubt they'll have seen me, watching.

Chapter 14

Liz

June, 2017
Wednesday 10:40pm

She's watching me, eyes bloodshot from lack of sleep, pupils deep like black pools. They are luminous eyes, almost like a child's, but her play at innocence doesn't fool me. There's something unsettling in them. Something dark. Her unwashed fringe hangs in clumps, obscuring her face as she shoves the bundle into my arms.

'Here. Hold her. I won't be a sec.'

She disappears, ostensibly to go to the bathroom but I suspect there's more to it than that. The bundle squirms in my arms and I feel a twitch of anger. How am I meant to help her when she won't help herself? Won't help her child?

I stand in the grubby kitchen with its cracked tiles and stained walls and the clock on the wall that says it is noon when it's morning. Sadness washes over me. What would it be like, to be here, alone? With this? I look down at the pale wisp of hair protruding from the blanket and cannot name what I'm feeling.

The kettle whistles and I jolt, startling the bundle in my arms. Her plaintive cry, now familiar, pierces the silence and instinctively I cradle her closer to my chest. With my free hand I lift the kettle from the stove then, using my elbow clear a space to set it down on the cluttered counter.

Over the acrid notes of smoke and filth, the smell of new life fills my nostrils. I bend down and inhale, and a primitive awareness brings goose bumps to my skin. I smile. The crying stops, and the downy, pink head turns until crystal-blue eyes blink up at me. Long lashes rest dark against skin so new I can see her veins. A hand appears, and tiny fingers, surprisingly strong, wrap around my thumb.

'Hello,' I whisper, charmed. She answers with a voluptuous giggle, and then I spot a mark – between her chest and her little rounded shoulder – and inhale sharply. It's a dark, purple thumb print, tinged yellow around the edges.

There's the sound of a toilet flushing and footsteps drawing near. Panic blossoms, and I clutch the precious bundle to my breast.

***

10:50pm

My senses return to me slowly. Cheek squashed against something musty and rough, mouth stale with smoke, I lift my head and groan. Shoving away the ratty old cushion, I gulp back a slug of water and blink out at the night.

The three rooftops across the creek are lit by silver light, and an answering glimmer paints ripples on the water's surface. Images of a nude Dee and a shadowy man seep into my consciousness, but I can't reconcile them with the darkness across the creek. The odd *plink* on the tin roof tells me the rain has dwindled, and the warm trickle of drool on my chin means I can't have been out long. Will I ever sleep properly again? I grapple with the thoughts that linger in between sleep and consciousness, and that's when I hear it.

Tap, tap, tap.

I frown and rub my eyes. Surely there can't be anyone at the door? I must be hearing things. But then,

Tap, tap, tap, tap, tap.

I sit upright, mind snaring on a hopeful thought. Adam! Maybe the road's been cleared and he's come home to surprise me. I check my phone – no missed calls, no messages. But then I remember there wasn't any signal earlier and – sure enough – there's only one flickering bar of signal now.

Tap, tap, tap, tap, tap, tap, tap.

Jumping up, I flick on the lamp and head downstairs. The stairs creak underfoot as I descend and my shadow dances on the wall. Has Adam forgotten his key? Or maybe it's not working. These locks are so old, my own key doesn't work half the time.

At the front door, I lift the blind on the little square window at the top.

'Adam?'

There's nothing out there but blackness pricked with stars.

I lean closer to the glass. 'Adam?'

Nothing. Just the clouds passing over the moon.

I open the door a crack, leaving the deadlock latched. Icy air rushes in, but there's no one to be seen. A cold feeling that has nothing to do with the night air steals through me. I close the door, turn the lock and am reaching up to draw the blind when a face appears at the window.

I stumble back with a shout. A white face stares at me and for a terrifying second I think I'm looking at a ghost. It's a moment before my brain makes sense of what I'm seeing and then I realise it's not a ghost. It's *her*.

'Oh gosh, it's you,' I gasp, clapping a hand to my chest.

Dee smiles and nods, an eager gesture, all big eyes and wild, dark hair. I make myself breathe before opening the door a fraction.

'Dee?'

'Yes, it's me. Sorry ... I know we've only met once, but I thought ...'

'No, no! Erm, it's fine. Are you okay?'

'I'm all right, I just ... Wait, Tim isn't in, is he?'

'Er, no. No, sorry. Adam's in Sydney I'm afraid and Tim, ah ... Tim passed away recently and we've come to tie up loose ends.'

Dee gasps. 'Oh! Oh, darling, I'm so sorry. How awful. Poor Adam. Poor you. Were you close to his dad?'

'To be honest I'd never met him. Adam and I only recently married.'

Dee nods and tilts her head. 'Oh, I see.'

It strikes me how odd it is to be having this conversation with a relative stranger through a crack in the door late at night. What on earth's possessed her to come across the creek so late at night to see someone she barely knows?

'How did you get over? Isn't the tide awfully high tonight?

'Yeah, but I've been boating this creek for years. And Rob's dinghy has a strong motor.' She smiles and I remember Pub Guy's comment about boat motors.

As I take in her pink cheeks and trembling lips, it dawns on me that she must be freezing. Appalled with myself, I unlatch the door and yank it open. 'I'm so sorry, you must think me terribly rude. Would you like to come in? I'm Liz, by the way.'

A grateful smile and a cold handshake. 'Yeah, thanks. Nice to meet you properly, Liz. And I'm the one who's sorry, showing up like this so late.' She shrugs off her coat and looks around for somewhere to put it. 'Is Adam home?'

I take her coat and hang it on the hat rack behind the door.

'No. As I said, he couldn't get back into town due to the road closure, so he's staying in Sydney tonight.'

She nods vaguely, looking around the cramped, dimly

lit hallway. 'It's so strange seeing it from the inside. Is that the kitchen through there?'

'Yes. Come through,' I say, turning on the kitchen light as I lead the way. The dining chair squeaks along the cheap linoleum as I pull it out and gesture for her to sit.

'Sorry, there isn't much room in here,' I say with an apologetic shrug.

'It's fine, I find it cosy.'

'It's a bit dilapidated, I'm afraid. Tim wasn't around much to maintain it, apparently. And then of course he got ill.'

'Oh yeah, right. I think I vaguely remember something about him being ill. Poor old thing. So have you moved here now, or did you say you were just passing through ...?'

'Just passing through. We're actually selling the place.'

Dee's eyes widen. 'Ooh, you should get a good price then. I guess you'd know that they're planning to put in a road and a bridge to Sandbar, that big town over that way,' she gestures to the back of the house. 'It's got a train line straight to Sydney. They're going to sell these places for a mint. Prices are skyrocketing at the moment, what with so many people moving up from Sydney and that train line coming in. That and the view, of course.'

'Yes,' I smile, 'That's what we're counting on.' I refrain from mentioning that, if the real estate agent is to be believed, we're certain to get an almost inconceivable sum for this run-down old place.

'So ... what part of England are you from?'

'London, East. Adam and I met there, where we both lived at the time. We'll be going back once the sale goes through.'

'I've always wanted to go to London,' Dee sighs. 'But we never got around to it. And now, with the baby, and everything going on ... I don't think we'll ever make it.' She seems to catch herself, ducking her head with a shy smile. 'You must think I'm super weird showing up here like this.'

'No ... well ... Are you ... is everything all right?'

Up close, I can see the toll the sleepless nights have taken in the sunken hollows of her eyes and in her tangled hair, though it does little to diminish her beauty. Every part of her is full, and the roundness makes her appear youthful. She has the kind of beauty you can't help but admire, that larger-than-life quality that leaves you a little awe-struck.

She shrugs and gives a funny little laugh. 'I'm all right. I saw lights on across the creek and thought I'd pop over and say hi ... You've been staying here, haven't you? I didn't know you were Tim's wife. I thought Tim's wife had run off with a Frenchman!' She claps a hand over her mouth. 'Sorry, that was a shitty thing to say.'

'Er ... I'm *Adam's* wife. Tim's son, Adam?' Strange, I think, to be confusing what happened between Adam's parents with Adam and me.

Dee blinks slowly and it's then I realise she's more than slightly drunk. 'Right, of course. The old man. I'm so sorry about that, by the way.'

'It's okay. Like I said, I'd never met him. And he and Adam didn't really get along, so ...' I shrug. 'Would you like a coat or something?'

'No, it's nice and toasty in here. Honestly, I was just after some ... company.'

I recall the loneliness I sensed in her, even from afar, and I can't help but wonder where her baby is.

'Well,' I say. 'I could use some company myself. Can I offer you something to drink? Tea? Wine?'

Dee relaxes back in her seat and gives me a warm smile. 'I'd love some wine, thanks.'

'Red or white?'

'White.'

I pour our drinks and hand her one and she grins and winks and clinks her glass with mine. 'Cheers.'

'Cheers!'

We sip and smile, and it feels nice having someone to share this space with. I was letting my imagination run away with me, jumping at shadows, but Dee's energy fills the room and warms it.

'I couldn't handle her tonight,' she says conversationally, apparently at her ease with glass-in-hand.

'Who?' I ask, already knowing.

'Ruby. My sweet little baby.' Her smile is tinged with sadness but there's a light in her eyes I've seen more than once before. That fierce, proud love, at once warming and overwhelming. The thought of ever having to feel it terrifies me.

'Sometimes she just screams and screams and it's all I can do not to tear my hair out.'

'It can be tough, having a little one.'

Dee's eyes flick to mine, suddenly alert. 'You have kids?'

'Um, no.'

'Oh,' her eyes turn dull. She chuckles darkly. 'You're cleverer than I am, then.'

'Is she in bed?' I ask, to change the subject.

'Ruby? Oh, yes, she'd have been in bed ages ago. She's over with Erica tonight.'

'Erica's your neighbour?'

Dee nods and I can't help thinking once again how strange it is for Erica to be minding Ruby's child after the fight I witnessed.

'Oh. Is your husband ... away?'

Dee's wine glass pauses on its way to her mouth.

'Sorry, I wasn't assuming you have a ... It's just Adam mentioned your ... um, I think he said his name is Rob?'

Dee takes a deliberate sip, her eyes not quite meeting mine. When she speaks again, her tone is flat. 'Yes. Rob's away on business. He left last week.'

'Oh, okay.' I take a nervous gulp of wine, my mind whirring. If Rob's not been around since Adam and I arrived, who was the man in the doorway? And where did the black eye come from? Although to be fair, it could be a week or so old if it was a bad one. It's almost invisible now. 'That must be tough, having to take care of Ruby all alone.'

'Yes,' she says vaguely, still in that flat tone. She seems suddenly weary. 'Very tough.'

Concerned by the direction of the conversation, I clear my throat. 'Ruby's very beautiful. She looks like you.'

Dee smiles, then. 'Thank you. She's such an angel. I don't deserve her.'

'Oh, I'm sure that isn't true.'

Dee sighs. 'It is.' She stares into the middle distance for a moment before shaking her head and sipping her wine. 'Want to see some photos?'

Without waiting for an answer, she takes out her phone and takes me through a reel of photos from newborn to recent.

'Look at those little booties,' she chuckles, pointing. 'Erica made them for her.'

Erica, again.

'She must be very fond of her then.'

There's a pause before Dee replies. 'Yes. Very.' I can't read her tone, but there's something off about it.

'Is she ... a good friend to you?'

Dee sighs. 'Yes. My only one, in fact. Slim pickings around here,' she shrugs, her expression inscrutable.

'Well, I'm glad you came to visit then. It's pretty lonely over this side.'

We smile at each other, and then our attention turns back to the baby photos.

'Gosh, she's so lovely. Picture perfect.'

Dee's eyes are moist and soft with adoration as she gazes

at the photo of her baby. While she may be struggling, being alone so much, it's crystal clear that she's in love with her child.

Suddenly her expression changes. She eyes me strangely. 'Hang on. How did you know what Ruby looks like? Have you been watching us?' Her words are direct, without preamble.

'Oh gosh, n-no,' I stammer the lie. 'We've met before, remember? At the pub? I know it was only briefly ... but, as I said, I also ran into Erica yesterday. She had Ruby with her.'

Dee exhales and shakes her head. 'Right, of course. Sorry. How stupid of me. This place can get to you, can't it? Make you paranoid.'

An unexpected shiver moves through me. I wonder whether I remembered to bolt the door. 'Yes. I have noticed that.'

'I suppose you're wondering about the bruise, then?' Again, her tone is conversational, but with an edge. 'I would be.'

'I hadn't really noticed.' I cringe inwardly as Dee chuckles; even I could hear how feeble that lie was.

'Walked into a door, didn't I?' she smirks, looking me in the eye as if daring me to challenge her. Then she shrugs, throwing back a slug of wine. I refill her glass and she gulps back half of that too. 'I'm teasing. Let's just call it ... a lover's tiff.'

My stomach sinks. 'Someone did this to you?'

Dee shrugs, swirling her wine.

'You know, if they did ... you can tell me.'

'Oh, for fuck's sake, really? I barely know you.'

We both freeze and Dee claps a hand over her mouth. Her eyes are wide. 'I'm sorry. I don't know what made me say that. And like I can talk, showing up here to a virtual stranger's house like a total loon. But it's not ... that's not what's wrong.'

'Okay. So what *is* wrong?'

Dee sips, peering at me over the rim of the glass. 'It's just ... well, to be honest, things have been getting the better of me lately. Rob's been ...' she trails off, lowering her glass. Her teeth worry her lower lip.

Remembering my training, I say, 'If you're in any kind of trouble, don't be afraid to say. Maybe I can help. I've had some experience with this sort of thing, you know.'

To my horror, Dee presses a hand over her mouth and lets out a strangled sob.

I stand so quickly my chair clatters to the floor and place my hand on her shoulder. 'It's okay. It's okay. Listen, Dee. I want you to answer a question for me. Do you feel safe at home?'

Dee hiccup-sobs and wipes her nose with the back of her hand. When she looks up at me, her eyes gleam with tears. She whispers one word. 'No.'

My senses go on alert. Is she lying about Rob? Is it him she's frightened of, or is it someone else?

'You know, you don't have to go back there if you don't

want to. Shall we go and get Ruby, and you can bring her back here to stay?'

'No,' she says, shaking her head fiercely. 'She's safer with Erica. And I couldn't bear it if anything happened to her. She's my baby. My *baby*.'

I'm about to question what she thinks might happen when her phone pings. She snatches it from the table and scans the screen with desperate eyes.

'Dee?'

'I have to go.'

'But, wait!' I place my hand over hers. 'What are you afraid of?'

Dee looks like a deer caught in the headlights. She stands quickly, tucking her phone into her jeans pocket. 'I have to go.'

'Was it the man in your doorway?'

She stops and looks at me over her shoulder, her face pinched and pale. 'What man?' she whispers.

'There was someone – a man – in your doorway earlier this evening. And then he just vanished. I'm sorry, I wasn't watching, but it caught my eye when you lit a candle and I couldn't help but see.'

'What did he look like?'

I shake my head. 'I ... I don't know. It was quite dark. I just saw a silhouette in the doorway. The one on the left side of the house from this perspective. I think ... I assume it's your front door?'

Dee's staring into space, nodding. 'Yes. But I always lock it,' she murmurs, almost to herself.

'Please, Dee. If you're in any kind of trouble, you don't need to go home.'

She clasps my hand and squeezes so hard her knuckles whiten and I almost pull away. 'I'm sorry.' She looks at me, lips pressed firm. Resolute. 'But I have to.'

And as she leaves, she does the strangest thing. She kisses me, her lips ice-cold against my cheek.

Chapter 15

Liz

June, 2017
Thursday, 2:15am

'I told you, I don't have time at the moment,' I say, my throat tight with frustration. It's not that I don't have compassion for the woman, but she's the cause of most of her own issues as far as I can gather, and I am already extremely far behind on my work. She shouldn't have just shown up here. That's crossing a line.

'Please,' she grabs my arm and a surge of anger fills me. 'I need your help.'

I shake her hand away and turn my back.

'No. PLEASE!'

***

I jerk awake, heart pounding. My skin is damp with sweat.

'PLEASE!' The shout comes followed by a high-pitched shriek.

I'm not dreaming, I realise as my eyes adjust to the dark. *The scream was real.*

I sit up and reach out for Adam before remembering he's not here. I peer at my phone – 2:15am – throw on my dressing gown and ascend the loft stairs two at a time. As I reach the landing, there's a clap of thunder and a millisecond later lightning streaks across the sky, illuminating the room. I shriek and skid on the floorboards in my slippers. Steadying myself, I rush across the loft and clamber onto the daybed.

I stare out into the darkness, listening. Nothing. I jiggle the window in its frame to loosen it, slide it open an inch and press my ear to the gap. The storm seems to have been a flash in the pan, because apart from the roar and churn of the king tide retreating, and the light of the full moon reflected on the water, all is dark and still.

Until a light blinks on across the creek, just to the right of Dee's house.

I fumble for the binoculars. A tall, solid figure is walking between Dee's house and the Haddads's house, dragging something along the ground. I squint and adjust the focus, but it doesn't zoom in any closer. Shit. Who are they and what are they carrying this late at night?

The figure hauls the bag over their shoulder with some

difficulty, and their body is turned towards me just as they disappear behind the Haddads's house. I recognise the face at once.

Samir.

Chapter 16

Dee

April, 2017
Friday, 5:52pm

The lights appear as we reach the top of the mountain. Brave Cove is a small town, really, but from up here it could almost be a city. I'm reminded of the buzz and glow of my Sydney days and feel the loss of a life left behind. Rob's eyes are on me, but I don't look at him. Ruby stirs and grizzles in her car-seat; the smell of baby shit wafts through the car and the spell is broken.

It's our anniversary. We haven't been to Pearls since before Ruby was born, and the gesture means Rob's trying, and I'm grateful. Because I've been on at him about how *suffocated* I feel cooped up with a four-month-old, and he's pretended to understand. He admits I 'do it all' but deep down I know – oh, no matter what he says I *know* – that's the way he thinks it should be.

But then tonight he looked at me with that old twinkle, and I could almost remember a time when I knew what sleep and sanity were, could almost forget my transgressions, the ever-present fear, and for a moment there was a spark of hope. But then Rob's mum got sick and couldn't mind Ruby, and now Ruby's fussy (she's always fussy), she's soiled her nappy twice and is overdue a feed.

We arrive late and Rob's smile is forced. The young waitress looks at me with my untidy hair, engorged breasts and tummy bulge with a mixture of pity and disgust and I want to tell her I was like her, once, and I didn't actually want this and I didn't ask for it and who the hell does she think she is?

But it's not her I hate, really. It's Rob. Because she's me a handful of years ago, and he's smiling at her the way he used to smile at me, while I'm struggling with a breastfeeding cover. *He* did this to me. *He* wanted this. So who the hell is he to sit there gawking at a pretty girl while I feed his child? It's as though *I* am the one responsible for the loss of the old days when, really, I wanted to stay there. I would have been happy to stay there.

But it isn't his fault. It's mine. I've done this, and I've trapped myself and I've doomed us both. And there's nothing anyone can do about it.

They're still talking and I'm battling the Velcro on the breastfeeding cover and Ruby's grizzling has reached the peak of its ascent, and I swear – *'Shit!'* – and the perky waitress glares and I've had enough so I throw the fucking feeding cover on the floor, yank down the strap of my dress and affix Ruby to my nipple. She sucks greedily and relief flows through me and for a moment there is peace and my mind is quiet. And then I realise they're all staring: the childless couple at the next table, the waiter walking past with a tray of champagne flutes, the man at the lectern by the door.

Our waitress smiles stiffly. 'May I take your order, *madam*?'

'I'm a bit busy,' I say between clenched teeth. 'Give me a minute?'

A silver-haired woman passes us, startling as she clocks my bare breast. 'Well, really,' she mutters under her breath.

'Sorry, what was that?' I say in a loud voice.

The woman scowls. 'You know there are appropriate *facilities* for that.'

I cock my head. 'I'm sorry, I thought I was using the appropriate *facilities*.' I look down at my breast. I smile.

The woman scowls and shuffles off. I take a slug of wine and bitterly relish in the widening of several pairs of eyes. 'Off you go then, old prude!'

Rob's eyes hold a warning glint. 'That was a bit rude, Dee.'

'Madam,' says our waitress, red-faced. 'This restaurant has strict policies. If you don't comply, I'm afraid I'm going to have to ask you to leave.'

'Are you serious?' I am furious. Humiliated. 'You can't ask me to *leave* because I'm bloody breastfeeding.'

Ruby senses my distress and tiny fists beat at my chest. Fire burns behind my ribs.

'Dee ...' Rob starts but when I glare, he shuts up.

'It's not that, madam. We have a strict dress code and behaviour policies; if you don't comply we'll have to ask you to vacate—'

'And if you don't let me feed my child, *I'm* going to have to ask *you* to *get fucked*,' I spit.

The girl gasps and I feel a burst of satisfaction.

Silence echoes and before anyone can react, Rob's grabbing my elbow and I'm being pulled along with Ruby on my hip and my left breast hanging out, and when we burst out into the cold night air I realise Rob isn't muttering under his breath. He's laughing.

***

8:20pm

Ruby's asleep; she passed out during the drive home. It's blissfully quiet, but there's chaos inside me. I swear at my shoes as I kick them across the bedroom, wrestle off my too-tight dress, fling my bra and underpants across the room. I stand, shoulders heaving. Livid.

Rob's in the doorway. I catch his eyes and recognise that spark and my chest fills in a way it hasn't in months.

'Dee ...' His eyes run down my body, then back up again to meet mine.

'What?'

'Delilah.' His voice is hoarse; he sounds broken. His eyes hold mine. 'You're still magnificent.'

My heart's thumping. I wait for him to come to me, as he used to. Three seconds, four. But just as I think he'll step forward and open his arms, a shadow passes over his face, as if he's remembered something. He turns away and walks from the room.

In the ensuing silence, I wonder about my husband, whose mildness I once mistook for compassion, until that loaded word sinks in. *You're still magnificent.*

Still.

Chapter 17

Liz

June, 2017
Thursday, 6:15am

It's dark although it's morning and I've barely slept – this day-bed is a bit worse for wear, but I've reached the point where it's futile to keep trying. I kept dreaming and waking, grasping at thoughts that refused to be caught. For a moment I think I'm back in our flat in London, and I reach out for the water bottle I keep beside the bed. But my hand connects with the cold, hard wall and I'm tossed back into the present.

I stare at the ceiling. My memory of last night is foggy; I think I took an extra dose of pills by mistake, but snippets from Dee's visit and the scream I heard reverberate around in my mind. The scream was real, wasn't it? I ran to the loft, but when I looked out of the window, no one was there. Until Samir showed up, that is.

It's possible someone was just frightened by the storm, and the scream was nothing more than that. Pub Guy probably has an endless stream of backpackers in and out of his bedroom, I think with a twinge of something I don't care to examine. I rub my eyes and sigh. But someone yelled *please*, didn't they? Or was that part of a dream?

The more I think about it, the less sense it all makes. Why would Dee come out here in the dark in the middle of the night to talk to a complete stranger? Unless she was expecting to find Tim? She did seem surprised to see me, and that Tim had died. I found it odd she didn't know that already. Isn't news supposed to travel fast in small towns? Then again, Erica hadn't known either.

And there are other factors that don't make sense. Would she really have risked coming across during a king tide, just for some company? It would have been so dangerous to cross the creek, even by boat, if Pub Guy is to be believed. It all seems so unlikely, and yet I can still feel the brush of her cold lips against my cheek as she said goodbye. And I can't shake the image of that unreadable expression in her eyes. For a moment I think it might have been pity, but why should she pity me? Most likely it's my own emotions reflected back to me. That's what got me in all that trouble in the first place.

But then there was Samir coming out of Dee's house ... Why would my mind conjure that up? What could he have been dragging that was so large and cumbersome?

A body, my brain whispers, and with that thought I throw back the covers and stumble out of bed. One thing I know for certain. I have to get out of this house.

***

9:50am

The air is like ice in my lungs. It's a shock – I didn't count on it getting this cold in Australia – and it wakes me up, propels me forward. I haven't eaten and my morning coffee is sloshing in my stomach with every step.

As I approach Cockle Street, a short woman is bustling towards me, arms folded across her chest, short blonde hair fluttering in the breeze like bird's feathers. It's a moment before I recognise her, and as I do, she's already passing me.

'Erica?'

The woman's head whips around. She stops, looks at me, and tilts her head to the side. She clearly has no idea who I am, even though we met just the other day.

Her hand is at her mouth, stubby fingers tapping at her chin. The nails have been chewed to the quick.

'Sorry! I'm Liz. We met the other day, remember ...?'

Erica appears agitated, her eyes darting over my shoulder. I turn around, but there's nothing there.

'Are you all right?'

I move towards her, but she rears up like as if under attack and, instinctively, I step back again.

'I'm sorry,' she mutters, eyes downcast. 'I'm in a hurry. I have to go.'

Her eyes connect with mine briefly before flitting away as she strides past me. I watch her walk the length of Cockle Street and then disappear around the corner.

I shake my head as I continue down the road. She *is* a strange one. The image of Samir outside Dee's house flashes in my mind, and I wonder if Erica's odd behaviour has anything to do with her husband.

Looking up at Dee's house now, grand and tall, windows reflecting the morning sunshine, I can almost imagine the whole of last night was a dream. This place is doing things to me. It's the isolation. The cabin fever. It's spending a night without Adam, without his gentle calm, waking alone in this place. I can't face the thought of sorting through the junk in the cellar today, can't fathom diving into the ocean of forbidden emails in my inbox, the endless Messenger check-ins from concerned 'friends', so I'm fixating on Dee and the baby. It's perfectly natural. Especially after what happened before.

Still. Dee had a bruise on her eye she didn't properly explain. And she seemed afraid. I'm certain I didn't imagine that. And then there was the man I saw – who, apparently, couldn't be Rob as he's away. Could she be lying? Protecting him, perhaps?

I hesitate only briefly before approaching the house. If Dee was in danger and I didn't bother to check, I'd never forgive myself.

I tread tentatively up the stairs to the porch, stepping over a child's rattle and a lone high-heeled shoe to reach the door. Strange to leave just one shoe there like that. It gives the impression that it has been abandoned in a hurry.

There's no doorbell, so I knock on the door and wait. When no one appears, I try once more but, again, there's no response. Not even a peep or the creak of a floorboard from within.

The door handle is an old-fashioned brass knob, embossed with a geometric art-deco motif. Quite pretty really, but somehow at odds with the rest of the architecture. Without quite knowing why, I reach out and place my hand over it. The metal is ice-cold and gives under my hand. The door opens inwards slightly, and I realise it's off the latch. Odd. Didn't Dee say she's always sure to lock her doors?

'Hello?' I call, pushing the door open further and poking my head through the gap. 'Is anybody here?'

I think I hear a faint creak, but it could just be the house settling. I step tentatively around the door and find myself in the living room. It *is* strange, as Dee said, to find yourself looking at the place from inside, and from the opposite perspective to how you usually see it. I get a funny sense of déjà vu as my gaze touches upon the familiar objects – the rows of book shelves, the vase on the coffee table. I have the strange sense of having entered the set of a play I've been watching, only to find the actors have left the stage.

To the left must be the stairs leading to the upstairs bedroom, I think, and across the other side of the living room must be the kitchen or the bathroom. There isn't a window facing the water on that side, so it's hard to say.

I step further into the room and, sure enough, to the left of the giant bookcase, is a short passageway. Beyond it, the first two steps of a polished wooden staircase are visible.

The creak sounds again, louder this time, followed by several more. They're coming closer. *Someone's on the stairs.*

'Hello?' I call, not wanting to startle whoever it is.

The creaks stop.

A funny little shiver moves through me.

'Hello?' I call again. 'It's only Liz from across the creek. I just wanted to check ...' I trail off. What if it isn't Dee? 'Erm. I just wanted to check that everything's okay.'

There's no response, and the silence gives me a chill. Why isn't whoever it is answering? I step backwards slowly until I'm back in the doorway. I'm about the clear the threshold when something clamps onto my shoulder.

I shriek and whirl around, my heart hammering in my chest. It's a moment before I collect myself enough to realise who I'm looking at.

'What are you doing?' Samir asks. His voice is deep and gruff; it's the first time I've heard him speak.

'I'm, uh ... I just wanted to come and check on Dee.'

'Ever heard of knocking?' Samir looks at me with large, dark eyes that give nothing away.

I give a nervous laugh. 'Yes, of course, and I *did* knock but no one answered.'

His answering silence makes me uncomfortable, yet I find I can't stop staring at his unusual eyes; the deepest of browns flecked with gold. He is actually quite a handsome man. Or at least he would be, if he had any manners.

'She must be out,' I say. 'I'll … I'll come back again later.'

In my eagerness to get away, I don't mention that I heard someone inside. Whoever it was didn't seem to want to be bothered, anyway.

Without saying goodbye, I scurry down the driveway, leaving Samir standing on Dee's front porch. As I reach the footpath I spot a figure across the road. The same scruffy-looking man standing in the same spot as yesterday. He turns his head and catches me looking. He winks and I turn and hurry away.

***

10:31am

The wind has picked up and has turned the air ice-cold, so I decide to skip the rest of my walk and head back to the house.

I've just cleared the bridge – low tide, safer – when a shadow crosses my path. I let out an involuntary shout, stumbling as I reach a sudden halt.

'Sorry, sorry.'

I look up and see a man – a mess of brown hair and

electric blue eyes. The guy from the pub. The zing of adrenalin fades and I bend over, hands on thighs, catching my breath.

'Scared you again,' the gravelly voice says with a hint of amusement.

'Yes. Thanks for that.' I push a damp strand of hair back from my cheek and run the back of my hand across my sweaty brow. I meet his gaze. 'What are you doing over here?'

There's the hint of a smirk on Pub Guy's lips. What on earth is so funny? Is he deliberately trying to intimidate me for whatever stupid, male reason?

'Oysters.'

'I'm sorry?'

'I'm collecting the traps.' He stretches out a brown, muscled arm and points to the mangroves growing amongst the rocks on the muddy shore. Occasionally, there's a hint of silver glinting in the murky water. Oyster traps.

'Ah. Okay.'

'Pub speciality. They thrive here in the creek; it's the best place to farm them. They pay me extra to lay the traps and collect them. Not many people willing to venture over this side of the creek. Not many *sane* people, anyway.' He looks me right in the eye, irises like lasers, and I stare back before glancing quickly away.

'I'm Zac, by the way.' He extends a muddied hand and I hesitate before taking it. His skin is warm and rough.

'Elizabeth. Liz.'

'Nice to meet you, Liz. Officially, that is. See you didn't take my advice about the creek.'

'The tide won't be coming in for a while yet,' I say, defensive.

He stares some more, making a strange grunting sound. 'Try the boat.'

'I don't know how.'

'Your boyfriend didn't show you?'

'Husband. And ... well, no. He didn't. But he told me about the footbridge. I suppose he thought that would be easier.'

Zac grunts, an indecipherable sound. I look at him, but his expression is neutral. It's then I notice a bulky, black plastic bag at his side.

'What are you looking for? I thought the oysters were over that side.'

'I'm ...' He stops and looks down into the water as if looking for the answer. 'Rubbish. You know, that sort of thing.'

I get the sense he's hiding something. Shaking away the feeling, I tell myself he's probably just fishing illegally or something equally harmless and stupid. I imagine the local fishermen wouldn't be too happy about him stealing their fish.

'Right. Okay.'

He exhales harshly. 'Sometimes people camp out here – illegally, right? – and they tend to chuck things in the creek. I do a bit of maintenance for the area – mowing, fixing bits and pieces, grounds-keeping, you know the sort of thing. One of my jobs is to trawl the creek for rubbish. Satisfied?'

There's something about the way he looks at me that makes my heart skip. Whether in fear or excitement I'm not sure. I've learned the two can be very closely linked.

'There can be some weirdos around,' he goes on. 'Not this time of year usually – it's too cold – but it's not unheard of for campers to set up illegally over here. We've had a lot of trouble with them lately. People who come over the mountain, wayward kids, drunks, druggies, trouble-makers. There's no one over this side, usually, you see. They think they can get away with it.'

The sweat on my skin has cooled and I rub my hands over my arms. 'Yes, I did see some ... *evidence* of that, the other day.'

'You see? I'm not trying to scare you. Just letting you know the score. What are you doing over here all alone, anyway?'

'I'm not alone,' I say quickly, forcing a smile. 'My husband's with me.'

Zac doesn't smile back. 'Is he? Can't see him.'

I frown. I don't like his tone, his *implication*. 'He's working down in Sydney. We're staying for a few weeks then we're heading back home, to London.'

Zac's answering silence riles me. What is it with the men in this town? 'He was trapped outside of town last night,' I feel the need to add. 'Because of the fires.'

'Right,' Zac nods, his expression giving nothing away. 'Well, if you're ever in trouble, give me a yell. I'm just across the creek.' He pauses, holding my gaze. 'If you scream loudly enough, I'll hear you.' And with that he flashes me a grin and trudges off, boots squelching over the sodden carpet of leaves.

It takes me a while to find my pace again. My heart's beating out a funny rhythm. Who does he think he is? And why does he get to me? Is he being funny, or should I be wary of him? I hate that I have to wonder.

Angrily swatting at twigs and vines, I emerge with relief from the damp, mangrove scrub and into the clearing outside Tim's house. There's a freshness to the air now; not a trace of smoke, nothing to indicate that yesterday the landscape was ravaged by fire, then flood, other than the occasional puddle.

A little thrill runs through me. Adam will be home tonight.

***

6:45pm

The power's been intermittent since the storm but I think it's staying on at last. I could do a little dance of relief! And Adam will be here any minute, which has me giddy with excitement.

I sit in the kitchen, which is the warmest room in the house thanks to it being so small and readily heated by the ancient Aga. From my position by the sink, I can see all three houses bathed in moonlight. Both Zac and Samir are hunched over dining tables having solitary dinners – I can tell Zac's is a TV dinner, even without binoculars – but Dee and Ruby are nowhere to be seen.

I sip my wine and run my fingers through my carefully blow-dried hair. I'm wearing lingerie underneath my favourite silk robe and have turned up the heat on the Aga, and in the bedroom, just in case.

As I sip and wait, Erica appears behind Samir and leans in to give him a hug. It's the first time I've seen her show him any affection. I do worry that Dee hasn't shown up, but it's hard to think of much else when I'm bursting out of my skin for Adam to come home.

***

7:25pm

I'm in Adam's arms the second he's through the door. 'Darling girl!' he peppers kisses all over my face before landing one right on my lips. 'God, I've missed you. What a shitty twenty-four hours that was.'

'I couldn't agree more,' I murmur into his neck, inhaling his familiar, comforting smell.

Adam steps back, his face alight with mischief. 'Hang on,' he says, disappearing back into the hallway. He returns with a flourish, brandishing a bunch of flowers – cheap, service station ones, but never mind – and wearing the most ridiculous grin.

'Happy anniversary!' he declares.

'What?' I giggle as he draws me to his chest and nuzzles my neck before kissing me long and slow. 'Mmmm,' I sigh. 'Not that I'm complaining – these are lovely, thank you – but what anniversary are we celebrating exactly? It was our year anniversary last month and we've been married only three and a half weeks!'

I take the flowers and look in the cupboards for a vase.

'It's a different sort of anniversary,' he says, waggling his eyebrows. 'It's a year since we first ... *you know*.'

'What? What other anniversary do we ... *Oh*.'

Having found a vase, I focus on arranging the flowers, but I know I'm turning pink. Even though my cynical side says this is all a bit cheesy and over the top, inwardly I'm thrilled. Adam has a way of making me feel like the only woman in the world, and while it's taking some getting used to, I can't say I mind it one bit.

'You're adorable when you blush,' Adam whispers in my ear, planting kisses down my neck.

'Stop it,' I whisper, sighing with pleasure.

'Do you remember having to stop five times so we could make out on the way back from the restaurant?' He bites my earlobe gently and I gasp. 'And my flat was only a five-minute walk away!'

'Do people still say "make out" these days?' I shiver as his hands slide up my waist towards my breasts.

Adam chuckles. 'Why don't you tell me, you young thing.'

I turn and kiss Adam urgently, my fingers in his hair, and he presses against me with a moan. I shrug off my robe and reach for him again, but he grasps my shoulders and holds me at arm's length.

'Wow,' he murmurs, his eyes moving over my body, lingering on every scrap of lace and exposed skin. If I weren't so aroused I'd have laughed at his naked admiration.

'Less looking, more touching,' I urge.

Adam's eyes lift to meet mine and they're sparkling with passion and mischief. 'Can't I do both?'

***

It's only once we've been holding each other for several minutes, our breathing slowing, skin cooling, that I register that I'm on the kitchen counter.

I giggle. 'That was ... unexpected.'

Adam lifts his head and gives me a lazy grin, his eyes still slightly glazed. 'Mmm. It was amazing.'

'Oh God,' I clap a hand over my mouth. 'I hope I wasn't terribly loud. Sound really travels across the water.'

'You were. As usual.' He winks and kisses me, lips moving languidly down my throat.

I let my head fall back to rest against the window pane, and when I tilt to the right I can see the only light still on across the creek is Zac's. He's standing in the window, staring out.

I shiver, suddenly cold.

If you scream loud enough, I'll hear you.

Chapter 18

Dee

May, 2017
Saturday, 5:14pm

The envelope trembles between my fingers. It makes a satisfying rip as I tear it in half, but I know it won't stop more coming. I peer out of the letterbox slot to see if he's back, but the street is empty.

Whenever an envelope arrives, I am quick to snatch it up before Rob sees it. It's my mess, and I'll be damned if I let him get involved. We're on shaky ground as it is and finding out just how deep the hole I've dug myself is would drain whatever remains of his respect for me.

Although I know it's irrational, I'm annoyed at Rob about what's happened. I'd done a pretty good job of cutting ties with my past, but his social media obsession would have made it pretty easy for me to be tracked down. He toned it down for a bit, when I asked him to, but it was the photo of us as 'proud home-owners' that would have given me away. It was only up for a bit – I made him take it down as soon as I spotted it – but that's all it would have taken. Oyster Creek is a small town and the photo showed our home in all its glory. You'd only have to come to town and drive around for a bit to find us. But I can't blame Rob really, of course. You can't live the kind of life I've lived and escape scot-free.

It feels like everything is unravelling. My mistakes are coming back to haunt me and I keep thinking of the past, and where I might have picked up the thread. If I could choose one moment in time to return to, when would it be? When did it all start? Or was it always inevitable that I would end up right here?

I'd certainly never have said yes the night Gus asked me to be his main girl. I'd have walked out of that seedy bar and found myself a nice waitressing job. Or any other job, really. It makes me shudder to think what my life would be like now if I'd stayed with him. And yet he's still managing to terrorise me from afar. Making his problems mine. Gambling was always the greatest of his many vices. And now he's in debt so deep they're using me to get to him. Unless one of us comes up with the money, I can only imagine what might happen. And I can't let anything bad happen – to me, and most of all to Ruby. I'll do anything to make sure she's safe.

***

My mind often likes to revisit the night I first met Rob, especially when there's tension between us. It's a hopeful sort of story, I suppose, or at least it was at the beginning. I owe him a lot. If it weren't for him, I might never have got out of there.

We met at a strip club – romantic, I know. I worked there, so I'm not one to judge. Rob was dragged there by friends, you know the type. It's all just a bit of fun, a standard alcohol-fuelled lad's night out, and there's always the guy who'll suggest it. The same guy, usually. Or a couple of them, egging each other on. I know their kind all too well. They're the ones in the front row, eating wings and buying rounds of shots, red-nosed and laughing too loud as they watch and sweat. The first to proclaim their girlfriend / wife / partner's 'cool with it' (real talk: she's *not*), the first to decree it a man's right, a basic need. The first to rate a woman he 'wouldn't touch' when you know five minutes later he's getting off in a bathroom stall, mind crammed with images of her.

Rob wasn't – isn't – like that. You think I wouldn't know if he was? But there are parts of him, parts put together by other men, by women, by society, that can't be fixed. I can see it in him now; the disappointment in his eyes, the disdain. The judgement. What is that saying? They want a lady in the street but a whore in the bedroom? Well, you can't have your cake and eat it too. I think he knows that now. Or, at least, he suspects it.

Even still, back then Rob was something new. A

revelation. A type I hadn't seen before, and one I didn't know existed. Not where I was from, anyway. And certainly not in the middle of a strip club on a Friday night.

My future husband sat nursing a glass of soda water while his mates grew steadily rowdier around him. I noticed him, staring into his drink, paying attention to his phone rather than the stage.

I was fascinated, curious, and somehow knowing he'd say no, I asked him if he wanted a lap dance. He just smiled and said he'd rather talk. And I thought *bullshit. What kind of line is this*? But that's what we did. Talk. For two and a half hours, and then an hour more in the parking lot outside. And then at dinner the next night.

Apparently, he was getting over some girl at the time, hence his mates' generous gesture of hauling him into a den of naked women, as apparently this is the antidote to male heartbreak. He never expected to meet someone, but from the moment our eyes met, he said he knew he'd found himself there for a reason.

He's the only one who's ever seen *me*. Beyond the mask. I suppose I never thought I deserved him. And maybe I proved myself right. You let people treat you how you think you deserve to be treated. That was always my problem. Still is. Men were always attracted to me for the wrong reasons, and I suppose I ended up placing my worth in men's hands, giving them too much power. Which is funny, because I always thought I was taking the power back, doing what I did. Exploiting their weaknesses for my own gain. But you grow up thinking you're nothing but a piece of meat and voila! That's what you become.

Rob treated me with respect, in the beginning. He still does, I suppose, but there's a distance – like he's on the other side of a growing chasm that I don't have the energy to jump. I feel him slipping further and further away and I find myself yearning for the days when it was just him and me. Before I'd let old habits interfere in our happiness, when we existed in a bubble of lazy Saturday mornings in bed, foot rubs, daily sex, restaurants and bars and pubs and picnics. Early morning hikes and moonlit swims. God, I had it so good. How did I not understand that before it was too late?

It's been different since Ruby. Sometimes I'm convinced he knows what I've done. I find my phone in places I haven't left it and wonder what he's seen.

I'm afraid. Afraid of what's coming. Every time I see a car parked outside the house, someone I don't recognise standing across the road, I panic.

I'll see *him* in the street, and he'll nod in greeting, lips curved in a grim smile, and hope he'll keep our secret.

I hear them fighting next door, muffled shouts through the wall, and I wonder if it has anything to do with me.

Chapter 19

Liz

June, 2017
Saturday, 7:34pm

It's been three days since Dee's impromptu visit when I'm woken by a sharp wailing. I jerk awake, heart pounding. *Ruby. Dee's back!* I scramble to a sitting position and throw back the shutters. The lights are on in the middle house, two squares of soft orange light above and below. I wait, but no one materialises in the window. It's like the lights have been left on by accident and nobody's home.

I go to call out for Adam before remembering myself. He's gone to town today; says he's putting in extra hours so we can be out of here sooner. *Sooner* can't come soon enough.

I rub my gritty eyes and sigh. I've gone and napped again so now I'll be sure to have another awful night's sleep. Did I dream the sound of a baby crying? I study the orange squares across the creek for a minute or two. Nothing. Perhaps Dee's in the shower or has gone out and forgotten to turn out the lights. I scrunch my nose, trying to remember if the lights were on last night too.

I know I'm over-thinking, but I'd feel better if I'd spotted her at least once since that night. I wish she'd given me her number so I could check she's okay. If my memory of the other night *is* accurate then maybe there's cause for concern.

I sip the half-empty glass of red I've left on the stool beside the day-bed when something flickers in my peripheral vision. There's a beam of light bouncing around in the Haddads's yard, and it takes only a moment to recognise what it is. Torch light.

Without thinking, I grab the binoculars and aim them at the window. I spot the torch light immediately, a conical beam in the dark, but the vision is out of focus and I can't see who's carrying the torch. My heart pounds as I adjust the focus and struggle to follow the bouncing light. The frame lands on a face, so close-up it gives me a start. Erica.

What's she doing out there in the dark? I watch as she walks with purpose through the darkness until the torchlight lands on a small structure. I recognise it as the shed that sits on the side of the yard closest to the creek. Erica disappears inside and a square of light appears. I adjust the focus, zooming in, but she never appears in the window. I wait for several minutes but nothing happens.

What on earth …? I have the urge to rub my eyes in a cartoonish manner. How does a person walk into a structure that small and not be visible through the window?

I'm about to lower the binoculars when they snag on movement from above. I lift my gaze and am eye to eye with Samir. With a gasp I pull back from the window. Shit. My heart is pounding; it felt like I was looking directly into his eyes, as close as if he was standing right in front of me.

Don't be an idiot, I tell myself. He can't see me. The lights are off and I'm all the way over here. He just happened to be looking in this direction.

From my vantage point, I can see Samir shake his head and run his hands down his face. He's probably just tired. And Erica didn't disappear, she's probably just fixing something or looking for something and there's more room in there than I think.

But the image of Samir dragging that garbage bag out of Dee's house, and the way he looked at me on the porch the day after, has my hands clammy and my throat tight and I can't shake the feeling that something terrible has happened.

He asked me what I was doing at Dee's house … but what was *he* doing there?

***

8:40pm

'I'm so sorry I'm later than I said,' Adam drops his satchel and scoops me up, kissing my forehead, my lips. 'What's been happening?'

'Nothing, as usual,' I sulk. 'Why didn't you call?'

Adam's brow furrows. 'What? I sent you several messages.'

'No, you didn't.' I glance at my phone. 'Shit. Bloody signal's out again. Fuck's sake!' I throw my phone on the couch. It bounces off one of the cushions and lands on the floor with a *thunk*. 'Adam, this place is driving me mad!'

Adam's jaw drops slightly, and I realise just how mad I must appear. He holds his phone out and I see that he's telling the truth. Just then my phone pings three times in a row and I lunge towards the couch to grab it.

'I'm sorry,' I say as I read his messages, and suddenly my lower lip trembles and my eyes sting. It scares me how quickly I can fear the worst. I suppose it's what happens when you have so much to lose. 'You did message. I didn't know.'

I step into his open arms, feeling exposed and more than a little foolish,

In the very beginning of Adam and me, I'd weighed the possibility, the likelihood, of cheating. Of course, I had. That's part of the elimination process when courting: *is this person going to hurt me?* And the men I'd had relationships with – dated briefly or slept with, more accurately – all rated pretty highly on the probability scale. But I'd convinced myself it didn't matter, that it would remain a *Non Issue* as long as I didn't get properly involved, as long as things didn't get *emotional*. Cheating didn't rate on my list of things to worry about.

Now, I can't imagine a worse betrayal, a single thing that could injure me more. I never realised how much fear comes with having so much to lose – or perhaps it was that I *did* realise this, unconsciously, after Mum and her transgressions which brought about my subsequent abandonment issues, and that was why I'd made it my mission to avoid commitment. To dodge the very possibility of being betrayed. Not wanting to be tied down by kids probably has something to do with that too.

I feel Adam's sigh more than hear it. 'Of course, you didn't, darling. There wasn't signal, as you say.' He pulls back and looks into my eyes. 'This is my fault. I've dragged you into all of this. If it weren't for what happened with Brett, I'd have had money, been ... been someone you could depend on. I've really fucked up, haven't I?'

'No,' I sniff. 'You haven't. None of that was your fault, and it's all going to be fine in a matter of weeks.' I glance at my phone and look up at him with a sheepish smile. 'I'm sorry about my ... well, I suppose they're good old-fashioned trust issues, really. After Mum ... Anyway. You've done nothing to make me feel that ...'

'Baby, I know. And I understand, really. Getting worried about not hearing from your husband when you're stuck in a place like this? I think maybe that's pretty reasonable for anyone. But I promise, I'm going to spend the rest of my life convincing you you're safe with me.'

'Shit,' I sniff and look away, embarrassed. 'How did I get so lucky?'

'I'm the lucky one,' Adam beams at me and plants a kiss on my lips. 'Now let's get you a glass of wine.'

'Oh God, yes. Did I mention you're perfect?'

Moments later, Adam hands me a glass of wine and a brown paper bag. 'I got you this.'

'Oh, what is it?' I reach into the paper bag and pull out a gossip magazine, an Australian version of the sort you find in every hair salon, which is the only time I'd ever bother to look at one. 'Oh. Thank you.'

'I know it's silly, but I thought a bit of gossip might help take your mind off things. You know, you could have a bit of a chuckle at all the celebs falling drunk out of nightclubs or being caught with their trousers down.' He winks and I force a smile so as not to appear ungrateful.

'Thank you. That's very ... thoughtful.' I shake away the feeling that this is the last sort of thing I would get for myself – it's only been just over a year, time still to learn each other's quirks and interests – and decide it actually *is* quite thoughtful, considering I'm in need of any distraction I can find.

Adam puts his feet up and sips his red as he flips through the newspaper.

It occurs to me to mention the night I spent with Dee – we didn't have a chance yesterday, what with all the sex

– but I don't want to spoil the mood. We sit in silence for a few minutes when Adam swears under his breath.

'What is it?'

I look over at him and he's staring at the newspaper as if it's a snake. He looks up at me with wary eyes, all his earlier contentment drained from his expression.

'What? Adam, what is it?'

'You might want to sit down for this.'

'I *am* sitting down. For God's sake, Adam ...'

Adam's face is grim. 'Dee's been reported missing. And the baby, too.'

I feel the blood drain from my face. '*What?*'

Adam nods. 'She was last seen on Wednesday, so it's been three days already.'

'Oh my God.' A wave of nausea washes over me. I knew it – I *knew* something was wrong.

'Are they looking for her? Why has no one reported it until now?'

Adam holds out the paper for me to see. 'It says here she was reported missing on Thursday morning, by a neighbour. I imagine some time has to pass before it becomes a priority for police. They're searching for her now.'

I take the paper with trembling hands and my gaze immediately catches on her name – *Delilah*.

Fears grow for missing Oyster Creek woman, Delilah Waters, 31, and her infant daughter Ruby, six months, who have been missing since Wednesday evening. Mother and daughter were last seen on a small footbridge that crosses the water at Oyster Creek at around 3pm by a neighbour.

The alarm was raised when Mrs Waters's friend and neighbour called in at the Waters' residence on Thursday afternoon for a scheduled babysitting arrangement and found the front door unlocked and no one at home. Mrs Waters has not been answering her mobile phone and it has been confirmed that no one within her circle of acquaintance has seen or heard from her since Wednesday afternoon. Last seen in a location known for its dangerous currents, and where several tourists have drowned in recent years, there are grave fears for both mother and child.

Mrs Waters's husband, who is overseas on business, has been informed of his wife's disappearance and is on his way back to Australia.

If you have any information regarding the matter you are urged to contact Brave Cove Police.

Dee is missing. I feel like the air has been knocked out of my lungs. My mind explodes with thoughts and memories, a jumble of everything that happened the night Dee came to visit, everything that's happened since.

I'm certain of one thing. Her 'neighbour and friend', most likely Erica, wasn't the last one to see her.

I was.

Chapter 20

Dee

May, 2017
Sunday, 4pm

He's there again. Does he think I can't see him sitting there in his beat-up car, or does he want me to know he's there? Another letter was pushed through the mail slot earlier. I tore it up without reading it. I already know what it will say. And I'm growing more and more fearful that time is running out; another reminder isn't any help.

I yearn to confide in Rob. I still crave him – for comfort, for stability. For love. Yet I know this is something I have to sort out on my own.

Sometimes he seems on the brink of saying something, and I ask him what's on his mind, but as soon as I do, he shuts down and turns away. My heart breaks a little each time. Although, in truth, I deserve the dismissal. He could do worse to me. Much worse.

I miss him. Miss us. I miss a time before I was nothing more than a milk bar to a greedy infant, when our days were long and lazy and our nights filled with laugher and love-making. But the time of 'me' has passed and now there's only her.

The man gives a little wave and I shiver and draw the curtains closed. I can't just sit here any longer. I fumble for my phone and call *him*. An answer after two rings, 'Hello?' Shit. 'Who *is* this?' But it isn't his voice, it's hers. I panic and end the call, my heart in my throat. It was so stupid of me to call the land line! I send a hasty text instead.

It strikes me that I need a plan for if the worst happens. What might become of Ruby if I'm gone? So I grab a pen and scrawl it across a notepad for several minutes, thinking carefully about each detail. I can't forget anything. When I'm done, I tear the page from the notepad and slip it into an envelope, then write Erica's name on the front. That's something sorted, at least. *Just in case.*

I pace the room, breathing to calm my nerves. My throat is parched and I wonder how long it's been since I've eaten or drunk anything. I go to the kitchen for some water but, in passing the fridge, change my mind. I take out a bottle of wine, clasp its neck and drink straight from its cold glass mouth.

Several gulps later I place the bottle back with trembling hands, reassuring warmth pooling in my stomach. I sigh and lean against the fridge door, tilting my head back. My back aches, my head aches and my breasts are full and sore, straining against the buttons of my blouse. I pray Ruby will have an appetite when she wakes or I'm going to have to pump again. I hate that thing. Makes me feel like a bloody cow being milked.

Behind my eyelids, I see Ruby's father's face. Shame swells within me and a tear slips down my cheek. What I wouldn't give to go back. To erase the past. But then I wouldn't have her. My sweet baby. My angel.

A smile touches my lips. I make my way to Ruby's room, open the door and tip-toe to the cot. The room smells of her: pure and milky-sweet. As always, my heart squeezes with a love so strong it's painful. I lean over the rail and brush my fingers over her soft, downy hair, her cheeks full and soft as rose-petals. If I can see him in her, I wonder if Rob can too. My stomach churns with acid and I'm suddenly aware of the sour taste of wine in my mouth.

There's a knock from downstairs. I glance at Ruby – still sound asleep – and throw on the silk kimono Rob bought me for Christmas.

'Oh. Hello.' I open the door to let Samir in. He looks over his shoulder, then closes the door behind him.

He takes one look at my face, steps forward and takes me in his arms.

I lean against his shoulder, a single sob escaping.

'It's okay, darling,' he whispers. 'We'll sort it out. Whatever happens, we'll sort this thing out.'

I smile up at him, but my lower lip quivers. 'I've made such a mess of things.'

His smile is kind and I'm reminded that that's my favourite thing about him. His unconditional kindness, despite his knowledge of what some people are capable of. It's a rare quality. One I thought I'd found in Rob, but it seems his love had conditions, after all.

'Is Rob coming home tonight?'

'I'm not sure. He doesn't really ... we don't really communicate much anymore.'

Samir's lips thin, his eyes unreadable. 'Call him. Make sure he'll be here. You know I would, only ...'

'I know.'

'But listen,' Samir says, his voice urgent now. He brackets my neck with the fingers of each hand, lifts my chin with his thumbs. 'If it comes to it, I can help. Just let me sort some things out – finances, whatever else. Okay?'

'It might be too late by then.'

The Haddads's front door slams and Samir winces. 'I'd better go. Sit tight, okay?'

'Wait!' I hand him the envelope. 'If anything ... happens, will you give this to Erica for me?

Samir nods. 'Of course.' He kisses me on the forehead and leaves.

I take out my phone and dial Rob. It rings six times before he picks up.

'Yes?'

'It's me. I was just wondering ... Do you know when you'll be home?'

Rob sighs, a world-weary sound. 'I'm not coming home tonight, Dee.'

'When then? I ... I miss you.'

'Dee ...'

'Ruby does too,' I whisper.

A pause. His next words sound strained. 'Soon. There are some things that need to be said.'

Chapter 21

Liz

June, 2017
Saturday, 9pm

I'm staring at the article, the words blurring together. *Mother and daughter were last seen* ... I struggle to swallow, struggle to breathe, as the gravity of it hits me.

'Oh, fuck.'

'What is it? Apart from the obvious.'

'*I* was the last one to see her, Adam. I was the last person to see Dee.'

Adam looks at me quizzically. 'What do you mean? When?'

'I saw her that night. *After* they're saying she went missing.'

'What? Are you sure, Lizzie?' Adam places a hand on my arm.

I yank my arm away. 'I didn't imagine it, if that's what you're suggesting.'

It irks me that Adam talks down to me sometimes, as if I can't be trusted to know my own mind. There were a couple of instances where I lost track of my meds, I'll admit, and maybe I did exaggerate a few things, like the time I thought the guy in the flat next door was stealing from us. But I'd been through a trauma so recently. It's only natural I'd become a little paranoid. He can't keep using the past as a reason not to believe anything I say. Thinking he knows best is a downside of the age gap, I suppose.

Adam looks hurt. 'I wasn't suggesting you were. I just meant are you sure it was *after* the neighbour saw her, or—'

'I'm sure,' I say, heading to the kitchen. Adam follows me. 'They're saying she was last seen Wednesday *afternoon*, but that isn't right. She came over. She was *here*,' I grab the already half empty bottle of red and top up his glass, then mine.

'God, yes, please,' Adam groans, plonks himself in a dining chair and takes a large swallow. 'Hang on, what? She was *here*?'

'Yes! She came over at around eleven, I suppose. She was a bit drunk and took me quite by surprise. I thought the knock at the door was you, at first, that maybe the road had been cleared and you'd come back, but then it was Dee at the door.'

Adam furrows his brow. 'How odd. Why would she come *here*?'

'I have no idea. She said she wanted company.'

'Why didn't you mention it before?'

I take a swallow of wine and pace the floor. 'I meant to! But then Thursday was our 'anniversary' and yesterday you were back ... Shit! I knew something terrible had happened.'

'What would make you think that?'

'Well, she seemed afraid, for one thing.'

'Afraid of what?'

I sigh. 'I'm not sure. She never said. But she had a black eye, and she was talking about things not being great at home.'

Adam takes a deep breath. 'Doesn't sound good, Lizzie.'

I shiver. 'Tell me about it.'

Adam stares out of the window, looking pensive. 'Shit.'

'I haven't been out today,' I murmur. 'I got started on some of the junk in the basement. They must have been here ... the police, searching. They think she was last seen on the bridge, so that's where they'll be looking. Come to think of it, I did hear a helicopter earlier.'

We look out of the kitchen window, but all the windows are dark in the middle house, and there's no sign of anything out on the water. 'Why aren't they out there now, searching for her?'

'Maybe the police have a lead that's taken them elsewhere. This newspaper is basically info-tainment – you know how they love to sensationalise things. If they were concerned she'd drowned, they'd be out there now.' Adam places a hand on my arm. 'Sit down, Lizzie, you're making me nervous.'

I can't sit down, I'm buzzing. 'Something bad has happened. I know it.' I stop and bite my lip. 'What do I do, Adam? Should I call the police? I saw someone. A *man*. In the house with her. That night. And then she was here. And her husband was away, so it couldn't have been her husband. Could it? *Could* it?'

Adam drags a hand across his eyes. He looks exhausted. 'Slow down, Lizzie.'

But I can't slow down. I feel as high as a kite. This is too similar for my liking. Too much like before. I slosh another dose of red into my glass and slug it as I pace the kitchen floor. 'What if I'm the only one who knows about this? I have to say something. Don't I?'

Adam blinks at me. He looks pale. Worried. 'Jesus, Lizzie. Yes. Yes, you have to say something.' He sips his wine and looks at me with knowing eyes.

'Oh God, it's happened again.' I whisper.

Adam reaches out and squeezes my arm. 'You don't know that yet. She's only missing, it could be for any reason.'

I nod, the back of my eyes stinging with tears.

Adam pulls me onto his lap. 'It might not be so bad, darling. She might have just gone out of phone range, "off grid" for a bit?'

'But she was afraid. Of what – or whom – she didn't

say. But I didn't imagine it. And there's something else. I heard a scream, later, during the storm. Around two I suppose? And I saw Samir ... He was dragging something out of the house. Dee's house. Oh God, what if it's him? What if he's killed her?'

'Hey, hey, calm down, baby. Why would Samir do something like that?'

'I don't know ... I ... I don't know. Maybe they were involved somehow? Like ... an affair gone wrong?'

Adam's eyes widen. 'Did she tell you that?'

'No, no. I just got the sense that not all was well at home and that maybe ... maybe there was someone else. She mentioned a 'lover's tiff'. And she did have that black eye.'

Adam stares blankly at the wall and I finally stop pacing and stand at the counter.

'I wonder when Rob will get back,' Adam says flatly. 'God, the poor guy. Imagine though, if you're right ... about the affair thing. Imagine if his wife's missing and'—he shakes his head—'and then to find out she was ...'

I perch on Adam's knee, put my arm around his shoulder and lean in. I know he's thinking of what happened with Brett and Beth and it still has the power to make my blood boil. Everything somehow ends up coming back to that. 'I know, baby.'

He looks at me, seeming confused for a moment. 'Sorry, that's not—' He tries to smile. 'I'm sure Samir had a perfectly legitimate reason to be there that night. And this has all been some kind of misunderstanding. That's the most likely explanation. Rob's away; maybe Samir was helping out around the house. Taking the garbage out or something.'

'In the middle of the night?'

'Sometimes people forget to put out their bins. Could you tell what Samir was carrying?'

'No. It was dark – there was a blackout here that night. I only caught a glimpse when an automatic light went on. It must have been solar powered or something. Or the power had come back on briefly. It was on and off the whole next day.'

I close my eyes and see a halo of red hair surrounding a cherubic infant's sweet, round face.

Gazing out of the window, I spot the bouncing light of a torch once more, and the little square of amber appears in the shed. And then another light, followed by several more, emerge from the scrub at the far end of the creek where the footbridge is. They dance over the water's surface, aimed downwards.

And then the unmistakeable, rhythmic *chop-chop-chop-chop* of a helicopter sounds in the distance, drawing nearer and nearer.

Adam's eyes meet mine, his expression grim.

They're searching for her.

***

Sunday, 9:55am

I called the police last night and they asked if I wouldn't mind coming in to make a formal statement. When we cross the water, there is police tape all around Dee's house, and people in high-vis gear are still scattered around the creek. But what if they're searching for nothing? What if she wasn't even anywhere near the creek that night?

Adam drives us to the police station, and we barely exchange a word on the way. I'm jittery with nerves, trying not to think about the last time I spoke to police. The two strong cups of coffee I had with breakfast haven't helped, and I'm a wired mess by the time we reach town.

The shirt I've worn is synthetic, some cheap H&M number, a stupid choice for today. The material doesn't breathe and I can feel the cold, damp patches beneath my arms, hidden – thankfully – by the jacket I've thrown over the top. This is what passes for winter over here?

'Relax, Lizzie, it will be fine,' Adam says. 'Just tell them what you know.'

'They'll probably want to speak to you too.'

'Of course, they will. It's just protocol. It makes sense that they would interview anyone living nearby. I imagine they didn't realise anyone was staying over the other side of the creek or we'd have heard from them sooner.'

'Thanks for getting in touch with us,' says a short, bottom-heavy police officer with sleek black hair pulled tightly back in a pony-tail. She smiles at Adam, then at me, and I recognise her voice as the woman I spoke to on the phone. 'I'm Sergeant Jamison.'

The man standing beside her introduces himself as Sergeant Harris. He's broad shouldered yet he stands with a slouch, as though carrying a heavy backpack. His expression is neutral, but his eyes seem friendly enough, even though he's barely spoken two words since I arrived. He has a long, bulbous nose – almost phallic – coated in an unhealthy sheen; I don't want to stare at it so I try to focus on his eyes.

'Yes. Er, no problem.'

Adam goes in first, as he needs to leave for work afterwards and, apparently, we need to be spoken to separately. I was hoping we could have done it together, it would have helped ease my nerves, but I'll just have to deal with what needs to be done.

Shortly after Adam leaves, I find myself on a hard-backed plastic chair, the kind you find in schools, in a small, square room with sparse furniture, fluorescent lights and no artwork or decorations of any kind on the walls or shelves. It strikes me as a cross between a hospital room and a depressingly small office.

'Mrs Dawson,' Jamison starts. 'Are you ready to begin?'

'Yes.'

Jamison smiles and presses a button on an ancient-looking recording device that reminds me of one my father had when I was a child. Honestly, are the police force too tight for more up-to-date technology? 'Can you confirm that you're aware that this interview will be recorded for the purposes of evidence in the missing persons case of Mrs Delilah Waters and Ruby Waters?'

I nod.

'For the tape, please.'

'Oh. Sorry. Yes.'

'Great. So, on the phone you said ...' Jamison flicks through a notepad. She's younger than I first thought. Mid-twenties, perhaps. 'You saw Mrs Waters on Wednesday night, the day before she was reported missing, correct?'

'Yes. I read in the paper that her neighbour Erica was the last person to see her, but that isn't true. I saw Dee much later than that. At around 11pm?'

I hate that I'm making it sound like a question, as if I'm unsure. The nerves are getting the better of me. The last time I was in a room like this, I was interrogated until I burst into tears. I don't realise I'm tapping my foot at manic speed on the floor until Harris eyes it pointedly. I stop and fold my hands in my lap.

'Okay,' Jamison says, meeting my eye for the first time. 'And can you describe, in your own words, the circumstances of your interaction with Mrs Waters on that occasion?'

'Yes, of course. Well, I was asleep, and I heard a knock at the door. I thought it was my husband at first, but that would be a bit difficult seeing as the roads were closed that night due to the fires and he'd been unable to get back into town so was staying in Sydney ...' I take a deep breath, aware that I'm rambling. I try to calm down. 'But when I answered the door, it was Dee standing there. I invited her in, and we shared a glass of wine together.'

'Had you met Mrs Waters before this occasion?'

'Yes, at the pub. But we barely spoke.'

'In that case, why do you think Mrs Waters might show up at a relative stranger's door?'

'I have no idea and thought it very odd myself. I had wondered whether she'd been expecting Tim to be there – that's Adam's father. He used to live there but passed recently, but she didn't seem to know him very well.'

'And how would you describe Mrs Waters' state of mind when you spoke with her?'

'Well, that's the thing,' I say, biting my lower lip. 'She was okay at first, a bit tipsy as though she'd been drinking already. But then after a while she seemed ... frightened of something. Or someone.'

Jamison glances over her shoulder at Harris, who still hasn't said anything, but I can't see her expression.

'What makes you think she might have been scared?'

'Well, several things really. She implied that she was having some trouble at home.'

'Are you able to recollect her exact words?'

'Um ... well, she had a black eye. It was faded, so it could have been from a while ago. When she caught me looking she said there'd been a "lover's tiff".'

I'm startled by the sound of Harris clearing his throat. When he doesn't say anything, I continue.

'I asked her if she felt safe at home and she said no. But she didn't say who, or what, she was afraid of ... I mean, she said her husband was away. So I don't know whether she meant him, or ... or someone else.'

'Did she give you any reason to suspect that someone other than her husband might have wanted to harm her?'

'No ... not exactly. But she got a text at about midnight, I suppose, and she had to go all of a sudden. I asked her if she was frightened of the man I'd seen standing in her doorway earlier, and she looked really scared then. She asked, "what man?" and I explained what I'd seen and then she said something about always locking her doors.'

Jamison holds eye contact with me for several seconds before writing something on her notepad.

'Where in the house do you think you saw this man?'

'In the doorway. The front doorway. It was open. But when I tried to look again, he'd gone and the door was shut.'

'How can you be certain? It's a fair way between where you were and the houses across the water. I can't imagine you'd be able to see anything very clearly.'

My cheeks flush hot. 'I, uh ... I had binoculars.'

Jamison nods slowly. 'I see.'

'I wasn't ... you know, spying or anything.' I laugh nervously. 'The binoculars happened to be there – they belonged to Adam's father. And when I saw someone in Dee's doorway, I suppose I ... I suppose I was curious.' I cringe inwardly at how that makes me sound.

'What time would you say it was that you saw this man?'

'Oh ... around 10pm, I suppose.'

'And he was there only for a moment and then disappeared?'

'That's right.'

'You're sure it was a man?'

'Yes. He was very tall and broad – almost filling the doorway.'

'And you didn't see any more of Mrs Waters or anyone else in the house until Mrs Waters arrived at your home at around eleven, correct?'

'Yes, that's correct. It was dark, there was a blackout. And then I fell asleep, so ...'

'I see.'

For a second I see the man standing in the doorway, the feeling of exposure when the power came back on, and my spine tingles.

'And can you remind us of what you saw later that night, after Mrs Waters left?'

'Well, at around two or three I think it was, I was woken by a noise. At first, I thought I was dreaming, but then I heard it again – a scream. Someone shouted "Please" and then there was a scream. I rushed to the loft upstairs – it's easier to see out from up there – and looked out of the window, but I couldn't see or hear anything else. Well, not until Samir appeared just outside Dee's house.'

'Yes, you mentioned you saw Mr Haddad'—Jamison

flips through her notepad—'dragging what looked like a full garbage bag from the Waters' residence and into his house. Is that correct?'

'Yes. But he didn't go into the house. Well, he might have done but I can't be sure. He disappeared around the other side of his house and I couldn't see anything else after that.'

'How can you be sure it was Mr Haddad you saw?'

'Well,' I tuck a strand of hair behind my ear, embarrassed. 'I had the binoculars. And I'd seen him before, in person at the pub one night, and later, through the window. I recognised him immediately.'

'I see.'

Harris pipes up then, his gravelly voice overly loud in the quiet room. 'You mention you'd had some wine with Mrs Waters earlier that evening. Had you consumed any more alcohol before or since then? Or any other medications or drugs?'

Heat creeps up my neck and into my cheeks. 'I'd had a bit of wine earlier. And I think I had another glass after Dee left. And I'd taken some sleeping tablets.'

'I see. Prescription ...?'

My cheeks flame. 'Yes.'

'Some of those prescription drugs can be pretty potent.' Harris says, levelling me with a frank stare. 'Would you say your account of events of that night are reliable, or might you have been intoxicated and confused at any point in the evening?'

A sudden flush of anger fills my chest. 'If you're suggesting I've made it up—'

'We're not suggesting anything, Mrs Dawson,' Harris says crisply. 'Just trying to ascertain an accurate account of events.'

Jamison shoots another look over her shoulder at Harris and turns back to me with an apologetic smile. 'Was anyone else with you during the evening? Anyone who might be able to verify your account of things?'

'No. I was alone in the house. Well, apart from when Dee showed up.'

'And, as far as you could tell, would you say that Mrs Waters was intoxicated at the point in time when she left your house, which you say was around ...?'

'Just after midnight. And, well ...' I feel disloyal to Dee somehow, but I know I have to tell the truth. 'She was a bit drunk, yes.'

There's silence apart from the faint whir of the recording device and the sound of Jamison's pen scribbling on her notepad.

A thought occurs to me, and I feel a sudden stab of fear.

'You won't ... you know, tell him, will you? Samir, I mean. You won't tell him where you got the information about him?'

Harris looks at me. 'Not if you don't want us to.'

There's a pause during which the only sound is Jamison's pen scratching on her notepad.

'I just wonder. If something did happen ... and he knows I saw ...'

'I'm sure there's no cause for concern,' Harris says. 'But if you're worried, there's no reason for us to disclose our source.' He flashes a brief, charmless smile that I'm sure is meant to reassure me, but it does the opposite. I have the sudden and intense urge to leave.

'Will that be all, or ...?'

'Just a couple more questions, and you'll be on your way.'

I slump back in my seat. 'Okay.'

'You say your husband stayed in Sydney on Wednesday night, is that correct?'

'Yes. That's correct.'

'Do you know where he stayed?'

I feel an unexpected jolt of fear. Is Adam a suspect? 'Yes. Yes, of course. He was in a hotel in Sydney. Like I said, he couldn't get back to town because the road was closed.'

'Do you know the name of the hotel? Approximate time of check in?'

'Yes ... well, no. He didn't ... I mean, he didn't give me the name. But he would have given you the details earlier, surely?' My voice sounds higher than it should, and my palms are starting to sweat. The memories of my previous police interrogation bubble to the surface.

'There's no need to get upset, Mrs Dawson. Your husband isn't under suspicion; we're just following protocol,' Harris says, sounding bored. He doesn't look up from his notepad. Twat.

Jamison leans into me, rolling her eyes in feminine solidarity. 'As Sergeant Harris says, we're just following protocol. We've checked with the hotel reception and it's been confirmed that your husband checked in around 8pm and checked out around 6am the following day. There's no need to worry.'

My shoulders sag. 'Thank you,' I murmur. 'I do know he said he checked in around 8pm – he called me just after. And he checked out early so he could be in a meeting.'

Harris shoots Jamison an irritated look but says nothing. Jamison shrugs and sits back in her seat. 'She should have the right to know she isn't in any danger,' she says bluntly, and I smile at her in gratitude. 'Well, I think that's about it then,' Jamison says, lacing her hands together and cracking her knuckles. 'Anything else you think of, however insignificant you think it is, let us know. It could help us find her.' She hands me a business card. 'My number's on here. You can reach me directly, anytime.'

'Thank you,' I say, genuinely appreciative at having been taken seriously. I'm about to ask whether I can leave when I'm struck by a thunderbolt of recollection. I can't believe I haven't thought of it before.

'There is something!' I exclaim. 'Something Dee said that night. She mentioned that Erica, her neighbour, was minding Ruby that night. But that doesn't make sense. Because didn't Erica say she last saw Dee and Ruby that afternoon on the bridge? Erica was the neighbour who last saw them, isn't that right?'

My heart rate increases as I realise this means Erica could have been lying.

Jamison frowns and Harris scratches his nose. When Jamison replies, she ignores my question. 'Hmm. That's interesting to know, Mrs Dawson. And you're certain Mrs Waters identified Mrs Haddad as the person minding her daughter, and not someone else?'

'Yes,' I wrack my memory to see whether she might have said anything else, but I'm certain she'd said Erica was minding Ruby. We'd had a discussion about how fond Erica was of her, and I thought it strange she was minding Ruby so shortly after they'd had such a terrible row. 'Yes. Yes, I'm sure.'

The officers exchange a look and then Jamison turns to me and smiles. She flips her notepad shut and Harris straightens, joints popping as he rolls his shoulders.

'Thank you for your time, Mrs Dawson,' Jamison says. 'You've been very helpful.'

She stands and I take my cue and stand, too.

As they're seeing me out, I turn to Jamison. 'Do you have any clues ... any idea what might have happened to Dee? And the baby?' I ask hopefully.

'We're following several leads,' she replies, her expression solemn. 'But at this stage, we're not at liberty to divulge any further information.'

***

Monday, 11:15am

As I walk down Cockle Street towards the creek the following morning, I gaze up at Dee's house. It's easy to imagine her there, easy to imagine everything's fine. The window must be open upstairs – the curtains are stirring in the breeze. I imagine she'll appear at any minute, Ruby on her hip, humming some nursery rhyme. Is the husband – Rob – back yet? There are no cars in the driveway. What a terrible situation to have to come home to. An empty house and a missing wife and child.

Out of the corner of my eye, I see movement in the window of the Haddads's kitchen but when I look up, the window is empty. And when my gaze returns to Dee's house, the blue and white tape catches my eye and my stomach sinks. Dee isn't just going to appear. She and Ruby are missing.

Pelicans are flying low above the creek's surface – eerily calm today – and the melancholy cry of the crows sounds in the distance. I'm nearing the entrance to the bush track that leads across the creek when I sense someone behind me.

I turn to see Zac, an oyster trap hanging from his shoulder from a thick rope, a beanie pulled down to his eyebrows.

'Didn't scare you this time.'

'Must be getting used to it.'

'Need a lift?'

I frown. 'A lift?'

He shrugs, his face remaining expressionless. 'Tide's too high to cross now. I thought I warned you about that.'

I sigh. I hadn't stopped to think about the tide this morning, which is quite stupid given the circumstances. I suppose I haven't been thinking clearly.

'Look, my boat's the same make as yours. Why don't I just show you how to use it and we can stop having this same conversation?'

I eyeball him, berating myself for not remembering to ask Adam about the boat. I'm not even sure it's in working order; it could be rusted through for all I know.

Perhaps noting my hesitation, Zac grunts. 'Last thing you want is to be trapped over there at high tide with no way out. Especially given what's happened.'

I feel a chill, as if someone walked over my grave.

'Your husband still hasn't shown you how to use the boat? He's not too worried about you, then?'

'Fine,' I snap, irritated.

Zac nods and turns away, but not before I catch his smirk. He trudges over the foreshore towards the water where a blue and yellow dinghy sits on the sand. The smell of fish stings my nostrils.

Zac throws the oyster trap into the back, drags the boat to the water and climbs in. 'Come on then.'

Trying not to breathe through my nose, I clamber in, steadying myself with both hands on the side as I find my balance on the wooden seat. I can feel my English complexion turning pink after my walk and wish I'd brought a hat.

The boat wobbles from side to side until I plant myself in the middle of the rear-most bench seat and before I have a chance to protest, Zac clambers in beside me. He smells of sweat and the sea but it's somehow not entirely unpleasant. 'Just flip this'—he shows me a switch on the motor—'and pull this, *hard*.' He guides my hand to a handle, which I yank back as hard as I can.

The engine splutters to life so suddenly I yelp and Zac chuckles. I hadn't realised these things even had motors. He shows me how to steer the boat and before long I'm getting the hang of it. 'You learn quickly,' he laughs.

'Why is that funny?'

'All that protesting you did earlier. Like you had something to prove. But now look at you.'

I don't know what to make of that so I say nothing, concentrating on the pressure of the water against the rudder and the way the light plays along the water's surface, changing when I change direction. In only a minute or so we're on the other side and I don't even have to ask how to stop; the boat lands on the sand and stops of its own accord.

Zac shows me how to kill the engine and when I get to my feet I can't help the grin that spreads across my face. It's going to be so much easier, now, providing Tim's boat works as well as Zac's.

But Zac's not smiling. He's staring at something over my shoulder. 'You heard about Dee Waters, then?'

The smile drops from my face. 'Yes, I did.'

'Don't hold too much hope of them finding her.'

I look at him sharply. 'What makes you say that?'

'Bit of a wild one, she was.' He doesn't say anything else. I feel a spark of annoyance – that seems to be all anyone can say about her. And I can't help but notice his use of 'was'. It gives me a shiver.

'So they tell me,' I mutter. 'Did you know her well?'

He shrugs. 'Well enough.'

Silence.

I sigh. He's a funny one: chatty one minute, silent the next.

A duo of plovers flies overhead, their cackles filling the air.

'She was struggling,' he says after a beat.

'Who? Dee?'

Zac looks at me as if I'm simple. 'That baby was always screaming. Kept me awake most nights; can't imagine how she would have coped.'

'But she had Rob to help, didn't she?' I probe.

Again, he stares like I'm stupid. 'Good old Rob.' He says in a tone I can't interpret.

I let out a frustrated breath. I don't know why I'm bothering. 'Well. Thanks for the ride.'

But it appears the conversation isn't over. 'Cops spoken to you yet? Haven't seen 'em over this side.'

I slant him a look. 'I just came from the station over in Brave Cove.'

'That right?' Zac eyes me squarely. 'You know something?'

Those electric blue eyes unsettle me and I find myself looking away.

'No.' I lie. I consider saying more, explaining, but why should I? If he can be evasive, so can I. And I don't know him enough to trust him. For all I know, he had something to do with Dee's disappearance. 'She probably just took off somewhere for a while.' I try to inject some commitment into the statement. 'You know what it's like when you have a new baby.'

Zac looks at me strangely and I inwardly cringe. Why did I say that? As far as I know, neither of us knows what it's like to have a baby.

A sudden image comes of a chubby toddler, clinging to her mother's leg – and then it's gone. I close my eyes as I stumble over the memory.

'Excuse me,' I say, avoiding Zac's gaze as I push past him towards the house. I can feel his eyes on me as I approach the back door. The wind picks up, wailing past, like a ghost. My skin feels numb.

When I reach the door and look over my shoulder, Zac has already gone. But when I lift my gaze, I see Samir staring out from the kitchen window.

Chapter 22

Erica

June, 2017
Sunday, 3pm

I don't need to work. I'm lucky that way, or at least that's what my sister likes to tell me. Samir's income is enough by miles for us both to live on. Which is good, because I'm used to my creature comforts; they're the only remaining comforts I have. If I had to give those up, too, I don't know what I'd do.

I work because I need to keep busy. And the hospital is just that – busy, busy, busy. It's perfect for me. Or at least it was, before the *Incident*. The incessant noise and the fluorescent glare grated on the nerves of my co-workers but not on mine. Those lights kept me awake, alert, their reassuring buzz an integral part of the symphony along with the hum of machines, the background chatter and the slap of shoe-soles on linoleum. The coffee was bad yet hot and there was never time to stop and dwell; it was all shuffle onwards, chatter with the other midwives, settle babies, answer calls.

It was only part time – three days a week – so the perfect work-life balance, really. And because the hospital is down in Sydney I sometimes slept the night at my sister's place after work. It wasn't just the convenience; it was being surrounded by the precious squeals and smells of my twin nephews, Jamie and Jake – their soft yellow curls like duckling down, the smell of bubble-gum shampoo after their splashy, steamy bath, the nostalgic aroma of mac and cheese or fish fingers or spaghetti bolognaise filling the house. I quite enjoyed the novelty of sleeping in my old childhood bedroom, even though I was still partly annoyed Sylvia had inherited the house (apparently I didn't need it, what with being married to Samir), and listening to the soft snores of my nephews in the next room, until one – or both – of them would wake and climb into bed with me. There was always something *happening*. Chaos kept the thoughts out. But now ... all that's gone. And all that remains are the thoughts.

It was inevitable, I suppose. Jeannie and Gaz were having problems, for one thing. Nothing too serious, as far as I could tell. Their main issue was renovating on a budget so tight they'd blown it by day one. It didn't help that they knew we had plenty of money and I didn't offer to help – I make a point never to lend money to friends or family; it's too troublesome – and then there was the fact that

Jamie and Jake had reached the Terrible Twos and their preschool was cracking down on their 'behavioural issues'.

I suppose it also had a bit to do with the *Incident* – the toll it took on me and how I wasn't handling it too well. And the fact that they had two toddlers and I'd been staying so often ... I don't blame them, really. They're a young family, decent people trying to make ends meet. They don't need me hanging around.

So now I'm spending time away from my sister and time away from my job and it's probably just as well because it was all getting too much and Samir was worrying about me being stressed and not having enough time to myself. Well, that's certainly not an issue anymore.

I wouldn't say I'm lonely. A bit bored, maybe, but not lonely. They've said it won't be long until I can go back to work and all I have to do is keep seeing Doctor Jones, sitting in that stuffy little office with the patchwork cushions and torn leather seats that smells like my grandfather's old study, smiling and telling him all's well, and I'm sure that in no time at all he'll be signing me off for return to work.

Then I can take a break from this house. From this street, this town. It's claustrophobic sometimes, living here. It can be so quiet my thoughts are like sirens and knowing everybody has its downsides, although it's nice having familiar people nearby in case anything goes wrong. Not that my closest neighbours would be much use, all tied up with their newborn as they are.

I can see her now, pushing that unsteady-looking stroller down the street. She doesn't take her out often enough, in my opinion – not that it's any of my business. I do know she's trying her best. I know it hasn't come naturally to her, that much is obvious. But honestly, a new mother going around dressed like that is a bit much. Surely she'd be more comfortable – and would be able to walk further – in proper shoes, not those ridiculous raised flip flop things (I don't know what they're called; I'm more of a sensible dresser) in this weather, and in a dress so tight I can see what she had for breakfast. She doesn't even look like she's had a baby, she's so skinny, though God knows she's got breasts until Tuesday.

I look down to find my hands pressed to my abdomen and I push down the sudden flash of anger. Yes, still, that part of me where You were attached aches. I swear there are scars in there I can feel, that bear your name. And yet, on the outside, everything has gone back to normal. Back to the way it was before, as if You never existed.

I watch as a plump arm is flung out of the side of the pram and my fingers itch for little hands to grasp. And, just for a moment, I allow the pain to burn and spread.

***

3:40pm

I can feel him behind me, though I haven't heard him enter the room. I stare out of the living-room window at the white-grey sky, tracking rain as it falls and fills the grooves and dips in the road. Dee's red hood is no longer visible – she and Ruby have disappeared down the road, probably on their way to the café for those croissants she likes. She should really eat some food with more nutritional value, especially since she's breastfeeding.

Four wood ducks – two male, two female – waddle across the lawn, prodding busily at the wet grass with their bills, wading through the deepening puddles. The water slides right off their backs.

'Miserable weather,' is all he says.

I silently disagree. I love this weather. It makes me feel like there's nothing more I should be doing than staying indoors with a book which – frankly – is all I have on my to-do list at the moment.

He steps closer until I can feel the warmth of his body against my back. Cold air rushes against my neck as he gathers my hair and lifts it, pulling it gently the way I like. I can feel his breath beneath my ear and I know what he wants. I shiver, though it's not with desire.

He presses his lips to my neck and I stiffen. 'Not now.'

Samir goes still. There's a silent beat before he pulls away and, in that moment, I sense fresh resentment.

'I should go, anyway.' His voice is tight, with embarrassment or anger I'm not sure. He releases my hair and his warmth disappears. With a strange sense of distance from my own body, I marvel at how little I know about my husband these days.

You always have to go, I think. To work, to your shed … and wherever else.

There's silence and as I turn I catch the pained look in Samir's eyes before he walks from the room. Guilt stabs at my gut and I'm angry at myself, because I'd planned on being nice today, maybe making a lamb roast – his favourite – and having a glass of wine or two together on the balcony, watching the sunset like we used to. I'd have all sorts of happy things to recount to Doctor Stone and he'd stop scribbling on his blasted notepad with that wrinkle in his brow, stop asking me how I *really feel* about things and just smile and nod when I explain that everything is fine. It was all just a misunderstanding.

But seeing *her* is a reminder, and it awakens something, rubbing the scars raw. It wouldn't have happened if she hadn't decided to walk in the rain, if I hadn't looked out of the window. I'd have turned to my husband and let him kiss me and let him put his hands on the body that housed You.

A shudder moves through me. I close my eyes and see the woman, curly hair wild, in her hospital gown, shrieking at me. She was making such a *terrible* noise. Was it necessary? Really? I'd have given her back; it's not like I'd *taken* her. It was my job to care for her, to soothe her when she was crying, to teach her mother the way of things. The stupid woman had fallen asleep … I mean, who can fall *asleep* when they have a newborn relying on them? Yes, it's wise to sleep when they do, but the child was *awake*. The child was *hungry*. And it's not like she had a husband around to help. She was on her own, so the responsibility fell to me. Is it any wonder I got so worked up afterwards? After what they're calling the *Incident?* The unfairness of it! It was all so ridiculous, almost a joke. And then to say I'm the one who needs help, to make me go and sit in that stuffy office and *talk* about it, when they should have understood, should have known I was just trying to help. Mothers need as much help as they can get. I'd just forgotten the time, that's all; I hadn't realised I'd walked that far from the room.

I was caught up in the moment – it can happen. Especially when you're tired and stressed, which I was, and that wasn't my fault – it was Dee's. And it's not really *that bad* that I helped feed her, surely. I know it isn't done, but the woman was near-mad with desperation to breastfeed her child so I fail to see it as a criminal act that I provided for that very need. Wet nurses need not be a thing of the past, in my opinion. I should have asked, yes, I understand that. Some people might think of it as a hygiene issue. But God, the silly girl – only young, too, just a baby herself – you'd have thought I'd *beaten* her baby by the way she reacted. For goodness' sake.

Shaking my head, I feel the familiar frustration bubbling up. I wasn't thinking straight. I misjudged things. I do admit that. But it was an innocent mistake, and it wouldn't have happened if it weren't for Dee with her endless calls and demands, her *neediness*. Knowing I'm always happy to help, knowing I can't say no. I wouldn't say no. Not because of her. Because of Ruby. That's why I do it. It's her who needs me. A helpless infant, blameless in all this. Innocent. But it had played with my mind, confused me. That's all it was. Confusion. It wouldn't have happened ordinarily. They know me at the hospital. They know what sort of person I am. How come they can't *see* that?

With a sigh, I turn from the window, but not before my gaze snags a flash of red. And as it does, my phone rings. I pull it from the pocket of my dressing gown to see a familiar name flashing on the screen.

'Please,' she says as soon as I answer, slightly breathless. I can hear the tears in her voice as I watch her pushing the stroller at a frantic jog down the street. 'I need your help.'

Chapter 23

Dee

June, 2017
Sunday, 4:40pm

Erica is prattling on about something to do with her work as a midwife but I'm scarcely listening. I thought I saw a light come on across the creek, but when I looked again all the windows were dark. Strange. It reminds me that I haven't seen a light on over there in ages; Tim Dawson must be away on holiday or something.

I sip my tea, longing for something stronger, but Erica isn't much of a drinker. I've never felt comfortable drinking around her; I know she judges me. She thinks I don't know her opinion of me, but I do. I know what everyone thinks. And, for the most part, they're right.

It's nice to have some company, even if it's just Erica. I'm grateful to her for helping me out; God knows without Rob around I'm barely making ends meet, although a meagre amount of money is appearing in my account every week, and Ruby is sleeping more which has helped matters.

It's pretty here; the Haddads's balcony affords a different aspect to ours with a clearer view of the mountains beyond the creek. It feels more spacious than our balcony somehow, although I know in truth they're identical. Everything is beautifully furnished: luxurious outdoor furniture, tasteful coffee table, rows of flower pots with colourful peonies all along the balcony rail. It's all Samir of course. His money, his taste. How he ended up with someone as dowdy as Erica has always been beyond me.

Still, I think as I glance over at her, watching as she speaks animatedly, there's a softness about her. With the setting sun illuminating her rounded cheeks, I see in her a maternal sort of kindness. Although she's most likely scarcely a decade older than me, I've always seen her as more of a mother figure. Poor thing; all those maternal instincts and no outlet for them.

'So it won't be long before I'm right as rain and back at work,' she's saying and she turns and looks at me expectantly.

I feel bad for letting my mind wander, so I attempt to engage. 'Yes, how's the stress leave going?' She still hasn't told me exactly why she's had to take time off, but I get the sense that something happened at work and it wasn't exactly her choice to leave. I wonder what she could have done? I can't picture her being anything other than hard-working and sensible, but we never really know what goes on in someone else's mind, do we? She's so upbeat about it all, yet I get the feeling she's withholding something, keeping her real feelings to herself. We all do it, I suppose. I would know.

She's frowning and I realise too late that I've said something wrong.

'As I said,' Erica says carefully, smiling now, though it doesn't reach her eyes. 'Once I've had this last session with Doctor Jones, I'm sure I'll be in the clear to be sent back to work.'

'Oh!' I say, surprised. Despite my inattentiveness, I'm almost certain she hasn't mentioned a doctor before. 'What ... sort of doctor? Are you ill? Is that why you're on leave?'

Erica hesitates, then sighs heavily. 'There was an ... incident.' She doesn't meet my gaze. 'It wasn't my fault. I was only trying to help, but no one will believe me.' She stops, straightens her shoulders, and smiles. 'But, as I said, one more session and I'm in the clear. It won't be easy, going back after everything, but I miss it so much I can't tell you. It's suffocating being cooped up here ...' she trails off, slanting me a guilty look.

'Yes,' I sigh, my heart sinking. *Tell me about it*. If Erica goes back to work, who will be around to help me? What will I do for company? I've come to depend on her more than I'd realised. The people I knew in Sydney – other dancers, people I knew in school, more acquaintances than friends – have long since disappeared from my life. I never knew my father and I don't speak to my mother, not since she turned a blind eye to what her sleazy boyfriends got up to at night.

'It's only three days a week,' Erica says as if reading my mind. 'And I'm still happy to mind Ruby whenever you like. You know that.'

'Thank you,' I reach out a hand and place it over hers. For a moment, as our eyes meet, and a current of understanding passes between us, I have the urge to tell her everything, to purge it all and have someone else bear the burden. But she stiffens, pulls her hand away, and the moment is lost.

'I haven't seen Rob around lately,' she comments, and there's something in her voice as she says it, aiming for casual but I can sense the edge. She *has* been edgier around me recently, I realise. How much does she know, or suspect? Not the whole, surely, or she'd have nothing to do with me.

'Oh, he's away on business. China this time, I think.' I try to smile but I can feel the stiffness in my cheeks.

When I look over, Erica is looking at me solemnly. 'If there's anything ... wrong, you can tell me, you know. I know how to keep a secret.'

I almost smile then, because I am certain she is someone who absolutely cannot keep a secret. Besides, which one would I choose? I have so many, none of which a woman like her could understand.

'Thank you, but everything's fine. It's just hard, on my own a lot.' As if I've reminded myself of this fact, I suddenly feel very tired. Ruby will wake from her afternoon nap shortly, and because she's teething I doubt she'll sleep through until any later than 3am.

My thoughts wander to a cool glass of wine and, though it's selfish, I can't help myself. 'Can you take Ruby tonight?'

I belatedly realise I've interrupted her, and she looks annoyed. I can hardly blame her. But I also know she won't say no. Because she thinks I don't know her secret, but I do. Samir told me. And I know she'd never say no to the chance to hold a baby in her arms, even if it kills her every time.

Chapter 24

Liz

June, 2017
Monday, 6pm

The sky is streaked with orange light and the water, dark and slick like a serpent, snakes through the bush and past the row of three white houses, rooves gleaming in the sunset.

The middle house is empty, of course. Knowing Dee's gone makes it appear abandoned, ghostly. I wait to hear the baby's cries, for a light to flicker on, a shadow to pass across the upstairs window. But everything is quiet and still. Only the branches of the pines on the foreshore stir in the mild breeze; only the squawks of the black cockatoos flying low overhead fill the silence. I keep Googling for news about Dee and Ruby's disappearance, but it's all different versions of the same thing. There's nothing to indicate foul play, though they're not ruling it out, and there are mentions of a couple of other people who drowned while crossing that bridge during high tide – a twenty-five-year-old woman and a fourteen-year-old boy. Both strong swimmers, apparently. No wonder Zac warned me about it, I think with a shiver. The thing's a bloody death trap.

If it weren't for what I'd seen and heard that night, I'd be thinking the same as everyone else. Considering where they *think* they were last seen – I've not seen any reports that mention the information I gave the police, which is strange – the most likely conclusion would be that she fell in and drowned. It was a king tide, after all.

Yet there's that familiar feeling of responsibility – that if there's something only I know, then only I can do something about it.

Ugh. I dig the heels of my hands into my eyes, frustrated by my circling thoughts.

The sun dips over the mountain and the sky darkens. Movement to the left catches my eye, but Zac's curtains are drawn. I can see shadows behind them, more than one. Is he with someone, I wonder, before pushing the thought away.

Erica appears in her kitchen window. She looks out, half draws the curtains, but I can still see in, see her waving her arms, shaking her head. They always seem to be fighting. Her anger seems at odds with the meek, anxious woman I've met. Samir's tall, dark figure emerges from behind the curtain. He puts his hands on Erica's shoulders but she shakes him off. Her head is down. Could she be crying?

Once more my thoughts drift to Samir coming out of Dee's house that night. Had he been the man I'd seen in the doorway earlier that night? Can I be sure *either* man was him?

What if Dee and Samir were having an affair? If Erica knew about it, it would explain why she and Samir are always fighting. What if Dee called it off and Samir got angry?

Still. Why would Erica keep minding Ruby for Dee if she knew she was having an affair with her husband? That part certainly doesn't add up.

God. I swallow more wine. My imagination is getting the better of me. I shouldn't over-think this. I've done what I had to do, all I *can* do. I went to the police and they will do as they should with that information.

So why doesn't it feel like it's enough?

I finish my glass, curl up amongst the cushions on the window seat, and close my eyes. As I'm drifting off I hear a thud and open my eyes to see a light come on at the bottom of the Haddads's yard.

I scramble to my knees and take out the binoculars, but it's too late. Whoever it was has gone inside and no one appears in the window. I stare out into the blackness for a while before exhaustion takes over and I curl up amongst the cushions and drift to sleep.

***

6:32pm

'Baby. Wake up.'

It's too bright when I open my eyes. Someone's turned on the light. I blink in the unexpected glare and Adam's face appears above me.

'What ...?'

He smiles, teeth bright white, and I'm gathered into his warm arms. I rest my head on his shoulder, inhaling his warmth, but he squeezes too hard – so hard I fear my ribs will snap.

'Adam,' I squeak. 'What are you ...? I can't breathe.'

'Sorry, sorry. Oh, baby,' he cradles me like a child, kissing my brow. 'God, I'm glad it's not you. I know it's selfish but ... you're here. You're safe.'

'What are you talking about?'

Adam pulls back to look down at me. I realise with a shock his eyes are wet. 'I heard a report on the radio.' There's pain – regret – in his voice.

I sit up. 'Oh my God. Is it ...?'

'No, no.' He touches my lips. His hand is trembling. 'Some woman found in the river two towns over. Description fitting you. A British tourist. And for a second, I thought ... I thought ...' He pulls me close and kisses my lips. His cheeks are damp.

'Adam,' I pull away, half laughing. 'Sweetie. It's okay. I'm here. I'm okay.' I notice my phone is lit up and I stare at the screen in disbelief. 'Fifty missed calls?'

'I know. I know, it's stupid,' he gives me a wobbly smile.

'Maybe it's the thing with Dee missing ... Maybe it's being apart from you so much. Maybe it's stress. I don't know ...' He rakes a hand through his hair and pulls his hand away, leaving it in spikes. 'Maybe a delayed reaction to Dad?'

'Oh, baby.' I run my fingers over his cheek. 'You've been through so much lately.'

He's shaking his head, a dazed look in his eyes. 'It was terrible. For one moment, I was convinced it was you.'

'It's not. I'm here.' I take his hand and place it on my chest so he can feel my heart beating.

'It's terrifying, isn't it?'

I touch his mouth with my fingertips. 'What is?'

'Loving someone so much.' He pulls me against his chest and I burrow my neck into the muscular space between his neck and shoulder.

Over his shoulder, beyond the open window, the Haddads's kitchen blinds are open. Samir stands in the window, staring out.

Chapter 25

Liz

June, 2017
Monday, 7pm

The pub is buzzing with commotion when Adam and I arrive. It's only 7pm – Adam rushed home early after that radio announcement – so we figured we might as well break up the monotony and spend money we don't have on a night out. Between his earlier scare and the whole Dee business (not to mention I was dying to get out of that house) we could both use a drink.

We receive a few side-eye glances from the locals, a nod or two from the friendlier ones, but no one greets Adam or seems to recognise him. I suppose it has been a long while since he's spent any real time here.

Zac's behind the bar and we lock eyes for a moment before I turn away. Everyone's crowded around the television in the corner of the main bar area. All are men, a mix of trade workers and fisherman; the only woman in sight is the young woman behind the bar. No wonder poor Dee didn't have any girlfriends around here. *Doesn't*, I correct myself with a shiver. Already I'm thinking of her in the past tense.

It doesn't take long to realise why everyone has congregated around the television; I don't recognise the man on the screen, but it's clearly a news report about Dee and Ruby's disappearance.

'Shh! Keep it down, will ya?' someone shouts and the cacophony of voices lowers to a dull roar. Adam's arm slides around my shoulder as someone turns up the volume; the man who is clearly Rob Waters speaks directly to the camera, his face filling the screen. He looks haggard, distraught.

'Please,' he says, wiping a tear from his eye. His lower lip trembles. 'If anyone has seen or heard anything ... or if anyone knows anything that could help us find Dee and my ...' he stumbles, clapping a hand over his mouth. For a moment I think he won't be able to continue, but then he coughs, wipes his eyes and regains control. 'If anyone knows anything that can help us find my wife and baby, please let the police know.'

It's pretty gut-wrenching to watch, and guilt lands like a punch in my stomach. I feel sick. *You've told the police what you know*, I tell myself. *That's all you can do.*

But you knew she was frightened, whispers another voice. *If you'd convinced her to stay with you that night, she'd still be here.*

'Reckon he did it?' I overhear someone say and I prick my ears up. Adam hands me a glass of wine and I sip it eagerly.

'Nah,' another gruff male voice answers. 'I knew him, saw him round the pub all the time. Wouldn't hurt a fly. I reckon she's done a runner. Probably found some feller elsewhere. Always was a bit of a tramp.'

I stiffen, and Adam strokes my back gently.

'All the more reason he might've done her in. You know what it's like when someone just snaps. Like that woman they found over in Brave Cove last year – seventeen stab wounds. *Seventeen*, mate! And the guy was her ex. Killed himself in prison after that. You never know what people are capable of.'

I couldn't agree more, I think to myself. Although after Rob's tearful plea for his wife and child's safe return, it's difficult to suspect him. Still, you know what they say ... It's always the husband.

'He's got an airtight alibi, mate. He was overseas when she disappeared; he's a pilot, ain't he? Heard it on the radio this morning. Bit hard to do away with someone if you're not in the bloody country.'

'Maybe it was that pretty-boy neighbour, then. Whasisname?'

'Who?'

'You know, the one who works here, flirts with any girl who walks in. Zac, is it?'

'Yeah, right. What about him?'

'Wasn't there somethin' going round that she had a fling with him?'

'Who?'

'*Dee*, you ding-bat. Who else?'

'Would you two knock it off,' a third male voice interjects. 'The woman's missing, and she's got a little one. Have some respect.' The voice lowers to a mutter. 'Pair of old gossips like I've never seen.'

The other men apparently have nothing to say to this, so the conversation dies away.

When I look up at him, Adam is staring at the group of men, his lips pressed in a thin line.

'Don't you think it's strange the reports haven't been updated?' I say to Adam.

'What do you mean?'

'Well, why aren't any of the reports saying when Dee was *really* last seen? I've told the police everything I know. Isn't it something they'd want the public to know in case anyone saw or heard anything later that evening? Isn't that kind of thing pretty important?'

'I'm sure they have their reasons, babe. There's procedures in place for this sort of thing. They'll be doing all they can.'

'It's just ... it changes things. If Erica *was* minding Ruby that night, she must have seen Dee when she gave her back. Either that, or she kept her overnight, in which case the bridge *wasn't* the last place Ruby was seen. Don't you think it's strange? Why would Erica lie about something so important?'

'Ouch, okay, let me wrap my head around this,' Adam sighs and pinches the bridge of his nose. 'Maybe they're questioning Erica as we speak. You said yourself you haven't seen her around.'

'That's possible,' I consent.

'Maybe Erica's not *lying*, but mis-remembering things. We have no idea what sort of person she is, whether she's a reliable witness or not.'

Grudgingly, I admit this is a good point.

'Or ...'

'Or what?'

'Well. It's possible Dee could have been the one lying about Erica having Ruby.'

I don't say anything, and we stand in silence as the implications of that sink in. I see Dee's frightened face in my mind's eye and can't bring myself to think that she would do anything to harm Ruby, despite Zac's implication that she wasn't coping.

Could Dee have left Ruby sleeping at home and was too ashamed to tell me that? That was a much more likely scenario.

'Look, I know why you'd feel this way about this whole thing, darling. I mean gosh, the similarities between what happened with Christy and her baby ...' Adam shakes his head. 'And it's lovely that you were so concerned for

Dee's wellbeing. It's one of the things I love most about you. But you didn't know her very well – neither of us did. We don't really have any idea what was going on in her life. So we're just going to need to wait and see what happens. I don't want you worrying yourself sick. Not after ...'

He sighs heavily and I can see how bloodshot his eyes are.

'God, I'm so sorry I've landed us in this mess,' he groans. 'What an epic fuck up.'

'No, *I'm* sorry,' I lean my head on his shoulder. 'I didn't mean to go on and on about it. You've got enough going on. And you're right; it's up to the police now.'

Adam gives me a weak smile. 'Until they find them, there's always hope.'

'Yes,' I agree, though I'm not sure I believe it.

As we leave, Zac catches my eye again. He smiles, but I don't smile back.

***

11pm

Later, warm and drowsy and snuggled up next to Adam, I feel his breath on the back of my neck as he leans in.

'I have some good news, at least,' he whispers, tracing my bare shoulder with his finger and kissing the back of my neck. 'In light of what's ... happened, and with all the commotion at the pub, I forgot to say.'

'Oh?' I arch my neck to give him better access and he presses a trail of lazy kisses along my neck.

I can feel him smile against my skin. 'We don't have to be here for the settlement. So as soon as I've finished up in Sydney, we're out of here.'

'That's brilliant!' I turn to Adam and beam at him in the semi darkness.

He chuckles. 'I thought you'd be pleased.'

'Pleased is an understatement.'

'The buyers are happy with their knowledge of the franchise and the staff have had most of their training sessions. If I put in a few hours this weekend, it would really speed things up.'

My heart sinks. 'You'll be working the weekend?'

Adam kisses the tip of my nose. 'Darling, you know what that would mean, don't you?'

'No.'

'It means we could leave as soon as the end of next week.'

I gasp. 'You're kidding!'

'Not even the teensiest bit.'

I smile but something feels off. I know I'm supposed to be happy; God knows I wanted to be out of here almost as soon as we arrived, but I can't quite reach the appropriate level of enthusiasm. Perhaps it's that Dee's disappearance is unresolved, and I'm struggling with the guilt that I should have done more to keep her safe. For all I know, I might be the only one who knew she was afraid, perhaps in danger. It seems too much of a coincidence that she felt unsafe and then went missing. And I don't feel I can rest easy until I know what's happened to her and to Ruby.

'Once we've set up in London, buy our dream house, make sure things are running smoothly after a few months, we can go somewhere special to celebrate, just the two of us.'

'That sounds nice,' I murmur, my heart not really in it. What a difference a day makes. Yesterday I couldn't wait to leave, and now? Now I feel there's something unfinished, something I'm meant to do before I go.

I think of the future stretching out ahead of me, and I can't feel joy just yet. Because there's a mother and child out there missing – two people who might not have a future at all.

Chapter 26

Liz

June, 2017
Tuesday, 10:02am

With the prospect of leaving this house sooner than expected, I've thrown myself into sorting out Tim's things. It's not the most exciting task in the world, but I've made pleasing headway and am finding that sorting the junk from the charity items is actually quite satisfying, not to mention a good distraction from thoughts of Dee and Ruby. I've only got to tackle the boxes in the loft before I can order a skip and take the rest to a charity shop.

Once my back starts to ache and I'm sufficiently covered in dust and grime, I rinse off in the shower and take a break for lunch. As I'm picking at a limp tuna niçoise I've concocted from the meagre contents of the fridge and a couple of marginally-out-of-date pantry items, I Google

Dee's disappearance on my iPad. As usual, no new information, which is not a good sign.

I find Dee's Facebook page and as I scroll through her profile, I almost choke on an olive. People are posting the most horrendous things. God, what is wrong with them? It's disgusting – despicable. They're calling her a whore (how original), because, apparently, she used to be a stripper. As if this is in any way relevant! She and her child are missing. Like that bloke in the pub said, they need to show some respect.

It seems everyone who ever knew Dee is coming out of the woodwork to have their say. People from her 'colourful' past in Sydney seem to be the only ones posting anything in her defence (it seemed she *was* once in fact a stripper, and possibly also a sex worker) but the general consensus from everyone else is that she was a troubled woman who never wanted children and most likely took her own life. Some are saying good riddance, that she would have made a terrible mother. One hideous human being, if you can call someone so devoid of humanity that, said the baby is better off dead than with her.

A shudder moves through me and I feel sick. Honestly, who do these people think they are? I'm filled with sudden rage. Why don't they leave her the fuck alone?

And that's when I see it. A post from Erica J. Haddad.

People need to stop demonising Dee's past. As a close friend I have nothing but sympathy for her. Some people just aren't meant to be mothers. I do hope she and baby Ruby are found safe and sound.

I seethe. What a low blow, sandwiching an insult between pretences of concern. There is something genuinely off about that woman.

I think of vulnerable, frightened Dee coming over to speak to a stranger in the middle of the night because she had no one else to talk to and the softness in her eyes as she looked at the photo of her infant. She wouldn't do anything to harm Ruby. I know it. She only wanted to keep her safe, she said so herself. *'She's safer with Erica.'*

But was she …?

***

7pm

The blinds are all drawn on the houses across the water, and I wonder if the police have spoken to Erica and Samir about what I told them, whether they're worried now that someone's been watching. Anyone who was out there that night could easily have seen me looking out when the power came back on, and logistically there aren't many people apart from me – and Adam if he'd been here – who could have seen Samir coming from Dee's house that night. He hadn't used the road, so he'd only have been visible from this perspective.

I sip wine and blow plumes of smoke out of the window

as I open a new Notes page on my iPad and start trying to pick apart possibilities.

1. *Dee and Ruby had an accident and drowned.*
2. *Dee deliberately killed herself and Ruby (I don't believe this for a second, despite it being the general consensus).*
3. *Dee has gone off somewhere and taken Ruby with her because she was afraid of someone.*
4. *Dee was having an affair and things got ugly. (Samir? Zac? Someone else?)*
5. *Erica isn't just 'misremembering' when she last saw Dee and Ruby, but is lying deliberately. Why would she do this? To cover for Samir or someone else? Or because she had something to do with the disappearance(s)?*
6. *Erica is covering for Dee and Ruby because Dee's run away from her husband and doesn't want him finding her?*
7. *Someone has murdered one or both of them. (An ex? A jilted lover? Rob? Rob was out of the country but has loads of money. Hit man?? But who would kill their own child?)*

Any scenario in which they've died is obviously terrible, but the last possibility is definitely the worst-case scenario. I just can't shake the feeling, knowing what I know, and having seen what I've seen in my line of work, that there's more to this than an accidental drowning or a suicide. Whether it's the worst-case scenario or not remains to be seen. But I know from experience that I have to trust my instincts.

A light appears in the Haddads's yard and my heart skips a beat. It's Erica again – I can tell by the height – and she's headed, of course, to the shed.

My mind snags on a memory. What was it Dee said about her? *Someone like her wouldn't understand.* What did she mean by that? There's definitely something off about Erica. Not only was she behaving very strangely on both occasions when I ran in to her, but there was that time I saw her shouting at Dee. Not to mention the business of her spending all that time in the shed at night and that awful message she posted on Dee's Facebook page. Dee said herself, Erica was very fond of Ruby. Maybe she was unnaturally fond of her, and jealous of Dee. I add one more thing to my list.

10. Erica has kidnapped Ruby and done something to Dee.

I almost laugh at how ridiculous that looks written down in black and white. But like that bloke at the pub said, some people, under the right amount of pressure, can simply snap.

Adam's words about Dee come back to me 'you didn't really know her. We don't know what was going on in her life.'

I didn't, I think. But I think there's someone who does. Maybe I should have a word with Erica.

***

Wednesday, 3:04pm

Adam is gone so I busy myself in the basement once more, then decide to head across the creek with a view to visiting Erica. There haven't been any search crews around today, but I've heard helicopters in the distance more than once.

As I'm about to get in the boat to cross the creek, I spot Zac hauling oyster traps from the water. I pull my leg back out and walk along the shore.

'Hi,' I say as I'm approaching so as not to take him by surprise.

'Hi,' he replies, not looking up from his task.

'Any news?'

'About what?'

I roll my eyes. 'What do you think? About Dee and Ruby.'

Zac straightens and wipes his forehead with the back of his forearm.

'Nope. You heard anything?'

'No. But I was wondering ... do you know much about Erica?'

'Erica?' He squints up at me. 'Is she the one married to Samir?'

I nod.

'Nope. Don't think I've ever met her. She's a quiet one, barely leaves the house. Had a run in with Samir more than once, though.'

I feel my heart skip. 'Oh?' I say, trying to sound casual.

'He's a real hard arse. Ex cop.'

'What sort of run-ins?'

Zac hauls another trap from the creek, splashing my ankles with water. He side-eyes me. 'That's between me and Samir.'

I exhale in frustration. 'What's with the mysterious-guy routine? I'm just trying to help, to figure out what's happened.'

'I'd leave that to the cops, if I were you,' Zac says, grunting as he heaves a trap on to the sand.

'Duly noted. Do you know much about Dee's husband, Rob? Were they ... were they having some problems?'

Zac's eyes narrow. 'What makes you ask?'

I shrug, aiming for nonchalance. 'Oh, just something she said in passing. And,' I add, dropping the flippant tone. 'She, um ... she had a black eye.'

Zac frowns. 'Well, I wouldn't know anything about that.'

'Okay ...' I say with a frown of my own.

'Look, I did overhear some fights. Hard not to, the houses being so close. But Rob has an alibi, if that's what you're getting at.'

Zac narrows his eyes.

'What is it?'

'Rob's been gone for a month. Left her and the baby.'

I gape at him. 'What? How do you know that? Dee told me he'd only been gone a week.'

He looks at me like I'm daft. 'Don't you think I'd have noticed if his car had been around?'

'Do you know why she'd lie? Did she ever confide in you about anything?'

He looks at me as if sizing me up. He hesitates. Then, 'No. Did she to you?'

It's my turn to size him up and then hesitate. 'No.'

'Look, Dee must have lied about Rob. Maybe she was embarrassed he'd left her. She was like that, you know. Always making things up.'

'Oh, and you'd know, would you?' Once more, I'm furious on Dee's behalf. The way people keep talking as if she's brought all this on herself. 'Why, did you and Dee have something going on?'

Zac barks out a laugh. 'You heard that rumour, did ya?'

'Ugh. There's no point talking to you, is there?'

Zac draws himself up to his full height and glares down at me. I feel a sudden shiver of fear.

'Look, *mate*. I think I've been patient with this detective game long enough. I've said everything I have to say to the police. Now why don't you run off and mind your own business.' He stands over me, his lips curved in a sneer.

I take a step back. 'You can't intimidate me,' I snap, jabbing a finger at him. 'You're nothing but a bully. I know your type.'

'And I know yours,' he spits, jabbing a finger back at me. 'Bloody snob.'

His eyes rake over me before he stalks away.

***

3:40pm

I'm still fuming by the time I reach Cockle Street, but my pulse quickens for a different reason as I pass Dee's house and approach the Haddads's property.

The house is pretty much identical to Dee's, only with a white picket fence and purple and blue hyacinths lining the perimeter of a perfectly square, neatly mown front lawn. The garage is on the opposite side to Dee's and the plantation shutters are ocean-blue instead of white. It's very pretty, obviously well maintained, yet somehow sterile in its perfection.

There are no cars in the driveway, but possibly they're locked up. Unlatching the gate, I walk up the path and take a breath, rehearsing what I'm going to say before knocking on the front door. There's no movement inside, so I try again. Nothing.

I sigh. All that energy spent psyching myself up and no one's here. I turn to head back down the path when I hear a creaking sound. After a moment it comes again, like a door with a rusty hinge. I cross the porch and peer around the side of the house, where the noise was coming from. There's a narrow path between the house and the fence dividing the Haddads's property and Dee's. A ways down, there's a gate that's been left slightly ajar, creaking as it moves in the breeze.

Glancing over my shoulder, I head down the path and call out a hello when I reach the gate. When no one answers, I open the gate carefully and slip through. The path leads all the way along the side of the house, and at its end is a stretch of lawn, more flower beds and a few gardening tools left lying around, and around the other side of the house is the shed.

A shiver moves down my spine. It's strange seeing it from this perspective; it's much larger than it looks from across the creek, more the size of a granny flat than a shed. Could it be that Erica has simply moved in there, that Samir and Erica are living separately? My gut tells me there's more to it than that.

My focus hones and I take a step forward, knowing without making a conscious decision what I'm about to do. I look up at the house, scanning the windows of both floors and finding them empty. Heart pounding, I cross the yard. As I near the shed, the door opens and I stop in my tracks. Shit!

Erica emerges, blowing her nose. Her eyes are downcast so it's a moment before she spots me. Her eyes widen and she quickly turns and shuts the door behind her.

'What are you doing here?' she says, furrowing her brow. Her eyes are red-rimmed and puffy as if she's been crying. Then, as if realising something, her expression hardens. 'This is private property.'

'I'm sorry, I ... I just wanted to ask you some questions.'

'Questions?' Erica eyes me quizzically.

Thinking on my feet, I blurt, 'Er, I just wanted to ask you ... You see, I saw Dee that night and she said you were minding Ruby.'

Erica cocks her head to one side. 'Sorry?'

'She came over on Wednesday night, but the thing is, it was around 11pm, after you said you last saw her. She came alone, and when I asked where Ruby was, she said you were minding her that night.'

Erica narrows her eyes. 'Well that's obviously wrong, isn't it?'

'I ... I don't know. Is it?'

'What are you implying?'

I lift my hands in supplication. 'I'm just trying to see whether ... whether Dee made a mistake, or ... I mean, she couldn't have left Ruby at home alone, surely?'

Erica shakes her head and sighs. 'Delilah Waters was a very troubled person.'

'So I hear,' I mutter.

'She wasn't coping with the baby. Didn't want her in the first place,' Erica's voice has a bitter edge. 'She should have known better. Why bring a life into the world if you can't care for it? God knows what she's done, run off or killed herself or something, but if something's happened to that child ...'

'With all due respect, Mrs Haddad, you can be troubled and still be a good mother.'

Erica looks primed to argue when suddenly her shoulders slump and she sighs. 'Yes. You're right, I suppose. I just ... I worry for Ruby. She's only a baby, innocent in all this.'

A cool breeze makes me fold my arms across my chest. 'She is. It's so sad.'

The leaves of the trees lining the fence rustle as a trio of magpies land in their branches. Erica looks towards them and smiles. 'I get cross with Dee sometimes, it's true. I just wish she knew how lucky she was. If I had what she had, I'd count my blessings every day.'

There it is again: the use of 'was'. 'What does Dee have that you don't?'

Erica sighs, a sad smile touching her lips. 'Do you know ... my David would have had his twenty-first birthday this year.'

A coldness settles in my stomach. 'Oh. David was ...'

'My son, yes. My first son. He died before he was born. A miscarriage.'

'Oh gosh, Erica, I'm so sorry.'

Erica gives a small shrug, but her lips are pressed thin. 'Then came Lucy, then Amanda. And ... and Sean.' Erica's lip trembles and she turns away. 'We lost them too.'

I gasp. Four babies. She lost four of them. It's unfathomable. Too big, too awful for words. 'That's terrible. I'm so very sorry,' I offer feebly.

I place a hand on Erica's arm and she stiffens. 'It is what it is. They're still with me as long as I think of them. I'm still ... still their mother, even if they aren't here anymore.'

'Of course, you are.'

'I planted one for each of them,' she gestures to the four trees. 'It sounds silly, but it makes me feel closer to them. Having something living to tend to, to talk to.' She shrugs. 'Samir thinks I'm mad, but it helps. It does.'

I smile. 'I can understand that. It must be hard sometimes, being around Ruby when you must miss your own babies so much.' Perhaps this goes some way to explain Erica's behaviour. I soften towards her as I imagine what she must have been through.

Erica looks at me strangely. 'It's not hard. It's wonderful. I love being around babies. I'm very good with them.'

'I'm sure you are! Sorry, I didn't mean ... I just wondered whether you might feel ... I don't know ... a bit envious?'

I glance at the shed and Erica's wistful expression evaporates. 'Not at all. I love Ruby, but I know the boundaries. I'm just helping out a troubled woman look after her baby.'

'Okay, okay. Sorry. That was over-stepping. It's very kind of you to help out.'

Erica steps towards the garden bed and reaches up to caress the leaves of the smallest tree. Her back is to me so I can't see her expression.

'It's a very large shed you have there,' I say, trying to sound neutral. 'It looks a lot smaller from across the creek. What do you get up to in there so often?'

Erica turns and looks at me sharply. 'What did you say?'

'Oh! I just ... I'm not being nosey, but I couldn't help but notice you spend a lot of time there, that's all.'

With narrowed eyes, Erica looks out across the water and back at me. 'Have you been spying on us?'

'No! Of course not. I only meant ...'

'So, let me get this straight. You've been watching us,

and now you're trespassing on our property.' Erica's hands are clenched at her sides.

'I'm sorry, I wasn't spying,' I lie. 'I was only—'

Erica holds up her hands. Her face is white and pinched with fury. 'I think you should leave.'

'S-sorry,' I stammer, stepping backwards. 'Maybe I could come back another time.'

'No!' Erica's shout is almost panicked. 'Please ... just leave us alone.'

As I turn to leave, I catch an emotion other than anger as it passes across her face.

Fear.

Chapter 27

Liz

June, 2017
Wednesday, 7:45pm

'You should have seen the look on her face. And then she kicked me out!'

Adam's chuckling into his wine glass as we sit at the dining table.

'It isn't funny!'

'Well you have to admit, it was a bit much of you, Liz.'

I sigh. 'Yes, perhaps. I feel bad for her. I do. I was insensitive,' I admit, chewing a fingernail. 'She's been through so much. Four babies! I can't even imagine how you'd survive that. But that being said, you have to admit it gives her a motive. I can't help thinking she knows more than she's letting on. And she really didn't want me seeing whatever's in that shed. When I asked her what she does in there, she properly panicked.'

'Maybe she's stolen the baby!' Adam crows.

I throw my napkin at him. 'Stop it. I can't believe you're joking about this.'

'I'm sorry,' Adam stops smiling. 'That was off-colour. Did you really accuse her of being jealous of Dee?'

'Not exactly. I feel sorry for her, but you should see what she's written on Dee's Facebook page. Totally inappropriate. And what if something *has* happened to her? Even if it was suicide. Shouldn't people have more empathy? Instead they're running around calling her a whore and a bad mother. It's disgusting.'

'Lizzie,' Adam reaches across the table and takes my hand in his. 'I can't say I disagree with you. But I'm getting worried. Spying on the neighbours, trespassing ...'

'It wasn't *really* trespassing ...'

'Lizzie, both of those things are illegal. You'll be lucky if Erica doesn't call the police.'

I bite my lip and take a slow sip of wine. Is he right? Am I crossing a line?

'In all seriousness, darling,' Adam says softly, the humour gone from his eyes, 'Can you please just try to leave this with the police? I'm *this* close to dragging you down to Sydney for the rest of the week. We have a bit of money now.'

'No! Adam, that's not for spending.'

'Then what else is money for?' Adam's eyes twinkle.

I roll mine at him. '*Saving*. Besides, we're not out of debt yet so it's not *real* money.'

'Fine, spoil-sport,' Adam pretends to sulk. 'Really though, I know this Dee business is awful, but we didn't know her and we have our own lives to live. The police are doing all they can. As for you and I ... we should be thinking about the future. We'll be out of here in a week's time, and just imagine all we've got to look forward to once we're home.'

'You're right,' I try to smile.

I look out at the Haddads's home, with the shuttered blinds. Something is going on over there, and I'm going to find out what it is.

***

Friday, 7:23pm

I head to the loft while Adam cooks dinner and gaze out of the window, though there's little to see. I've not caught sight of Erica or Samir – not even Zac – today, and there's nothing of interest popping up in my Google searches. The Haddads have been at home all day, so I haven't had the opportunity to try to find out what's in the shed, but they've got to go out sooner or later, surely. Do either of them even work? One or both of them always seems to be around.

All news reports and articles are *still* saying Dee and Ruby were last seen by the water late the previous afternoon. I don't understand why the police haven't told the media the truth.

The newest articles all seem to be about Dee's 'sordid'

history, which doesn't appear to have any correlation with her disappearance, or any relevance at all, apart from giving people an excuse to bad-mouth her.

Between Dee's history as a drug user (apparently), previous mental health issues (where's the proof of this?) and her absent husband (it seems that's come out now), people are ready to believe it was a murder-suicide. Erica is quoted as having said Dee hadn't spoken to her about any suicidal thoughts, but she admits that she, and everyone, knew Dee wasn't coping with the baby.

What a bitch, I think. I'm not without empathy for her – what she's been through is unfathomable – but talking to plants as if they're your dead children is just odd, and on top of that, having experienced loss like that gives her a motive. She clearly thinks Dee is an unfit mother. And she's definitely behaving like someone with something to hide.

I rummage in my handbag and find the card that Sergeant Jamison passed me as I was leaving the station and slip it into my pocket. If I do see anything suspicious, I know who to call.

As if on cue, movement draws my eyes to the window and there it is again, the now familiar light of a torch crossing the Haddads's yard. I press the binoculars to my eye sockets and peer out. It's already adjusted to just the right distance to see someone enter or leave the shed. Sure enough, it's Erica again. She's holding something – a satchel? – which she lifts from her shoulder as she enters the shed, glancing over her shoulder before shutting the door behind her.

A scary thought enters my mind. What if she really *does* have Ruby in there?

'Boo!'

I shriek as I'm grabbed from behind and warm arms enfold me.

'You scared the shit out of me!' I exclaim, turning just enough to whack Adam on the shoulder. 'You must have crept up the stairs like a ninja.'

'Still playing spy, are we?' he teases, tucking a strand of hair behind my ear and kissing me on the cheek. Then he laughs. 'Oh, I see.'

'See what?'

He turns me so I'm facing left just in time to see Zac crossing the landing towards the bedroom – bare-chested, as usual.

I giggle, feeling my cheeks heat up. 'I wasn't ... oh gosh. No, look over *there*.' I steer Adam back to the right. 'The light is on in the shed again and Erica just went in there. And she was carrying this bulky satchel.'

'Hmm,' Adam kisses the side of my neck. 'She's probably just getting supplies for when she kidnaps you and locks you in there to punish you for trespassing.'

I laugh, but a shiver comes with it. 'Stop it. You don't think ... you don't think they *really* could have kidnapped Dee and the baby or anything do you?'

Adam sighs. 'Honestly, darling? No, I don't think that.'

'But it's not *impossible*, is it?'

'Nothing is impossible, but you said yourself you could hear the baby crying from across the water. The shed's even closer to us than Dee's house. Surely we'd have heard something by now if they were keeping a six-month-old in there.'

'You're right,' I say, knowing I'm not going to get any further with getting Adam onside. 'I'm being ridiculous. Let's eat, I'm famished.'

Adam might be able to joke about this, but he didn't see the fear in Dee's eyes that night. Despite his mother's absence and what happened with Beth and Brett, he's had a fairly sheltered existence. He hasn't had to inspect and analyse the darker side of human nature, as I have in my line of work.

And, an unwanted voice whispers, *he can be just the slightest bit condescending, can't he?* Sometimes I think he doesn't take me seriously enough. But I'm not as dumb as my hair colour and cup size make people think. Adam may be more inherently practical, but I've always been intuitive, and it's rarely led me astray.

The one time I didn't trust my instincts, I sorely paid for it.

Chapter 28

Erica

June, 2017
Monday, 3pm

Light sparkles on the creek's surface like diamonds in the sunlight. I sip my wine, a blood-red shiraz from our trip to the Hunter Valley, the getaway that was supposed to get me 're-energised', allow Samir and me to 'spend some quality time together'. I'm not sure what we took from it, other than a car boot full of wine.

The shiraz washes sharply over my tongue as the sun sinks behind the mountain. Forty bucks a bottle and I can't for the life of me understand why. I don't really understand wine. Never have. It's Samir who's the connoisseur. They all taste the same to me.

The sky changes from blue to purple to pink and I remember how, on winter evenings much like this, Samir and I would bring blankets out onto the balcony and snuggle up together on the outdoor lounger to drink expensive wine and watch the sunset. Once, we made love out here under the night sky, even though I'm sure the Dawsons were staying across the water and could have seen us if they'd happened to look out of their window. We were so caught up in the moment, we didn't care.

We were so happy here in the early days. Who wouldn't have been? This place is paradise, as they say. And we were young, still in that entitled phase of life when you can't imagine anything truly terrible ever happening.

When we met, I was nineteen and Samir was twenty-four. A lifetime's difference in age, it felt then, giddy as I was – as only silly young girls can be – with the thrill of having caught myself an older man. Now forty and forty-five, it's like the gap doesn't exist. Samir was always solidly built and, though he's spread somewhat, he's kept his shape. Only when I see the salt and pepper at his temples and the creases in his brow do I think of it, and then I look at the lines on my own face and wonder if there's any difference between us at all. Sometimes I'm sure I look like the older one.

My parents thought I'd won the jackpot with Samir. They were Catholic, old-fashioned, eager for their daughters to marry young and start having babies. So when a man started paying attention to their somewhat chubby, previously invisible, daughter, they were thrilled to bits. I was pretty surprised myself. Though I wasn't *unattractive*, I was the 'sensible' one, the quiet one. Not particularly bright or clever or interested in much apart from cooking, but well-behaved, dependable, *solid*. Whereas Jeannie was pretty and high-spirited. It didn't matter that she was as thick as two planks of wood and twice as silly, she was the one who attracted all the boys, though she never had any intention of settling down with any of them. Well, not until Gaz, who she didn't meet until she was thirty-two. Which was ironic because all I'd ever wanted was to find someone to start a family with, and she'd never wanted kids. And now look at us.

To my surprise, and despite my grandparents' disapproval, my traditional (and let's face it, borderline-racist) parents didn't seem to give a hoot that Samir wasn't *white*. It helped that he was Catholic – and wealthy, of course, whereas my family were working class through and through. It also didn't hurt that he was beautiful: dark, soulful eyes, a film-star smile and a thick head of dark curls. But it was his gentle nature that won them over. His calmness and willingness to 'do his duty', to work hard, settle down and start a family. That's like crack to Catholic parents. One taste of him and they were addicted. Even Jeannie said she'd marry him if I didn't, and she didn't even *believe* in marriage back then.

Samir wined and dined me and made me feel like a woman. And he didn't let me – or my parents – down. The day before my twentieth birthday, when we'd been dating only seven months, he proposed with a two-carat diamond solitaire ring at the restaurant he'd taken me to for the occasion.

I was the first of my friends to marry. Nowhere near the thinnest, nor the prettiest, I was a blushing twenty-one-year-old bride with my life ahead of me, a brand new house in paradise and a handsome husband. It was more than I'd ever dreamed of. I could hardly believe I'd outdone my pretty, popular sister and her silly, shallow friends.

We did everything the right way. We saved ourselves for marriage and the first time we made love, he undressed me like he was unwrapping something precious. He tried to make sure it didn't hurt, and even though it did I didn't care because I loved him, and we were married and nothing could spoil the dream I was living in. Everything was perfect.

When we found out I was pregnant, it seemed things couldn't get any better. I was still so young and it felt like life had nothing but delights in store for me. It seemed I'd been blessed in every possible way. Samir was so overjoyed he looked like he might explode with pride. It never occurred to me that I'd peaked too young and the only way left to go was down.

How proud I was! I glowed. I beamed. I watched mothers with their children and smiled, knowing someday soon that would be me. Samir couldn't keep his eyes – or his hands – off me. I felt like a goddess. I felt like I'd done the most womanly thing a person could do: I was becoming a mother.

The first time I lost a baby I was only a few weeks in. I didn't feel anything much, apart from some cramping. It was just a globby red mess that oozed out during a shower, and at first I didn't know what had happened. I'd heard about spotting during pregnancy and thought that must be what it was, only really bad. But when I talked to my friends, I realised what had happened. And I felt the void where the baby had been in more than just a physical way.

The second time I was a bit further along and didn't find out until my second scan that the baby was dead. Emotionally I was raw, feeling I'd failed – failed myself, failed Samir – and that my body had turned against me. But there was still hope. I knew we didn't have any problem *getting* pregnant, and – as I told myself back then – that was the hardest part. We just needed to *stay* pregnant.

When it happened again at four months, that time nearly broke me. Because by then I was showing, I'd felt the baby move and felt a closeness I'd not felt the previous times. I'd had numerous additional scans to ensure everything was progressing as it should, and I had hoped this time would be different. We'd thought of names and we knew the sex – a little girl we named Amanda.

And then the impossible happened. I carried You to term.

I loved them all, of course, because they are all my children. But You. You were different. I held you in my arms, even though you were already dead by the time you were born. Nothing can ever wipe that memory from my mind. No number of years can dull the intensity of the pain I feel every time I re-live the shock and loss, how empty my arms felt once you were taken away. How broken and sore my poor, battered body had become, and all without reward.

Sean was the name we'd chosen, and that's what is on your gravestone. But to me you'll always be You, the name I called you during those precious months when I carried You inside me. Now I am a mother without a child. But I always have your memory, and no one can take that from me.

After trying for a decade, I didn't have it in me to do it any longer. When I lost You, something inside me died too.

Chapter 29

Liz

June, 2017
Thursday, 10am

I'm half way down Cockle Street on a jog when I spot Zac crossing the road. He waves and I slow my pace, eyeing him warily as he approaches.

'I shouldn't have said what I said,' he says without preamble. 'I'm sorry. I've been a bit ... on edge.'

'I'm sorry too,' I say grudgingly. *Yeah, sorry not sorry*, I think. But I don't want to make an enemy of Zac, particularly as I don't quite trust him yet.

I study his face. Are you a bit *on edge* because you know something you're not saying? I wonder. But he seems sincere, and it's a bit hypocritical of me to judge when I'm holding my own cards so close to my chest.

'Look, I need to show you something,' Zac says, gesturing in the direction of the creek.

'What?'

'You'll see.'

He leads the way through the bush and over the bridge, and I refrain from pointing out that he's not using the boat. I suppose he's familiar with the movements of the tide, having known this place as long as he has.

'You seen this?' He asks a short way into the bush over the other side.

'Oh.' I stop in my tracks. It's a campsite similar to the one I spotted last week, only in a slightly different spot. There are more beer cans and rubbish scraps, only there's one noticeable difference: the embers are still smoking.

'Someone's been here recently.'

'Yeah.' Zac looks at me and I shiver.

'Just wondered if you'd had any trouble lately? Sometimes these types of folk like to steal stuff too. Your locks secure? You got a smoke alarm?'

'Um ... I think so. I'll check with Adam.'

'Anyway, just thought I'd warn you.'

I smile. 'Thanks. Listen, while I have you, have you noticed anything strange happening at the Haddads's lately?'

Zac shrugs. 'Don't think so.'

'It's just ... I can't help feeling there's something off about Erica. She's so ... jumpy and nervous all the time. And you know the shed at the side of their house? She's always in there, even late at night.'

Something crosses Zac's face. 'That *is* a bit weird. Still, it's not a crime, is it?'

'No, I suppose not.' I sigh. 'Is ... is there anything you know that you're not saying?'

Zac grunts. 'I know what you're thinking. But you can trust me. I haven't had anything to do with Dee, other than some gardening and fix-it stuff Rob wanted around the house.'

'Oh, I wasn't ...' Zac raises an eyebrow and I laugh nervously. 'Okay. Well, maybe I was. Everyone's a suspect and all that.'

Zac doesn't smile and I clear my throat. 'Uh, that's good to know.'

'I was at the pub down in Brave Cove that Wednesday night – worked a long shift from midday to midnight and stayed with a friend in the next town over. You can check if you like. The cops already have.'

'No, I ... I believe you,' I say, secretly wondering whether that's the truth.

'I'm a lot of things, but I don't go sleeping with other people's wives,' Zac says gruffly. He holds my gaze long enough that heat floods my face and I turn away.

'Right, well I'll be off,' he says, heading towards the bridge. 'One more thing, though,' he says over his shoulder. 'I'd be careful snooping around the Haddads's place.'

I pull my coat tighter to my chest.

'What do you mean?

'Like I said, he's an ex-cop. He's got some connections. But just make sure you stay out of his way, yeah?'

He doesn't give me a chance to respond before he starts trudging off.

Chapter 30

Erica

June, 2017
Tuesday, 3:15pm

I'm booked in with Doctor Jones for nine tomorrow morning, and I'm hoping it will be our last session. Honestly, there's nothing I enjoy less than sitting around being forced to talk about personal matters with a complete stranger. It's invasive. Unnecessary.

What exactly is it he needs to hear to convince him I'm perfectly fine? I've mentioned Dee, of course, hoping he'll see what a good neighbour and friend I am and how capable I am of taking care of babies and mothers. But he wants to talk more about my relationship with Dee and with Ruby. He keeps bringing it up, wanting to know how being around them makes me *feel*, and all of a sudden we're talking about why Samir and I haven't had children of our own and I end up telling him more than I mean to. I don't understand how he does it.

Dee's been acting strangely lately. I get the feeling there's something she's not telling me – apart from the fact that I'm fairly sure Rob's run off, which, frankly, I saw coming from the day he brought her up here. How someone could abandon their child is another matter, however. I simply can't understand it. But fathers are different, I suppose. It's not the same connection.

She called me last night in hysterics, saying she just couldn't cope any longer. Of course, I rushed over there and took Ruby for her. It's not the poor child's fault her mother's a wreck. But, in all honesty, I'm starting to get quite cross about the whole situation. Not about Ruby, of course, but between being stuck here day in, day out and Dee's assumption that I've got nothing better to do than be at her beck and call, I've been growing increasingly frustrated.

I called the hospital to ask whether I can come back to work soon and the new nurse – I don't know her name, but she was very rude – snapped that that was up to my 'shrink' to decide.

I've been trying to stay positive, but then the smallest thing goes wrong – like a dropped stitch or a broken glass – and anger bubbles to the surface.

I try very hard not to judge Dee, but she doesn't make it easy. Women can be very good at judging each other, especially mothers. I know that. And I'm not perfect. We're not supposed to do it, and most won't admit it, but we do. But sometimes it's justified. Some women just don't make very good mothers. And Dee's one of them. I was *born* to be a mother and yet nature made *her* one. Where's the justice in that?

I know being a single mother isn't easy. But it's not an excuse, is it? I could do it alone. I know I could. There's no question of it; when you want something badly enough, you'll do anything. That's what a real mother would do. She's not hard done by. She's just selfish.

Samir comes into the living room as I'm jigging Ruby on my hip, admiring her halo of soft red hair as she giggles and coos.

'Oh,' he says as he comes up beside me. 'I hadn't realised ...'

He turns to go, but I call him back. 'Look! She has two teeth now. Aren't they precious little pearls?'

Samir's smile wavers as he looks down at Ruby. After You died, we both had trouble being near babies and children for a while. But although it's bittersweet, I revel in it now. Yet Samir always finds an excuse to leave the room whenever I'm minding Ruby.

This time I manage to convince him to hold her and, once he recovers from the initial shock of having an infant in his arms, his face softens in a smile that warms my heart. I never tire of witnessing the effect that babies have on people. As I watch my husband holding Ruby in his arms, I glimpse the life I'd always dreamed I'd have. And I think of how much I loved him, once, until it all became about one thing. Something that never came to be.

After a minute or so, Samir clears his throat and hands her back, a suspicious shine to his eyes. He leaves the room without a word.

I watch him go with a heavy heart, leaning in to bury my nose in Ruby's hair. It's then that I smell something familiar; a distinct fragrance that isn't baby shampoo or nappy rash cream or sweet baby skin. It's perfume.

Ruby often smells of perfume, of course – mine, her mother's. But I've given her a bath – Dee doesn't bathe the poor child often enough – and she hadn't smelled of perfume until Samir held her.

The arms that cradle Ruby begin to tremble. Because I know who that perfume belongs to.

Chapter 31

Liz

June, 2017
Friday, 3:02am

Moonlight filters through the gap in the curtains and casts a silver stripe across the bed. I'm unsure if it's the cold that's woken me, but my bare feet feel frozen and I'm shivering under the bedclothes.

I'm debating whether to get out and find some socks or snuggle up closer to Adam and risk waking him, when the rhythmic creaking of floorboards underfoot sounds from the hall. Adam on his way back from the bathroom, probably. I'll get those socks after all.

I'm about to swing my legs over the side of the bed when I hear it. A soft snoring, coming from Adam's side of the bed. I reach out a hand and, sure enough, my fingertips find a warm body.

My mind jumps to the image of the smoking campfire

and my heart starts to thunder. Through the roaring in my ears, I listen for the footsteps but they've stopped.

I tap Adam urgently on the shoulder. 'Adam!' I whisper. 'Wake up!'

Adam groans softly and rolls onto his back. 'What ...?'

'Shhh!'

Adam seems to sense the urgency as suddenly he's sitting upright.

'There's someone out there,' I whisper. 'I heard footsteps. I thought it was you ... but you're *here*.'

Adam places a finger over my lips and we sit in silence, waiting.

Nothing. Then, after a beat, the distinct click of the front door closing.

'Shit! Did you hear that?'

'No. Hear what?'

'That was the front door!'

I jump out of bed and rush down the hall. I'm about to try the handle on the front door when I stop. I don't know who's out there. What if they're dangerous?

I lift a corner of the blind on the little window at the top of the door and stand on tiptoe to peek through. In the moonlight, through the mist, I can just make out a figure on the shore, climbing into a boat.

Adam appears behind me and I grab his arm.

'Look!' I hiss. 'There's someone out there.'

The figure begins rowing away, disappearing in and out of clouds of mist.

'I don't see anything,' Adam squints beside me.

'What? Keep looking. There's someone out there, rowing across the water.'

Adam rubs his eyes 'Lizzie. I don't see anything.' He sounds a bit annoyed.

'Look, I'll prove it.' I turn the door handle and push, but it doesn't open. 'What the ...?' I try again, pushing harder this time. It doesn't budge. I shove my body against it, swearing under my breath.

'Lizzie ... Liz! Stop!' Adam takes me by the shoulders and whirls me around to face him. The whites of his eyes gleam in the moonlight. 'It's *locked*.'

I stare at him in disbelief. 'No, that's impossible. How—?'

My heart thrusts itself against my ribs. Oh God, maybe he's right. Maybe I am losing my mind.

'Look.' Adam lets go of my shoulders and turns the lock on the door. He tries the handle, and the door creaks open. 'See?'

When my husband turns towards me, his eyes traveling over my face, it's not just concern I see in his eyes. It's fear.

Chapter 32

Liz

June, 2017
Friday, 10:15am

I'm trying not to think about last night, but my mind keeps wandering to the shadowy figure crossing the creek. Adam hasn't mentioned it again. I know he thinks I'm mad and have imagined the whole thing, but I can't convince myself he's right.

I'll admit, this business with Dee has stirred some things up for me, but I'm not delusional. I can concede Adam may be right that the sounds I heard in the hall may have just been the house settling (it *is* run down and rather creaky) and there's no denying the door was locked from inside, but I didn't imagine the figure crossing the creek. Adam probably wasn't able to see it due to the mist and the fact that by the time he got there they were too far away.

The ocean side of town is almost an entirely different landscape: an endless stretch of beach gives way to choppy, slate-grey sea and distant, misty mountains. As I jog the beach, it dawns on me that Dee and Ruby have been missing for over a week. I'm starting to wonder if they'll ever be found.

I researched what happens to drowned bodies, and because the lungs act like sponges and fill with water, the body sinks, at least in the beginning. The ocean's a big place and there was a king tide the night they disappeared. If no one started looking for them until days later, who knows how far out to sea they could have ended up?

It's possible Dee's just run away, of course. But wouldn't it be tricky to stay hidden for so long when the whole state is looking for you? Dee didn't strike me as someone with a grand plan.

I've been keeping an eye on the Haddads's place, but I haven't seen an opportunity to find out what's in the shed. One or both of them always seem to be at home during the day, and night-time isn't an option as Erica is always out there. I'm *not* imagining that there's something in that shed that the Haddads don't want found. I just need to find out what it is.

The wind bites into my cheeks as I begin at the southernmost side of the beach and I have to raise the hood of my windbreaker and draw the string around my face. It's colder than I ever expected it would get in this part of the world; it's the wind from the ocean and the moisture in the air that exacerbates it.

It's not until I'm halfway along the shore that I notice anything amiss. A handful of fishing boats can be seen in the waters surrounding the pier situated directly opposite the pub; that's true of any given day.

But today something's different. There's a small crowd of people on the shore and, as I draw nearer, it's clear they're all looking at something in the water.

My heart rate increases with my pace and when I reach the edge of the crowd I can see what they're looking at. At first, it doesn't register. What I'm seeing can't be real; I simply can't process it. It's as if time slows, and the sounds around me are drowned out as if I'm under water, then all of a sudden time speeds up again and everything comes into sharp focus. I fall to my knees.

'Get that hook out of my wife!' a male voice is screaming, raw with grief. Between the shifting bodies of the people who've gathered around me, I can see a tall man standing with his shoulders heaving. He's staring out at the ocean, his face the picture of anguish. I recognise him from the television.

Rob Waters.

'Oh my God.' I bend over and throw up violently on the sand. Spots dance before my eyes and for a moment I think I might faint. I wipe my mouth, retch, then fumble for the water bottle at my hip.

Voices murmur around me and then, out of the blue, Zac is there kneeling beside me. He prizes the bottle from my trembling fingers, removes it from the holster and unscrews the cap.

His eyes are haunted, his face is grey, but his voice is calm. 'You've had a bad shock. Let's get you home.'

***

In our kitchen, defrosting by the Aga, I find I can barely remember the journey back to the house. Was I carried? Did I walk?

Zac and I stare sightlessly out of the kitchen window, holding stone-cold cups of tea. Neither of us drink or speak.

'Got anything stronger?' Zac says after an immeasurable length of time.

I startle from my trance. 'Oh. Yes. Wine?'

'Got any whiskey?'

'No, I'm afraid not. Oh, wait. Tim might have had some, let me check.'

Minutes later, we're eyeing each other over the rims of our whiskey tumblers.

I'm feeling the effects of the whiskey, but my mind intermittently dances with horrors that shake me back to reality.

'That was pretty fucked up.' Zac says.

My skin feels numb. 'I can't believe it,' I murmur. 'I thought something terrible had happened, but that was ... that was ...'

'I know.' Zac polishes off his whiskey and helps himself to another. He offers me the bottle and I take it and top up my own drink.

'I'd still hoped ... you know, that she'd be okay.' Something warm trickles down my cheek and it's a moment before I realise it's a tear. I swipe it away and take a deep swallow of whiskey.

'Yeah.'

'Who ... who did that to her?' I shudder, unable to shake the image of Dee's body, pierced through by a fisherman's hook, being hauled from the water.

Zac raises one eyebrow. 'You don't think it was an accident?'

I eye Zac, wondering how much to say. I sense an ally in him, somehow, but I don't know who to trust, let alone my own instincts.

I shrug. 'It just seemed to me that she was ... I don't know, scared of someone.'

Zac meets my eye. 'Any idea who?'

I shake my head. 'I'd just got the sense ... that not everything was okay at home. That she didn't feel safe. But Rob was away, and he has an alibi. I ... I don't know.'

'Anyone else you got your eye on?' He asks, and there's a hint of challenge in his tone.

I meet his gaze. 'You know there is.'

Zac shrugs and the gesture irritates me. 'You know what I think about that.'

I exhale sharply. 'Zac. If you know something, and don't

want to say because you're worried about the cops, or whatever it is, this is more important than that. Dee is dead!'

Zac eyes meet mine. 'I don't know anything.'

I hold his gaze until it grows uncomfortable and I look away.

Zac inhales and exhales slowly. 'Look, mate. This is shit and all, but don't you reckon ... I mean, she was pretty unhappy as far as I could tell. Maybe she just lost it. Maybe it's like everyone's saying, and she's just gone and ... you know ...'

That's what someone would say if they'd had something to do with it, I can't help but think.

I wrap my dressing gown tighter around my body, 'I just ... I know I don't know her. I only met her twice. But she loved that child. It was so obvious. It just doesn't ... It doesn't add up.'

There's silence apart from the shriek and cackle of birds as they cast their silhouettes across the darkening sky.

'What do you reckon's happened to the baby?'

I close my eyes against a thrust of pain.

'I don't know.'

'Yeah,' Zac mutters. 'Me neither.

***

7pm

The shock dissolves to grief once Adam's home and the tears all come at once.

'I can't bear it,' I sob into his shoulder. 'I still thought maybe ... I was hoping ... and Ruby. Where is *she*?'

'I wish you hadn't had to see that, darling. It must have been ghastly.' Adam holds me close to his chest and I can feel his heart beating fast against my ear. His face is ashen.

I gulp back another sob, reach for a tissue and swipe at my eyes and nose. 'She'll be drowned too, won't she? If she was with Dee – and she would have to have been – she'll be gone too. It's just so unbearably sad.'

'They haven't found her yet. There's still hope.'

I pull out of Adam's embrace and sink into a chair, suddenly exhausted.

Adam's watching me with concern and something else I can't place, but I'm too overwrought to analyse anything right now. All I can think about is Dee and Ruby. All I can see is Dee's pale, bloated body pierced through by that hook, her dark, wet hair adorning her body like a mermaid's. An image of a baby doll with seaweed for hair flits across my vision and I shake my head quickly, willing it to disappear.

'I'm not sure this will help,' Adam says, reaching for a bottle of red from the wine rack and pouring two glasses. 'But I sure need a drink.'

He hands me a glass and I tip back my head and gulp it back in three swallows. It burns the back of my throat and makes my eyes water, but in the moments when the warmth spools in my stomach and spreads through my veins, it's worth it.

'Here,' Adam offers up his palm in a manner you would offer seeds to a bird. In his hand are two small pills. One is my sleep meds, the other I recognise as the Valium Adam was prescribed for his fear of flying. 'I was saving them for the flight back, but I think you might need one now.'

I don't argue, swallowing them back gratefully with a swig of wine.

'You know, darling, it's only a matter of days and then we can get out of here.'

I nod and smile, trying to reach the appropriate emotion, but I can't get there. Because I know I can't leave until I find out how Dee ended up dead, and what's become of baby Ruby.

***

Saturday, 12:01am

Adam has managed to persuade me to come to bed, and even now, though my body is weak with exhaustion and the Valium has loosened my limbs, my mind won't stop whirring. I pretend to sleep until I hear Adam's breathing slow and even out, then I creep from the bed and up to the loft.

The middle house itself seems ghostly now, as if in echo of the fate of its owner. I don't blame Rob for not wanting to stay there. Who would, after everything? Every room and every possession would be a reminder of them. Whatever was going on between him and Dee, no one with a soul could bear what that man has lost.

'I'm so sorry, Dee.' I push my face into a musty pillow and allow myself to succumb to wracking, silent sobs. I can't shake the guilt, the grief. I could sense she was in trouble. If only I'd persuaded her to stay, she'd still be here.

An owl shrieks outside the window, startling me back to the present. I shiver as I stare out into the night. All the windows are shuttered, even Zac's. But there's a light in the Haddads's backyard, as ever. A tiny square of orange. The shed light.

I take out the binoculars. There's a face at the window, dark hair and a strong jaw. Samir. He's in profile, head bent forward as if looking down at something. He brings a hand to his mouth, and if I didn't know better, I'd think he was crying.

What if everyone's looking in the wrong direction when the truth has been right in front of them all along?

'Was it you?' I find myself whispering.

And as if he's heard me, he looks up.

Chapter 33

Liz

June, 2017
Saturday, 10:02am

There's no sign of life in the Haddad residence. I've had the binoculars aimed at the property all morning and I'm fairly sure that, as of twenty minutes ago, no one is at home. Erica was packing a bag in the bedroom earlier, so I wonder if they've gone away somewhere. Before I change my mind, I throw on my windbreaker and head out of the door.

I'm being smarter about it this time, so instead of going along Cockle Street, I take the boat and moor it on the shore in front of Zac's place, where it can't as easily be spotted. I check my pocket to make sure my phone's in there; it could be useful if I find anything worth photographing.

I head along the shoreline until I reach the bottom of the Haddads's yard. Zac's warning rings in my mind, but

I shove the thought away. For all I know, he has his own agenda. Besides, there are some things that are worth taking risks for.

There's a low wire fence along the perimeter of the yard, but it's poorly maintained and there are gaps in places. My heart pounds with every step as I approach one of the gaps and carefully step through it. I creep up to the side of the shed and peek around the corner. The house looms above, its windows like unseeing eyes. It's difficult to tell with sunlight glinting off the glass, but the house appears to be empty.

I wait for a couple of minutes to be sure, then go around the front of the shed and try the handle. Locked, of course. I don't know why I dared to hope otherwise.

'What do you think you're doing?'

I jump at the sound of the voice and whirl around.

'You again?' Samir growls, eyes blazing as he looks down at me. Instinctively, I step backwards, stumble, and he grabs me by my upper arm and hauls me upright. 'Hey! Get your hands off me!'

Samir stands over me, his expression unreadable, and it's then I realise he's holding a long shovel in his other hand, coated in soil. I eye it warily, my pulse quickening.

'This is the second time you've trespassed on our property,' Samir says, his voice dangerously soft. His hand is warm on my shoulder. 'We won't stand for it again. Next time we'll call the police and have you charged. Do you understand?'

He raises the shovel, and I cower. Seeming to realise what he's doing, Samir lowers it once more and releases my arm.

'I know you're hiding something in there,' I say, rubbing my arm where he grabbed me.

Samir shakes his head. 'That's ridiculous.'

'Then why is Erica out here every night?'

Samir seems to falter, but then his face darkens. 'Been spying as well as trespassing, have you? I don't have to tell you anything. And I suggest you leave now.'

Something in his tone tells me I should do as he says. I turn to cross the yard when something catches my eye. It's Erica in the kitchen, her back to the window. I squint against the sunlight, trying to see more clearly, and that's when I notice it. Something about the way she's moving, like she's dancing or swaying. Or rocking.

***

4:39pm

It's getting dark, and Adam's not home yet even though he said he'd be early. I don't really understand what's left for him to finish down there, but I suppose he knows what he's doing.

I watch as lights come on across the creek. Samir appears in their kitchen window. He stands staring out for a minute, and instinctively I reach for the binoculars. Just as I manage to adjust the focus, he reaches out and pulls the shutters closed.

Damn it! I search the other windows in the house but they're all closed too. My focus lands on the sliding glass doors that lead to the patio; they've been left ajar. I swing the binoculars in the direction of the shed when suddenly Samir's face fills my vision, his eyes staring straight at me.

I give a shout and jerk backwards. He's standing at the bottom of his yard, past the shed and near the fence. He's staring straight up at the house in a way that sends an unpleasant tingle down my spine.

With slow, deliberate movements, he steps over the fence and onto the foreshore where a small, white boat is moored. He gets in, his eyes never leaving the house, and starts the engine.

'Oh shit,' I whisper, my heart beginning to pound.

He's coming in this direction.

I turn and bolt down the stairs and down the hallway to the front door. I check it's locked and double bolt it, lifting the blind on the little window to peer out.

Samir's closer still and my heart somersaults. With trembling hands, I take out my phone and am about to dial the police when the boat changes direction and heads to the right, in the direction of the ocean.

***

7:17pm

'Should I say something to the police?' I ask Adam after recounting the events of the day.

'Why?' he asks. 'Because Samir was in a boat?'

'No. Because he threatened me!'

'Well, you were trespassing sweetheart,' Adam sighs, looking tired. 'And he hardly threatened you.'

'He grabbed my arm, and he ... he had a shovel! Zac warned me about him, said he'd had run-ins with him before. He said he was dangerous and I should stay away.'

Adam rubs his eyes. 'Well, maybe you should listen to him.'

'It's too late for that now!'

'Liz,' Adam's tone is sharper than usual. 'You do understand that what you did was illegal and, frankly, dangerous. You don't know how people will react when they find someone sneaking around on their property.'

'That's why I'm so scared.'

Adam runs his fingers through his hair. I notice for the first time that a few grey hairs have appeared just above his ears. I feel guilty that all of this is taking its toll on him too, but I can't just let go of it if Erica and Samir are somehow involved in what happened.

'Look. He didn't actually come here, did he?'

'No.' I fold my arms across my chest. 'But he was trying to scare me. I know it. My instincts are telling me the Haddads have something to do with what happened, Adam, and I can't ignore it this time. I won't! I won't go through that again'.

'Liz ...'

'You didn't see Dee that night, Adam. She was scared!

Maybe it was of Erica or Samir. A jilted lover, or a jealous wife ... I don't know. But something isn't right here. Something doesn't fit. I know they're hiding something!'

'For God's sake, Liz, can you hear yourself?' Adam shouts and I flinch. He's never raised his voice at me before.

Adam grits his teeth and lowers his voice. '*None* of this means the Haddads have got anything to do with what happened to Dee. She was found in the ocean for Christ's sake. You said yourself she'd been drinking, and you heard a scream later that night. The fact is she probably just fell in the creek and drowned. Or she's taken her own life. I'm sorry, Liz, I know this is hard for you, but this has got to stop.'

'If it was suicide, why would she scream?' I whisper.

Adam closes his eyes and sighs. 'Lizzie, please listen.' He puts his hands on my shoulders. 'There are endless reasons why she might have screamed. Falling into the water being one of them. Maybe it wasn't even her you heard. Can you admit that's a possibility?'

I nod my head.

'Even if it wasn't suicide. Don't you think it's possible she simply fell? Or had an accident in the boat?'

'They didn't find her boat floating around out there though, did they? And it doesn't explain where Ruby went. She wasn't with her when I saw her.'

Adam closes his eyes, a muscle feathering along his jaw. And I know it, now. He doesn't believe I saw her at all.

'Please, Adam. I'm not crazy. I just know, in my gut, that Samir and Erica have something to do with—'

'You're wrong!' Adam's tone is so sharp is startles me.

'Why won't you believe me?' I whisper. 'Something strange is going on. Don't you think it's weird that reports are still saying that Dee and Ruby were last seen on Wednesday afternoon when I've told the police that's not true. Zac said Samir used to be a cop ... What if he's got connections, if there's some sort of cover up ...?'

'Liz.'

'If you can explain to me why the police would withhold a vital piece of information from the public, I'll stop talking about it. I promise.'

Adam's expression is solemn, almost sad. He looks defeated. 'I know why,' he says. 'I tried, Liz, I really did. I tried to protect you from this.' He rubs his eyes and I notice the shadows beneath them. 'Call the police,' he says, handing me his phone. 'Then you'll see.'

Eyeing Adam warily, I search my handbag and find Sergeant Jamison's card. She answers after four rings.

'Jamison.'

'Sergeant Jamison, it's Elizabeth Dawson from Oyster Creek. We spoke last week about ... about Dee and Ruby?'

'Mrs Dawson, yes. How can I help?'

'Well ...' I glance at Adam who's watching me with an unreadable expression. 'It's just that you said to call if I thought of anything that might help. And ... well, I think there's something going on with Dee's neighbours, the Haddads.'

'Oh?' Jamison sounds surprised. 'What do you mean, exactly?'

'Well, there's what I told you, about Samir coming out of Dee's house carrying a bag the night she disappeared. And a day or two before I saw Erica shouting at Dee out the front of her house.'

There's a pause on the other end of the line. 'Okay. And do you know what they were arguing about?'

'They weren't arguing – it was just Erica shouting and Dee standing there taking it. Dee was holding Ruby, so it was really rather awful. I couldn't hear what they were saying but Dee looked very upset.'

'I see. Well, thank you for letting us know, Mrs ...'

'No, that's not all! The strangest thing is that Erica has been going into the shed in their yard at the strangest hours – even the middle of the night. I have the feeling she may be hiding something in there.'

'And how do you know this exactly?'

'I've been watching them.'

'I see. With ... binoculars?'

'Well, yes.'

'I see.'

There's a long pause on the other end of the line.

'Look, I know how that sounds, but don't you think this whole thing is suspicious? Erica can't have children, so maybe she's become obsessed with Ruby and is jealous of Dee. When I went to see if I could speak to Erica or Samir they shouted at me and told me to get off their property or they'd call the police.'

When Jamison speaks again, her tone is that of someone cajoling a child.

'Mrs Dawson. We appreciate your interest in the case and your efforts to help with the investigation. But I'm afraid I have to inform you that Mrs Haddad has reported you for harassment.'

'What?' My mouth opens in shock. I look at Adam, but he looks away.

'And Mr Haddad was in his full rights to ask you to leave his property as you were in fact trespassing.'

They're sounding just like Adam, I think with dismay.

'Okay.' I say, my voice weak.

'Mrs Dawson,' Jamison's tone is gentle. 'We know what happened in London, with your client and her child.'

I inhale sharply.

'We've spoken to your husband, and out of concern for your well-being and that of everyone involved, we strongly advise you against involving yourself any further in this case.'

My mind spins. I feel off-balance, sick.

'You may as well know, as it will be all over the media tomorrow, that the post mortem on Mrs Waters has come back and there's no evidence of foul play. It's been confirmed as an accidental death by drowning.'

I let the shock sink in.

Death by drowning. It was an accident. Just an accident.

I was wrong, after all.

Again.

Chapter 34

Liz

November 2016
Wednesday, 12:04pm

I just want to save my little girl. Please.

I shove the note into my pocket and thrust open the office door, bracing myself against the icy wind. My heels click along the pavement like a metronome, the sound keeping time with my pounding heart.

Please don't be too late.

The moment I heard her voice on the phone, I knew I'd been wrong. It's hard to fake that kind of fear. But if that hadn't convinced me, what I heard next would have. A man's voice, snarling the most horrific things, and a baby's cries. Cries of pain that I knew would haunt me for all of my days.

I can't believe it's come to this, that I could have missed the signs. She didn't qualify for a women's refuge as she wasn't in a domestic violence situation. Except that she was. And I failed to realise that.

Please don't be too late.

My hand hovers over the doorknob. The speed that catapulted me here has vanished; time now moves in a drunken stagger. I'm too late. My body knows it, telling me with the frenetic beat of my heart and the moisture in my palms. I smell it in the quiet of a house that has never before known silence.

My muscles twitch to run, but as in a dream, a nightmare, I'm pushing open the door, quaking as I follow the crimson trail that mars the shabby carpet. Thinking, wildly, that perhaps it's only paint. Hadn't she been talking of renovations? Sprucing up the old sunroom? It's a groundless hope, confirmed when I find them, with abrupt finality, not in any of the bedrooms, but curled together on the kitchen floor.

The brutal beauty of the scene winds me. They could be sleeping, were it not for the dark liquid pooled around them, reflecting a flickering, fluorescent halo. She, on her side, matted hair copper-streaked, body curled around the infant. Both are deathly still. Both are as white as the frost spidering across the window pane above them. Mother and child, locked in an eternal embrace.

I don't feel my knees hit the floor. 'Oh my God,' I whisper as the world fades around the edges. 'Oh God, what have I done?'

Chapter 35

Liz

June, 2017
Saturday, 9:49pm

Their names were Christy and Bella Hill, and I'm the reason they died.

Squeezing my eyes shut, I throw back a pill with a slug of wine, withdraw the slip of paper from between the pages of the abandoned thriller and stare at it, fingers trembling.

I just want to save my little girl. Please.

I release a deep, shuddery breath. The words are faded, the paper aged and worn, though it's been little more than half a year. The last words Christy Hill would ever write. And I ignored them.

I push the scrap of paper deep into my pocket and swear I can feel the heat of it against my leg. I'm supposed to have burned this, along with the print outs of the emails she wrote me, the tangible reminders of my failure. That was my therapist Tanya's advice. She said I'd worked through the guilt and there was no sense continuing to relive it. But I haven't worked through it yet – not even close.

Because it turns out I'm one of those women, after all. Or I was, at least. The first to blame the victim – thinking she's exaggerating, making things up for attention, for money – when, all along, the real culprit was staring me in the face.

Christy Hill was a twenty-two-year-old former drug-addict and she had a seven-month-old baby named Bella. She'd named her after the heroine in the *Twilight* novels. She'd escaped a domestic violence situation, or so she said, but there was never any evidence of abuse. She was trying to claim benefits as well as the single-parent allowance. She'd applied for government housing. The husband claimed he was innocent, and that Christy was framing him. He claimed she'd cheated – whether she had or not was never proven – and was trying to pin a wife-beating label on him to get him out of her life so she could move on with her new lover.

You only had to look at the girl – troubled background, young, uneducated, former drug addict, history of attention-seeking behaviour, too pretty for her own good. And him – wealthy background, expensive education, well mannered, well spoken. General consensus was Christy had planned it all, to get what she could out of the situation. She was deceitful, conniving. Vindictive. *A bitch.*

I had been in charge of Christy's case. We're required to take any allegation of domestic violence seriously, so we went through the usual procedures and Christy was instructed to contact me if she was in any trouble. Which she did. After the last time police were dispatched to her home and her husband, who was supposedly threatening her, was nowhere to be found, I got fed up. Our case-loads are sky-high and we are under-staffed and under-funded. I was heavily involved in another case and it was eating up all my time and energy. It's no excuse. But that's what happened.

Christy's last plea for help – a note slipped under my office door – went unanswered. A neighbour had heard the commotion and phoned the police, but they were too late.

They found me at the scene. I don't remember any of it, but I'm told I was found kneeling by the bodies, appearing to be in some sort of trance-like state. To this day, I have no idea what came over me. I was arrested, and released later once they'd ascertained who the real – and sole – perpetrator was. The baby's father and Christy's ex, Jared Owen, was found in the back shed, trying to gas himself in the car. He didn't succeed and, after a full confession, was locked away for life for double murder. I was charged for not having immediately reported the crime. One of the most shameful experiences of my life.

It was revealed in court that Jared had killed the baby first to punish Christy. *The baby first.* What kind of a monster is capable of that? I've never stopped imagining what that poor woman witnessed. I don't know the feeling first hand, but biology is a powerful thing. And we're programmed to be bound to our young, to protect them. It was evident in their final embrace.

Jared was distraught, screaming over and over that he didn't mean to do it. That's why, watching Rob break down on the shore when Dee's body was found, I couldn't be sure it wasn't guilt that was the cause of his grief. If he didn't have an airtight alibi, I wouldn't be sure.

Jared's confession meant I didn't have to provide much evidence, but my time spent in interview rooms detailing Christy's case file was the most shameful of my life. To have to admit she'd come to me the day she was murdered, and I'd done nothing ... I wanted to disappear. I wanted to die. Because of me, a woman and an innocent child were dead.

All right, I didn't take a knife and stab them to death. That's what my therapist loves to remind me. It wasn't my fault, it's solely the fault of the perpetrator who decided to take that action. And I knew that – should have known that; it was my *job* to know that – and there was something I could have done about it. And I didn't. I *didn't*.

I take a long, deep swallow of wine and let the tears fall, let the ache unfurl and spread. I haven't let myself do this in a long time, but now I let the grief crash over me like a tidal wave. I don't even hear Adam come in.

***

11pm

I listen to the thump, thump of Adam's heart as I rest against his chest. His fingers stroke my hair and I succumb to the gentle rhythm of both. You always hear a heartbeat described as soothing, but I've never felt that way – at least not until this moment with Adam's gentle fingers in my hair and the calming effects of Valium doing their work. Listening to someone's heartbeat has always made me think of our mortality – of blood, and organs, and how suddenly they can malfunction and life can be turned off, like a switch.

It's had to come to this, and I accept it now. Adam and the police are right. There's no other explanation. I've been projecting all along, imagining things that weren't there. The bump in the night. Maybe even the entire evening with Dee, although I doubt I imagined that.

Even the sinister-looking campsite and Zac's warning. There was no danger there, after all. On his way home, Adam had run in to the guy who'd been camping there; he said he'd been sleeping rough as he didn't have the funds to camp at a proper site. He seemed harmless, Adam said. He asked whether it was him I saw in the boat that night and he said he was night fishing for bream as it's the best time to catch them. Nothing sinister about that at all.

I suppose part of me knew I was grasping at straws, but after what happened I've been so desperate to make amends that I suppose, unconsciously, I was looking for ways to do that.

Dee and Ruby reminded me of two people I could have saved. I think they did from the moment I first saw them together, although I didn't realise it then. That scene, mother and child in a pool of blood, lives in my mind so clearly that I feel like it still exists, so real that I could open a door and step back into the memory. And I suppose until I can find a way to accept what happened, and forgive myself, it will always be with me.

Dee is dead and any moment now they will probably find Ruby's body. There's nothing anyone can do to change that.

Chapter 36

Erica

June, 2017
Monday, 5:16pm

I sit on the couch with my head in my hands, shaking all over. I can't believe what I've done. I don't know if she'll ever forgive me, and if she doesn't I'll never see Ruby again. The thought fills me with a fear as intense as physical pain.

It was those messages that started it. After I smelled her perfume on Samir, I did the sort of thing my mother taught me never to do. She said it was in a man's nature to stray and, as wives, it was our job to turn a blind eye and make sure they were dependant on us so that they would always come home. They would keep paying our bills and putting food in our children's mouths. Condoning infidelity isn't particularly Christian, if you ask me, but people rarely ask for my opinion.

So I looked through his phone and, sure enough, there

were a stream of messages between Dee and Samir, dating back weeks. My blood ran cold and I felt physically sick. Suspecting what I might find was nothing compared to the terrible reality of actually finding it.

I'm not an angry person by nature. I've always prided myself on my ability to stay calm in stressful situations. That's what made me so good at my job. Dealing with women in the throes of labour and juggling newborns day in, day out takes a lot out of a person, and those with short fuses generally don't last long. You can understand it's not everyone's cup of tea being overworked and undervalued – not to mention underpaid – and yet you're expected to do it all with a smile. Always giving while others take and take.

Apparently, I am a giver. That's what we talked about in my session today. Doctor Jones said it's only natural I'd reached a point where I could give no more. He knows about how Dee depends on me – I've told him that much – and he knows what happened at work from the reports. I *touched* on my history of infertility, just to see if that was what it would take to get him off my back, and he said it was understandable that in my line of work and with Dee's dependence on me for help with Ruby, that I would feel resentful. He thinks that it goes a long way to explain the *Incident* at work. I didn't tell him the whole truth. Some things are private, and I couldn't bring myself to share it with a stranger when I hadn't even told Samir.

The final straw was the news I'd received the morning

of the *Incident*. I'd been to the doctor about some women's issues and was told that I was suffering from primary ovarian insufficiency. In other words, I was going through early menopause.

I'd known for a long time that I wouldn't – or couldn't, more like – have children. We could have tried IVF, but it seemed pointless because the problem wasn't that I couldn't *get* pregnant, but that I didn't seem to be able to carry a baby to term. Not alive, anyway. Doctors couldn't tell me why and said there was still a chance I could carry a healthy baby to term, but I didn't have it in me to face losing another child. Five times is enough. And I'll always have You, my sweet, darling Sean. No one can take your memory from me.

Being sure I couldn't have children but hoping there still might be a possibility is very different from knowing once and for all that it is impossible. All that loss and feeling that I'd failed as a woman came flooding back; I felt like I was drowning. And after talking to Doctor Jones, the weight of what I'd left unsaid was crushing.

I waited until I got home to cry. I'm a private person and don't like showing my feelings to others, particularly strangers. But I didn't survive over a decade of grieving You to just keel over and give in to my grief. I owe You more than that.

Doctor Jones suggested it might make me feel better to express my feelings, and he gave me some phrases to use that were 'assertive' yet respectful, rather than passive.

So I did what he said. I decided to take control, to stand up for myself. Samir was out and not answering his phone, so I decided I'd deal with him later.

I didn't mean to shout at Dee. It was meant to be a calm, civilised discussion in which I let her know in no uncertain terms what she'd done with my husband was wrong and that it had hurt me very deeply. I would give her a chance to apologise; I wasn't sure I could forgive her, but I'd at least hear her side of things.

That's not how it went at all. The things I said! All the names you could ever call a woman; some I'd never uttered aloud before. It was like a dam broke, and then out it all came. All the years of suppressing the pain, the loneliness, the sense of failure and loss – I heaped it all on Dee. Poor Ruby was in so much shock she didn't even cry at first. To think she saw me like that! It's unforgiveable.

Dee told me I'd got the wrong end of the stick and that I'd better speak to my husband. I don't know what I expected. For her to confess. Apologise. But I hadn't anticipated she'd deny it. And that just made me angrier.

When Samir came home, I shouted some more. But then he explained. He told me the truth about why he's been going over there, and the relief of it was so exquisite I burst into tears. I ran into his arms, and for the first time in as long as I can remember, we just held each other.

But now I keep reliving the things I said to Dee, and I'm frightened by the intensity of my own rage. I don't recognise the person who could have said those things;

it's as if someone else took over my body. Poor Dee looked so defeated. I'm a terrible person to do what I've done. Maybe they were right to send me to Doctor Jones.

I have to put things right. So, I pick up the phone and dial Dee's number.

Chapter 37

Dee

June, 2017
Sunday, 5:49pm

'So what have you been doing all month?' I try to keep my tone casual, but I can hear the rise in inflection on the word 'doing.'

There's an elephant in the room. The reason he's left remains unsaid, although we both know what it is.

'Can we get to the point?' Rob says, dodging the question. 'It's been a long day and I could really use some shut-eye.'

'You know you can always stay here,' I try, gesturing in the direction of our bedroom.

Rob's lips harden into a thin line and I regret my words. I'm coming off desperate, already.

'You don't want to be here,' I say flatly.

A muscle twitches in his jaw. 'Not particularly, if I'm honest.'

Though I can hardly expect any different, the rejection still lands like a punch. I turn away and take a long swallow of wine.

Rob runs a hand over his three-day growth and sighs. He's perched awkwardly on the barstool in our kitchen as though he doesn't belong there, in a place he's sat every morning for almost three years.

He looks like shit. His hair is unwashed and his skin has a greyish pallor. He looks like a grieving man and, suddenly, his pain hits me like it's my own, so sharp it splits me in two.

'How is Ruby?' he asks. He avoids eye contact, his gaze focussed on his tatty fingernails.

'She's fine. She's, uh ... she's actually sleeping most of the night now.'

Rob's eyes widen and I grin. He gives a weak smile in echo and I realise there will never be anyone like him for me. There is no other person who feels about Ruby the way I do. No other person who thinks of her as the most precious being in the universe.

'That's amazing,' he's beaming for a moment before his smile turns sad. 'We thought that day would never come. God, those early days when she screamed all bloody night ...'

'Which you mostly snored through,' I say, rolling my eyes.

Rob acknowledges that fact with a sheepish smile.

'Do you want to see her?'

I watch an internal battle play across his features. And as I watch him, I remember how dear those features are to me.

'Okay,' he croaks.

We go to her room and he looks down at her. I recognise, feel in my own heart, the love I see in his eyes, and I share in those emotions flitting across his face: awe, fear, adoration. But then his eyes tighten at the corners, and they start to glisten and something inside me knows. It just knows that we're never coming back from this. Even still, I have to try. Because he and Ruby are everything. How did I never realise they were everything until it was too late?

'She looks exactly like you,' he whispers, a touch of awe in his tone, but I can't interpret the full measure of his meaning.

'So I'm told,' I whisper back with a smile, longing to reach over and take his hand.

We hold each other's gazes, and time stands still for a moment.

I open my mouth to tell him, to confess and beg for his forgiveness, but a shadow passes over his face, and the atmosphere shifts.

'What did you want to see me about, Dee?' he asks once we're back in the kitchen. 'You made it sound pretty important.'

'Oh. Do we have to get onto that right now? I was hoping we could ... I had some dinner sorted. There's some more wine in the fridge. I thought maybe ...'

Rob's face turns stony. 'Thought we could what?' His tone is dark. 'Just forget everything for the night? Pretend everything's okay?'

'No. But ... I've missed you.'

'Well,' Rob pushed his chair back and stands as if to leave. 'That's your doing, isn't it?'

'What exactly is it you think I've done?' I shout.

He looks incredulous. 'Are you serious? You know exactly what you've done, Delilah. Or more like *who* you've done.' He points out of the window accusingly.

Amidst it all I cringe. The vulgarity doesn't suit him.

He looks on edge, ready to say more. My mind races. Does that mean he doesn't know about Ruby? That it may still be salvageable? Cheating is one thing. Some people can come back from that; they must. But if he knows the worst of it, we're done for.

There's white-hot fury in his eyes but then he closes them and takes a deep breath.

'You asked me to come, so here I am. What is it you want, Dee?'

There's one last chance, specific to my skill set. I grasp at it, hoping.

'You,' I tell him, truthfully. 'You. You're all I want.' I throw my arms around him, clasp the back of his head in both my hands and stare up into his eyes, willing him to believe me. To forgive me. He doesn't move; his body is as rigid as stone, but he hasn't pulled away.

'Do you still love me?' he asks softly. The pain in his eyes is more than I can bear. 'Did you ever?'

'I always have, and I still do.' I know my words sound hollow, trite, in light of it all, but I mean them. 'I always will. That's why I hoped ... I'd hoped ...'

Time stands still, and I know that no matter what comes next I'll remember this moment forever. I close the distance between us and press my lips to his.

For a moment, there's no response. But when I stroke his face, Rob lets out a sound that's half whimper, half moan and then he's kissing me, hard and fast like he's been starved for me.

Then, out of nowhere, he shoves me away.

'What are you ...?'

'I can't,' Rob gasps, looking at me with pain and anger in his eyes. 'I have to go.'

He turns away from me, but I grasp his forearm. And pull him back 'Please,' I whisper, reaching for the last weapon in my artillery. 'What about Ruby? She misses you. How could you do this to her?'

Rob gapes at me. 'How could *I* do this? Believe me, none of this is how I wanted things to go. *None* of this was up to me!'

'Please,' I sob, desperate now. 'Please just tell me so I can understand.'

'You *know* why.'

'No, I *don't!*'

Rob reaches into his coat pocket and thrusts a piece of paper to in my face.

'I had to be sure,' he says, his voice dangerously soft.

When I look up, his eyes are filled with a kind of rage I've never seen before.

'And now I am.'

Chapter 38

Dee

June, 2017
Sunday, 6:30pm

The floor rushes up at me. I land on my arm, pain like lightning shooting up from my elbow and wrist. My gasp echoes in the room.

He's staring at his hands, his mouth agape. The anger has vanished. His face is a white mask, drawn tight with horror. He looks at me and the expression in his eyes morphs from regret to conflict.

My throat closes against speech. There's too much, and yet nothing, to say.

Rob turns sharply to face the window, as if worried someone's seen, but the shutters are drawn. He turns to face me, and his eyes are haunted.

I can't move or speak. I stay where I fell, pain pulsing through me, the area around my eye on fire. The slip of paper lies on the floor just out of reach, the words DNA TEST RESULTS at the top of the page glaring like a neon sign. The words burn into my corneas, but I don't feel anything yet. I'm in shock. Numb.

'Fucking hell, Dee,' Rob rasps. His hands are shaking. 'Look what you made me do.'

Even under the glaring exposure of what I've done, his words light a fuse. I burn. '*Made* you do?' A croaky laugh escapes then dissolves into a cough.

Rob's shaking his head and I see it in him, the hypocrisy, the devil on his shoulder convincing him what he's done is okay, that the cause justifies the means. He laughs bitterly. 'You know I'm not like that, Dee. I'm *not!* You made— I've never done it before. Never! Even though ...' He clenches his hands and my cheekbone throbs in response. 'They all warned me about you. I didn't listen. I should've listened. Now look! Look what's happened!'

He's looking around maniacally, as if something in the room can save him, as if he can find something to dig his way out of this. And I can't believe how something – someone – I thought was so strong has crumbled this easily.

Ruby chooses this moment to break into a wail. There's no lead up, no slow build, just her shrill keening piercing the air.

Rob's head jerks towards the cot. And in that moment the numbness evaporates. I feel a flash of fear. 'No,' I shout, but it comes out as a whisper.

Ruby's cries escalate and my heart thunders against my ribs. Rob tears his gaze from the cot and my fear turns to pain – deep, searing pain made richer with shame. My husband's face is the picture of agony.

'I'm sorry,' I sob as I try to push myself up with my arm. 'Rob. Oh God. I'm sorry.'

Rob's face is white, his jaw clamped shut, teeth exposed in a tragic imitation of a smile. A spot on his neck jumps with his pulse. 'Why?' he says through his teeth, a tear bursting from the corner of one eye and running down his cheek. '*Why?*'

Ruby has gone silent and all I can hear is the roar of blood in my ears. A catalogue of memories flutters through my mind: Rob on bended knee, eyes bright with fear and hope, his feet entangled with mine in bed, the first kiss of the thousands he placed on Ruby's brow.

I double over with the pain I deserve to feel, the pain I wished I could take from him. 'It was only once. Just once. I'm sorry. I'm sorry.' My voice is dead. 'I love you.' I can't look at him.

I don't even hear him leave.

Chapter 39

Liz

June, 2017
Sunday, 4:55pm

It's the third cup of coffee I've made, and the third I haven't drunk. I pour the tepid remains down the sink and stare out across the water. In the growing dark, the three grand houses seem ghostly, and I have to turn away. Two more days and this place will be just a memory, and I can try to put everything that's happened behind me. I'll make an appointment with Tanya again, with a view to working through some things. It's high time I put some demons to rest.

I pass the fridge on my way to the bedroom and automatically reach for the handle. I hesitate, shake my head, then make my way down the hall and into the bedroom. I let myself fall backwards onto the bed and lie there for a while, staring at the cracks in the ceiling. There's a patch of mould above one of the cornices and I can hear something scuffling behind the wall. A rat, probably, I think with a shudder. We can't get out of here soon enough.

I reach for my iPad and enter the passcode, frowning when I am denied access. I try twice more only to receive the same message that my password is incorrect. It's then I realise it's Adam's iPad; he must have taken mine by mistake.

I head to the loft and pick up the thriller I'm struggling to get into, but after five minutes I realise I'm not taking anything in. Sighing, I roll onto my stomach on the daybed and peek through the curtains. Zac's lights are on, as are the Haddads's, but – of course – the Waters's home is in darkness. I wonder whether Rob will return, or whether he'll sell and find somewhere else. That's what I'd do, if I were him. I draw the curtains closed and tell myself to think of something – anything – else.

Without knowing quite how, I find myself back in the bedroom. I fluff the pillows, straighten the duvet and slip on my dressing gown. The iPad stares at me from its position on the bedside table. Something's scratching at the corners of my mind, and although I know it's in my best interests to ignore it, I also know I won't.

I carefully pick up the iPad and recline on the bed with the device held above my face. I try the passcode we share for our joint bank account, but it doesn't work. Then I try our wedding anniversary – nope. I go to 'switch user' and find the guest login. Apparently, Adam's neglected to put a password on it as I'm immediately granted access.

I feel a twinge of guilt at using his device without his permission, but there's also an inexplicable frisson of excitement, like when I used to snoop around in my mum's things before she left because I suspected her of having an affair (I was right), or as a teenager when I'd occasionally slip a tenner from my dad's wallet while he was out of the room – that hyper-awareness that at any moment I could be caught.

I open Facebook, but it's logged in as Adam. I'm about to log out when a Messenger alert pings. Trying not to look, but unable to help myself, I see it's written in Chinese characters, probably Mandarin as Adam's been learning the language in the hopes it will help him to liaise with overseas clients and China will potentially be one of his biggest markets.

I hover the mouse over the 'log out' icon when another message pings through. This time, it's an image: a young Asian woman in lingerie posing seductively for the camera. It's clearly an amateur mirror-selfie and not professional soft porn.

Warmth floods my chest and spreads up to my face. Surely this is just some click-bait designed to lure random men to a porn site – I know it happens to me now and then. Without hesitation I click on the message and a conversation reel comes up.

My heart is thudding out of time. What the fuck? There are messages dating back to January, and Adam has been replying to nearly all of them. Obviously, I can't understand what they're saying, so with trembling hands I copy the most recent message from the woman and Google 'Mandarin to English translator'. When it pops up I paste the text into the window and close my eyes. When I open them, my heart sinks.

You are so sexy, I can't wait to make you naked. When will we meet?

There has to have been some sort of misunderstanding. Adam wouldn't encourage some other woman like this. What has he said in response? I clutch at the hope that maybe it's been about business until now, and she's got the wrong idea and sent him these messages. I copy one of Adam's previous messages and paste it into the translator. The translation isn't perfect, but the meaning is clear.

Only a few more weeks and we can meet again. Can't wait to see that beautiful body again.

My skin flushes hot then cold. This can't be right. *Again?* My stomach lurches at the implications of that one word. There must be a mistake. A mistake that will end up being a funny anecdote at social occasions when we're back in London. We're planning a future together. We're buying a house, starting a business. He adores me. I adore him.

But those are the exact words he's said to me.

Everything goes out of focus and for a second I think

I'm going to pass out. I stand on shaky legs and run, tripping, to the bathroom. I just make it before I throw up, acid bile and the mushy remnants of the crackers I had as a snack sticking to the sides of the bowl. I press my cheek against the cool seat, my mind a blur of thoughts.

I sit up and look in the mirror. My skin is pale and blotchy; my eyes stare wildly back at me. *We have it all planned. We're in love. Happy. How can this have happened? How can he have done this?*

I stare at the iPad that's still in my hand as if it is the enemy. I have to make sure. So, deliberately, I go through the messages, pasting the text of at least five of them into the translator. All of them are sexually explicit. There are naked photos of him, of her. It's stomach-turning. Sickening. The last message is dated yesterday.

I glance at my phone. Fuck. It's 5:30pm; he'll be home soon. What the hell am I going to do? What will I say? Instinctively I go to call Adam, the person I reach out to in a crisis, and then the weight of it all hits me so hard I throw up again, so violently my throat burns.

The iPad pings and a text message appears on the screen. I'm confused for a moment before I realise the message is intended for Adam. It mentions something about contracts, so presumably from someone involved in the business.

Adam's phone must have synched to his iPad. I scroll through his messages.

My whole body goes hot, then cold.

There's no name, just a number. And the message:

When can you come over?

It's dated the night Dee went missing.

If you don't come now, I'll tell her everything.

I press my hand to my chest, unable to process what I'm seeing. I scroll back through the messages until I find the words 'she's yours' and click on the photos attached. I click and click but it's pixelated and won't load properly. 'Come on, come on ...' I mutter under my breath.

And then I hear the front door slam.

Chapter 40

Dee

June, 2017
Wednesday, 1:55am

I take a deep swallow of wine as I pace the living-room floor. Where is he? He said he was five minutes away, and that was before I came back from across the creek.

He's so unreliable. When I didn't hear from him all day, and it got until bloody ten at night, I decided I'd take matters into my own hands. I sent him a message warning him that if he didn't meet with me soon, I'd tell his wife everything. And then I dragged the dinghy out of the garage and took myself across the creek.

Admittedly, it wasn't one of my best plans. I'd been drinking, and the tide was dangerously high, almost reaching our back fence. A storm was due; I could feel it in the air, and, as proof of my premonition, it's starting to drizzle now. It had seemed, at the time, the only way left to confront him, as he didn't seem to be taking my requests seriously. But it's worked out better this way. Much, much better.

I can see why he's so desperate to protect his marriage. Liz is the type of person you like on sight. She's lovely-looking, of course, but not in an intimidating way. Warm and sweet yet self-assured. She was so welcoming, despite me showing up drunk so late at night. In another lifetime, we might have been friends.

The second Liz answered the door, I knew I couldn't tell her the truth. That I'd do whatever I could to protect her from it. She's innocent in all this, and I've wrecked enough lives already. I might have made some mistakes, but I'm not vindictive. I don't like causing pain.

But Adam doesn't need to know that. The threat of me telling Liz everything and spoiling his plans for his perfect little life is real, as far as he knows.

It's not her I'm out for. It's him. And freedom. At long last, freedom – for me, for Ruby.

Adam showing up across the creek when he did ended up working to my advantage. I'd run out of options to keep the threats at bay, and Rob clearly wants nothing more to do with me, so when I saw a light on across the water and recognised Adam as one half of the couple in the window, I did some Googling.

Turns out Adam got married a few weeks ago, so I figured the woman in the window was his wife. A pretty decent bargaining tool. And with the recent death of his father and the sale of the house going through, knowledge to which I'm now privy thanks to Liz, he'll soon be rolling in money. With the price houses around here are going for at the moment, the amount I need won't even leave them skint.

I check my phone. Still nothing. For God's sake, hurry up! I'm going to be shattered when Erica brings Ruby back tomorrow. Topping up my wine, I sip and pace, telling myself that it will all be worth it in the end. I may have lost Rob, but I still have Ruby. She's everything, and I'll do anything to protect her. After tonight, my baby and I will finally be safe, and we can get out of this place. Start over somewhere new.

The knock at the door startles me so much I trip, and a generous slosh of wine escapes the rim of my glass and lands in a puddle on the floor. I must be more nervous than I thought. I grab one of Ruby's onesies that's drying on a clothes horse and quickly mop it up before answering the door.

'Hi,' he says, his face a study of indifference. From his expression, you'd think that by simply showing up he is doing me a favour.

But even though his arrogance pisses me off, I'm reminded of why I was tempted. Even as distant and as solemn as he's looking at this moment, there's something about him.

Rob and I were going through a rough patch after several failed attempts at fertility treatments, and because I was refusing to try IVF he'd grown distant and sulky. It's not an excuse, of course. But with Rob sullen and away for work a lot, running into Adam at the pub one night and having a few drinks felt like a holiday compared to the tense, silent evenings I'd been sharing with my husband.

Adam's one of those people who has that ability to make you feel like you're the most fascinating person he's ever met. That night, he made me laugh, and his obvious appreciation of my opinion, and – let's be honest – my appearance, made me feel noticed, wanted, when recently all I'd been feeling was that I was lacking in all the ways a woman can be lacking. I wasn't maternal enough; I didn't want a family to take care of; I wasn't the doting little wife staying at home baking, or whatever the fuck it is housewives do. I had no designs on joining any book clubs or yoga classes or community groups and I found life in this quiet little town, frankly, boring as fuck.

Adam made me feel like being childless and pursuing my own interests was a valid way of life. That motherhood should be a choice, not an obligation. We swapped opinions on why having children was the stupidest thing you could ever do, how it was like signing the death certificate for your own freedom.

I confessed that it seemed I was infertile, and that IVF was probably our only way to have children, and he told me that was lucky. Free contraception, he called it, and at the time, after more than a bottle of wine, I found this the funniest thing I'd ever heard.

We shared another bottle at my place. One thing led to another, and a month later I found out I was pregnant.

I guess it wasn't me who was infertile, after all.

***

'Come in.' I open the door and gesture for Adam to enter.

He shakes his head. 'No.' He nods towards the windows facing the creek. 'Liz might see.'

'It's late. I'm sure she's in bed by now.'

Adam's lips press thin. 'I'd rather not, thanks.'

'I'll close the blinds.'

'Outside. Please.'

I sigh. I'd really rather stay inside, especially after Liz mentioned she saw a man in my doorway, but I suppose I'll have Adam for protection. Maybe I'll see if Erica will let me stay over once Adam's left. I'll have to deal with Ruby's nightly wakings, but at least I'll feel safer. 'Fine. Just let me get my coat.'

Moments later I'm following Adam down the street towards the entrance of the creek. He's got his hoodie pulled over his head as if he's trying not to be recognised. There are no lights on in any of the houses, and the few streetlamps on Cockle Street do little but cast eerie shadows along the road, so I don't know what he's so worried about.

'Why are we going this way?' I pull my hood over my head against the chill. I'm a bit wobbly on my feet and, despite the sobering effect of the cold, quite a lot drunker than I'd thought. 'It's dangerous. Look how high the water is.'

Adam stops halfway across the bridge, so abruptly I bump into him. 'Liz thinks I'm spending the night in town because of the road closure.' He turns to face me, moonlight painting his skin silver. 'So I'd prefer it if I wasn't seen.'

'Ha. The perfect alibi. Well done.'

Adam doesn't smile. 'It would have been the truth if you hadn't started with your threats. I'm just lucky the road was reopened or you'd have gone and told your little story.'

'It's not a story, Adam. It's the truth.'

'It was just the once, Dee. It meant nothing. I love my wife. Are you really prepared to ruin two lives because of something that was an *accident*?'

'Oh, that's rich. *I'm* the one whose life has been ruined because of that accident, Adam. Until now you've got off scot-free.'

'You told me you were infertile!'

'I thought I was! But you knew I didn't know for sure. There were two people involved that night, if I recall correctly. Two people who decided not to use protection.'

'Fine, whatever.' Adam mutters. He sounds bored. 'Look, how can you even be sure she's mine?'

'Rob went and got DNA results. Ruby isn't his. And there's only one other person it could be.'

'Are you sure about that?' he sneers.

'Fuck off,' I hiss. 'You're one to talk. And yes, I'm sure. Are you sure she's your only illegitimate child?'

Adam steps forward and grabs my wrist. 'Stop fucking around, Dee.'

'Stop it, you're hurting me.'

He doesn't loosen his grip. 'Look, I don't play games, so why don't you cut the crap and tell me what you want?'

'Money.'

Adam doesn't say anything for a moment. Then he barks with laughter.

'Money? You're delusional. I don't have any money.'

'Bullshit. The house is for sale and I know how much a place around here is worth.'

'You can't blackmail me, Dee. I won't stand for it.'

'Look, Adam,' I change tack, trying to appeal to his humanity. 'I'm in trouble. I wouldn't ask otherwise, but ... my life's in danger.'

Adam laughs. 'You expect me to believe that? Whatever trouble you've got yourself into is your mess, not mine. You're not getting money out of me, Dee. It's not going to happen.'

Anger fills my chest. 'You don't get a choice. If you don't help me, I'm going over right now to tell your wife everything!'

Adam grabs my shoulder, his face an inch from mine.

'Don't you fucking dare.'

I try to pull away, but his grip is like iron.

'Let go of me! For fuck's sake Adam, you're hurting me ...'

'Say you're not going to breathe a word to Liz.'

I stare him in the eye. 'I'm going to scream it from the rooftops if you don't give me what I'm owed,' I whisper.

Adam glares, teeth bared in a snarl. 'You do that, and I'll fucking kill you.' His grip tightens on my arm and I cry out. 'Stop. PLEASE!'

For a moment conflict clouds Adam's expression. But then his eyes change. In the moonlight, they are as hard as glass. 'Whatever you say.'

He releases my arm so suddenly I stumble backwards, one foot tripping over the other. There's a brief weightlessness and then suddenly I've hit the water, my shout piercing the night air. The cold is all consuming; it's like being submerged in ice. I don't even make it back to the surface before the strength of the tide starts to pull me in the direction of the sea.

All of a sudden I'm being seized by the shoulders; looking up through the murky water I can make out Adam's silhouette. Thank God, I think. But something's wrong. And then I realise he isn't pulling me up. He's holding me down. I struggle against his grip, but he's stronger than I am. He holds me firmly and the more I struggle, the harder he pushes down. I hold my breath as long as I can, but my head starts to ache and dizziness takes hold. After a few minutes I feel faint and I can't stop the reflex to gasp for breath.

Images flit through my mind at shutter-speed as the world fades around the edges. The paths I could have chosen, the ones I did choose; it doesn't matter now. All the threads of my life have led to this.

An angel's face fills my mind. Sweet and pure with hair like fire and the brightest smile I've ever seen.

Chapter 41

Liz

June, 2017
Sunday, 6:02pm

I splash my face with cold water and try to slow my rapid breathing, then switch off the iPad so that when it's turned back on it will revert to login and Adam won't see what I've looked at. I can hear the creak of the floorboards in the corridor, the squeak of linoleum that means Adam's in the kitchen, and I assess how long it will take for him to reach the bathroom. I quickly apply some mineral powder to my flushed cheeks and a sweep of lip balm to my lips.

'Lizzie?' Adam's voice carries through the house. I suppress a sob, wipe my eyes and run a brush through my hair. Nope. I still look properly ill.

'Liz?' Adam's head appears around the door and his

smiling face immediately crumples with concern. 'Jesus, are you okay?'

'No,' I say, not having to feign my misery. 'I've ... I've been throwing up all afternoon.'

'Oh, darling. Can I get you anything? Some tea ... or dry toast or something?'

I shake my head. 'No, I'm okay. I think it was the leftovers I ate for lunch.'

Adam makes a face. 'Ugh. Poor you. Will you be wanting dinner, or ...?'

The thought of food makes me want to retch. I shake my head vehemently.

'Okay, well, perhaps bed then? I was hoping to have a shower ...'

I nod, eyes flitting nervously to the iPad and back to Adam. I force a smile. 'Sure, of course. Just let me get out of your way.'

'You're not in my way, sweetheart,' Adam's smile is so warm and sincere I almost burst into tears. How can this be happening? How can everything I thought was real be a lie?

'Let me help you up.' He reaches out for my hand and, when I grasp it, he pulls me to my feet, kisses me on the cheek and murmurs into my neck. 'I can't wait to start our new life together. It's going to be perfect.'

'Yes,' I manage, my voice coming out suffocated. 'Perfect.'

His eyes travel to the iPad and then flick to mine. He retrieves it from the floor.

'Have you been on the internet today?' His tone is casual, but I can detect an edge. He places the iPad on the sink.

'No, darling, why?' I ask, shooting for a breezy tone as I try and fail to still my shaking hands.

'Oh, just wondering if there's been any more news on Dee.'

I analyse his words for any trace of guilt but can't detect anything. He's good; too good.

I force a laugh. 'Didn't you tell me to try not to think about Dee anymore? I'm being good, remember? No Googling. No dwelling.'

He comes towards me, clasps my face in his hands and it's all I can't do not to shudder. 'Good girl,' he kisses my lips. 'I'm glad you listened to me. For once.' He winks and I wonder how, until now, I couldn't have seen through the pretence.

'I couldn't even if I wanted to, anyway,' I say, hoping he doesn't notice the tremor in my voice as I smile up at him and push his hair back from his face. 'I don't know your password. Remember?'

'Haven't I given it to you?'

I shake my head.

Adam's body softens and his features relax.

'We'll have to remedy that then, won't we?' He kisses the tip of my nose. 'We're going to be spending the rest of our lives together; I don't want there to be any secrets between us. It's the date of when we first met.' He smiles at me and I could swear his eyes are full of love. But what does that mean? Can someone capable of what he's done also be capable of love?

He draws me in to his arms and I pray he doesn't notice how damp I am all over. 'Okay, sexy. I'm going to have a shower.'

Chapter 42

Liz

June, 2017
Sunday, 6:59pm

I wait outside the bathroom door until I hear the water running and the change in pitch that means Adam's stepped beneath the stream. Adam's work bag is propped against the wall at the foot of the loft stairs; I rummage through it until I find his phone, then tiptoe up to the loft.

My hands are shaking so much I can hardly press the on switch. The phone is password protected – shit! – but then I remember Adam's code for the iPad and try the date of when we first met. It works.

I scroll through the messages until I find the one I'm looking for.

She's yours.

This time, the photo loads instantly.

If I didn't recognise the cherubic face, I'd recognise the background from my nightly voyeurism. The wallpaper, the book shelves, the wedding photo on the mantlepiece.

Ruby.

My blood runs cold. The room tilts.

***

A strange sense of calm settles over me at having my suspicions confirmed. It's surreal to see it now; if I'd known to look for similarities, I'd have spotted them instantly. The shape of her nose, the curve of her bottom lip. All undeniably Adam. I don't know long I've been standing staring at the screen before I realise I can no longer hear the shower running.

'Lizzie?' Adam's voice floats up the stairs.

Jolted back into motion, I dash over to the window and peer out, trying to judge whether I'd survive the leap. It's too late to make it back downstairs.

'Lizzie!'

I look around desperately before stashing the phone under a cushion on the day bed. My heart is pounding by the time Adam appears at the top of the stairs.

'There you are!' He clocks my position and wags a finger at me. 'Spying again? I thought we'd cured you of your voyeurism.'

I don't trust myself to speak, so I smile and shrug.

'Are you feeling any better? It's freezing up here,' Adam shivers. 'Why don't we get you somewhere warm?' He crosses the room and wraps me in his arms. Unconsciously, I stiffen.

Adam pulls back and gives me a strange look. 'What's the matter?'

I shake my head, willing my words to come out normally. 'Just ... stomach cramps.'

Adam looks sympathetic. 'Poor darling. Perhaps we should get you to bed.'

I nod and Adam smiles and offers me his hand. I take it and let him pull me to my feet. The movement jostles the cushions and I hear a tell-tale *thunk*.

I freeze and Adam turns and gives me a curious look.

'Let's go,' I say clutching my stomach, not daring to look down at the floor.

Adam looks down, then back up at me. The phone has landed face-up, the picture of Ruby still filling the screen. His face pales and he looks like he might speak but then his lips close and he gives me a funny little smile.

'Not just spying on the neighbours, but on your husband, too?'

My face flushes white-hot. 'N-no. Of course not. I was only ...' My brain is malfunctioning and I can't get any more words out. My gaze flits to the stairs and, his eyes on me, Adam steps to the side, blocking the entry to the stairwell.

'Lizzie. I can explain.'

I shake my head. I don't want to hear what he has to say, but at the same time there's a shred of hope that maybe it *can* be explained. That maybe it was all some big misunderstanding and he'll go back to being the husband I thought I knew.

Adam drags a hand over his mouth. 'Look. I might not have been completely honest about something, but I need you to know that it was because I was trying to protect you. I see now that I should have been honest from the start, but it's too late for that now. The truth is I *have* met Dee a couple of times.' He looks down at the phone. 'But this isn't what you think. She was trying to blackmail me.'

'Why would she do that?'

Adam stares at me with his warm, brown eyes. 'The child isn't mine, Lizzie, I swear. Dee wanted money, so she lied to me to try to get it.'

I search Adam's earnest face and for a moment there's uncertainty, and hope. Could Dee really be trusted, or was she mentally unstable? Could she be making the whole thing up for attention ... or money? But then I remember. I remember seeing Adam in Ruby's features. I remember the messages with that other woman. He's lied to me before. He's lying to me now.

'Why would Dee even *say* that Ruby could be yours, Adam?'

Adam hesitates. Then he seems to settle on a thought, and he steps towards me. 'Liz, angel, you know how much I love you. It's only ever been you. With Dee, it was just the once; it meant nothing. Dad had just been diagnosed, and I was here alone and everything was so fucked up. Dee and I met by accident in the pub one night. We had too much to drink and one thing led to another …'

I wince and turn away.

'It was a drunken mistake, sweetheart. I promise, it meant nothing. It never ordinarily would have happened. It was a one-off, a monumental fuck up.'

Liar, I think, shivering with the force of my anger.

'That message is dated the night she disappeared; she's asking you to meet her. Did you? Did you see her that night?'

Adam pales. 'What? No, of course not! I was in Sydney, remember? I promise you, Lizzie.'

'Don't call me that,' I shudder. 'How can I trust you? You've been lying to me this whole time!'

Then it hits me. I clap a hand to my mouth to smother the gasp.

Plovers. I could hear those horrible, squawking things in the background when I spoke to Adam on the phone the night he was supposedly staying down in Sydney. Tim's bird book says they're native to this area and are rarely found elsewhere.

'You were here. That night. You were in town.'

Adam's face tightens. 'No. I was in Sydney. The police checked, remember?'

'I could hear plovers, Adam. In the background, when you called.'

'What? That's ridiculous. What's that got to do with—'

'They're native to the area. *This* area.'

Adam looks at me in disbelief. Then he sighs heavily and shakes his head, his eyes full of pity. 'That's what you're basing all of this on? *Birds*? How can you even be sure they were plovers? They could've been any sort of bird. And, I'm sorry to play this card, but you know you haven't exactly been thinking clearly lately.'

'Don't tell me I don't know what I know,' I say through gritted teeth, furious despite my fear. '*You're* the one who's been messing with my head this whole time. Making me think I was imagining things when you've been hiding the truth from me.'

Adam's eyes widen and, if I didn't know better, I'd think he was genuinely outraged. 'How can you say that? I've never lied to you. Well, only about one small thing but that's because I thought you might be in danger. Dee was unhinged, you only had to look at her to—'

'Did you meet with her?' I ask softly.

Adam blanches. 'Liz. Darling, what are you implying?'

'Did you see Dee that night? Before she died?'

'I've *told* you. I was in Sydney!'

'You're lying!'

Adam holds up his hands. 'You need to calm down. You *know* the road was closed, Liz. You *know* I'm telling you the truth.'

'You've been lying to me this whole time! Was it you

Dee was afraid of? Was it you she got a text from and had to leave so suddenly?'

Adam shakes his head. 'I can't believe I'm hearing this! How *could* I have met with her? Come on, you *know* me, Lizzie.'

I look at the man standing before me and it's as if the parts of him that were once so familiar don't fit together anymore. I don't recognise him. He is a stranger to me.

'I thought I did,' I whisper as a hot tear rolls down my cheek.

'Lizzie.' Adam's eyes are desperate. 'Please stop this. I never met with her. I promise you!'

I bend to pick up his phone and tap the screen a few times. 'Then how do you explain this?' I hold the screen up to his face so he can read the final text he sent Dee the night she went missing.

I'm here.

Adam lets out a sound that is half groan half shout. 'Fucking hell! Yes, okay! *Okay!* I met with her. I *had* to. The bitch was fucking threatening me! Saying she'd tell you everything if I didn't meet her that night. I was trying to protect you. Protect the life we're building together.'

I squeeze my eyes shut. It's one thing to suspect, and quite another to hear it from his lips. My whole body is shaking. 'You were trying to protect *yourself*.'

'No! Lizzie. Baby. Please,' Adam holds out his hands, his eyes wet with crocodile tears. 'Think of everything we have ahead of us. You don't want to throw that away over a silly mistake, do you? I thought I was doing the right thing!'

'You're the one who's thrown it away!' I spit, shocked by the strength of my own fury. 'Your mistake has cost us our marriage and Dee's life!'

Adam's face turns white. 'You think ... you think I killed her?'

'I don't know!' I choke on a sob. 'I don't know what to think about anything anymore!'

'I'm not a murderer, Lizzie. I can't believe you would think that ...'

'How can I believe anything you say?' I shout, unable to stop now.

'You *know* me.'

'Stop saying that! I don't! I fucking don't! I have no idea who you are!'

Adam's eyes gleam wet. 'Please don't do this, Lizzie.'

'I'm not doing anything!' I throw up my hands, defeated.

'Look, angel,' Adam's tone changes to the calm, reassuring one that used to soothe me. 'I know this is a lot to take in. I've made mistakes. I can admit that. But we love each other, don't we?'

I don't answer, letting his question linger in the air.

'There's one thing I want to know.'

'Anything. I'll tell you anything you want to know, Lizzie.'

I raise my eyes to meet Adam's. He looks hopeful, but I know there is no hope. Surprisingly, I feel nothing. 'Was Ruby with her?'

Adam looks momentarily confused, then disappointed. He shakes his head. 'No ... no, Dee said she was with Erica.'

I glance out of the window into the darkness. So Erica *was* lying. And so was Adam. He's lied about everything. To hide what he's done. To protect himself.

When I see the light come on in the shed, see Erica's silhouette in the window, the pieces fall into place.

'I'm calling the police,' I say, retrieving Adam's phone from the floor. 'You're going to tell them what you saw, and we're going to tell them Ruby's alive and well and has been under our noses the whole time.'

Adam's face closes. 'I'm afraid I can't do that, Lizzie.'

Chapter 43

Liz

June, 2017
Sunday, 7:30pm

Adam takes the phone from my hand and slides it into his pocket.

'Don't you understand what would happen if people found out about this? If they knew I obstructed the course of an investigation by withholding information? I'd be arrested. I wouldn't be able to go back to the UK.'

I stare at the man I'd thought I loved more than anything and feel nothing but hollow.

'Did you kill her?' I whisper.

Adam tilts his head back and squeezes his eyes shut. 'For the love of— *No*. I didn't kill her! How many times do I have to tell you? How could you think I'm *capable* of such a thing?'

'Then what happened?' I ask, unmoved.

Adam cradles his face in his hands and moans. 'God, Lizzie, it's been so hard keeping it in. It was terrible, an awful, awful thing to happen. Dee was drunk, shouting. She was saying such heinous things, making threats ... She was going to ruin everything we've worked so hard for. We argued. She ... she *fell,* okay?'

'Oh my God,' I take a step backwards. My eyes sting with tears. 'Did ... did you push her?'

'No! Fuck! She fucking fell and I ... I tried to save her, but the tide was too strong. She was already too far out ...'

I'm trembling as I try to read his expression but it's like the Adam I knew has vanished. 'Why don't I believe you?' I whisper.

Adam's eyes flash with hurt, then an expression I've never seen in them before. A shiver runs through me. 'I didn't kill her,' he says very softly. 'Can we get that straight, Lizzie? It was an accident.'

The way he says it makes it sound like a threat. And then I see something that makes me go cold. There's that tell, the muscle twitching in his jaw that he always gets when I catch him out in a lie. Like how many drinks he's had at the pub, or what happened to the chocolate I put in the cupboard. Innocent things. Or so I thought.

He's lying.

Ice washes over me. I try to make sense of reality as blood roars in my ears and the room closes in on me.

Adam's watching me carefully. 'Lizzie? Are you okay?'

Fear rises. I glance at the stairwell, gauging the gap between Adam and the stairs. If I made it past him, how long would it take me to reach the front door? Outside, Zac's light comes on and his silhouette crosses the top floor.

If you scream loud enough, I'll hear you.

'How ... how did you get back into town with the road closed?' I ask, biding for time.

Adam shrugs, his eyes trained to my face. 'I kept tabs on the traffic announcements, and the second the road was open I drove up. I knew I couldn't leave it any longer or she'd tell you everything. When you said she'd come here, I thought that was it. I thought the game was up,' he gives a humourless laugh. 'In the beginning I thought maybe you were toying with me, trying to see if I'd confess something you already knew. But you genuinely didn't seem to know anything. Only that Dee was scared of someone. I parked the car over in the bushes where no one would see it and walked to Dee's house. It felt like the perfect opportunity; you'd think I was away, so if you did happen to see anything through the windows – God, I knew you were so fond of watching the bloody neighbours – you'd assume it was someone else.' The way Adam's speaking, it's like telling me is a relief.

I keep waiting for the pain to come, but it's like I've gone numb. Perhaps it's shock. It feels like I've stumbled into some alternate universe, like none of this is real. And yet, somehow, it makes perfect sense.

'We can come back from this, baby,' Adam reaches for my hands. His eyes search mine and I fight the urge to recoil. 'It was just one night; she was ... needy. You know what I'm like, Liz. I felt *sorry* for her.'

I shudder. It's inconceivable that he thinks my main grievance is that he slept with someone else, not that he murdered them.

'She's always been like that,' he continues, warming to his theme. 'Desperate to be loved. I never understood what Rob saw in her. I suppose he thought he could save her.'

His naked derision for the woman he killed makes me want to be sick. I pull my hands from his grasp and take a step back. 'Can you answer one question for me, Adam?'

Adam looks wary. 'Of course.'

'If it really was an accident, why didn't you go to the police? Or call out? If she really just fell and was swept away, she might have been saved if you'd called for help.'

Adam hesitates before arranging his features in an earnest expression. 'Lizzie, listen. I was sure she was already dead. What else could I have done? If I called the police I would have had to tell people the truth, and I wanted to protect you from that. Liz, please understand. I did what I did for us! Dee was going to destroy all our plans ... The house we want to buy, the business ...'

Your plans, I realise dimly. It's never had anything to do with me.

'I still want all that with you, darling. Don't you want everything we've planned for? We could start over, put all this behind us. Dee's gone now; it's terrible, but there's nothing we can do. There's no sense in ruining our lives too, is there? When you think about it, it's almost ... a blessing. The poor woman was so unhappy ...'

I half laugh, half sob. 'Oh, so it's a good thing, is it, that she's been put out of her misery?'

'You know that's not what I meant.' Adam says, softly.

It's getting dark – lights are coming on across the creek. I think of the families in town beyond, families getting ready for dinner, putting their children to bed. I think of Dee, of a baby without a mother, and something simmers inside me. This could be my only chance.

I hesitate before saying, 'I know.'

Adam looks at me with surprise.

'All right,' I say, offering him a small smile.

His eyes glint with hope. 'All right what?'

'We could start again. Pretend this never happened.'

Adam's face relaxes.

'Or at least, we might have been able to. Except for the fact that you *killed* her! You fucking killed her, Adam!' The volume of my voice is startling.

Before he can react, I plough my shoulder into his chest. Adam's startled eyes meet mine and he teeters for an instant before falling backwards. What follows is a sickening series of thuds as Adam falls down the stairs and a final, wet *thunk* as he hits the floor below.

Then silence.

I creep over to the top of the stairs and peer down. Adam

lies on his side at the foot of the stairs, one leg twisted at an unnatural angle. 'Oh my God,' I whisper as my pulse pounds in my ears.

'Oh fuck. Oh God.' I look around wildly. What am I going to do? The drop from the window is too far. There's only one way out. What if he wakes up? I won't be able to fool him twice. I look around for a weapon but, after my clearing efforts this week, the loft is almost bare. Then I remember the binoculars – they're made of solid, heavy metal. I find them under the cushions and creep back over to the stairs.

Adam hasn't moved. I wait for a moment, listening. Is he breathing? I tip-toe down a couple of steps, wincing as they creak. I squint. I can just make out the faint rise and fall of his chest.

Fear and relief course through my veins. I'll have to be quick; I don't know how much time I have. I creep down the remaining stairs, holding my breath as I reach the last one. Adam's prone body lies diagonally across the landing, between the last stair and the hall leading to the front door.

I take a deep breath and balance myself on the bottom stair, a little squeak escaping as I manoeuvre my other leg over Adam's body and place it as lightly as I can just beside his hip. The floorboard creaks and I grimace as I shift my weight onto my other foot and half step, half jump over him.

My breath rushes out and I'm about to make a run for the door when something closes around my ankle.

I shriek, looking over my shoulder to see Adam on his stomach, staring at me with red eyes and blood dripping down the side of his face.

I kick my ankle free and run down the hall, unlatching the door and stumbling out into the cold night air. I can hear a rhythmic clunking and turn to see Adam rising from the floor and staggering forward.

I clamber into the boat, turn on the engine and pull the string but my hands are so clammy I can't get a grip. 'Fuck!'

Adam appears at the door, dragging one of his legs as he crosses the lawn and reaches the shore. The engine starts as he approaches and the boat zooms in to life, carrying me out into the water.

The boat is driving at an angle and too late I realise there's a weight at the back. A glance backwards confirms it: Adam is clinging to the side of the boat, his red eyes boring into mine.

I scream and search frantically for any signs of life across the water. Zac's in the window, but he's not looking in this direction. 'Help!' I scream, waving my free arm frantically. 'Zac! Help me!'

The boat rocks and I turn to see Adam haul himself up so his neck and shoulders are above the boat. I shriek and shove him with my free hand, but he doesn't budge.

'Help!' I scream, but when I look up, Zac has disappeared from the window. 'No! Zac! Zaaaac!'

'Hey!' a voice shouts from the shore. 'What's going on?'

Adam startles and slips downward as his grip loosens. I rear back and kick out my leg as hard as I can. My foot connects with Adam's jaw, and there's a sickening crack. Adam goes slack and slides down the side of the boat and into the water.

The boat continues to plough across the creek and, when I look over my shoulder, I can just make out Adam's fingertips as they disappear below the water's surface.

People are gathered on the shore and when the boat meets the sand and comes to a halt, I see who they are.

I crawl out of the boat and onto the sand with a sob. Zac kneels beside me and puts a hand on my back. 'Are you okay?'

'I don't know,' I gasp. 'He tried … he would have killed me.'

Zac looks out across the water. 'Who *was* that?'

'My husband,' I say, teeth chattering and body trembling with cold and shock.

I dimly register the scratchy texture of wool and a faint, flowery smell as a jumper is placed over my shoulders. And another scent. Baby powder.

Erica looks down at me with round, worried eyes. 'Come inside, let's get you some dry clothes and a hot drink.'

Chapter 44

Erica

June, 2017
Thursday, 8:15am

Dee isn't answering her phone, and when I come through the shared gate between our houses and knock on the door, she's not answering there either.

We *did* agree I'd drop her off at eight. Not that I mind, but now I'll have to keep Ruby with me while I wait to hear from Dee. It's the irresponsibility – the *audacity* – that irks me. She really doesn't deserve this darling child. If she were mine, I'd take so much better care of her.

I sing softly as I finish tending to my flowers, making sure to water them just the right amount – I think I over-watered Lucy the other day and she's looking a bit soggy – when the baby monitor crackles and I hear Ruby's little coos and murmurs. Ah, she's awake at last.

I head back to the shed – well, the nursery now, really,

but we've never fallen out of the habit of calling it the shed – and pick Ruby up from her cot. She grins when she sees me, and it makes my heart swell.

I sit her amongst Your toys, smiling as she gurgles and chatters to one of Your stuffed teddy bears. It really is the perfect playroom; we had it set up perfectly for You. The previous owners had the space converted into a recording studio, which turned out well for when I needed to come in here to cry and be sure no one could hear me. It also means Ruby doesn't disturb Samir, or the neighbours for that matter, which is a plus.

I was going to spend the cold winter months in here with You, keeping You warm, using my body to feed and nourish You, as I did when I carried you in my womb, but I suppose having Ruby here on occasion to enjoy the beautiful space we made is some small consolation. They let us have You for a short while, and I brought You in, showed You our house and Your playroom. Samir doesn't like to have Your toys and clothes in the house anymore, so they've all found a home here. There's even a single bed in here now, set up because I love to be amongst Your things. And it's useful for when Ruby spends the night; I just curl up in here beside her cot.

She's getting so big now; gurgling and babbling away. She's so chubby and soft; I could just spend days tickling those perfect, pink feet.

'Where is your mama?' I murmur, smiling as Ruby

passes me her favourite stuffed toy; a blue rabbit that has purple spots for some inexplicable reason.

And she looks up at me with those round blue eyes and a cheeky grin and utters a word that makes me lose my breath.

'Mama.'

Chapter 45

Liz

June, 2017
Sunday, 7:59pm

The four of us sit around the Haddads's dining table holding cups of tea that remain full but have gone cold as we wait for the police to arrive. I look out into the night. The lights are all still on across the water, and for some reason the sight makes me unbearably sad.

'He might still be alive.'

Zac's staring out at the water. 'I doubt it,' he murmurs. The ripples have faded, the surface now still and quiet.

I don't know whether I'm in shock, but my teeth have stopped chattering and my body has stopped trembling and now all I feel is numb.

'He killed her,' I hear myself say, to no one in particular.

'Who?' Zac asks.

'Adam.' A single tear slips down my cheek. 'He killed

Dee. He said it was an accident, but it wasn't. I know it wasn't.'

Zac stares at me, slack-jawed, and Erica and Samir are both white with horror.

'My God, she was murdered?' Erica claps a hand over her mouth, muffling what sounds like a sob. Her eyes are as round as saucers.

'I'm sorry,' I say, my voice sounding distant, small. 'I didn't know. He's lied. All along. He's lied about everything.'

'Wait. Who's lied? Do you mean your husband?' Samir's tone is urgent, and I swear I can see a glint of moisture in his eyes. '*He* killed Dee?'

I nod. 'He confessed. Well, more or less. And there's evidence. Text messages between him and Dee. They had an affair. Ruby was his. He said Dee was trying to extort money out of him. But I don't know what to believe. He's lied about so much. I knew all along something was wrong. I knew Dee would never do anything to harm her baby. She loved her,' my voice cracks. 'She loved her.'

I'm aware that I'm rambling, repeating myself, but I can't seem to stop. It's like by speaking the words I'm making sense of them, passing on some of the burden. I want people to know. I want everyone to know. Dee is innocent. I can't bring back her life, but I can clear her name.

There's a low sound and it takes a moment for me to realise it's come from Samir. He's moaning, his head is in his hands, fingers raking at his hair.

The three of us stare at him in shock.

'I thought it was my fault,' he says, dragging his hands down his face. 'I thought I'd been too slow, that the bastard had finally got to her.'

'What do you mean?'

Erica puts a hand on her husband's back and rubs it up and down. In a distant part of my brain I wonder at their newfound closeness.

'It's never been your fault, darling,' she whispers to him.

Samir looks up at us, eyes brimming with tears. 'Dee was in trouble ... An ex of hers was in debt to some dodgy characters. Fucking bastard,' Samir's fists clench and Zac slants me a look but Erica doesn't even flinch.

'If her ex didn't pay his debts, they were going to hurt Dee. Maybe Ruby and Rob too. The coroner's report came back saying it was an accident, but I knew what had really happened. Or at least I thought I did.' He swipes at his eyes and Erica hands him a tissue.

'It's okay, Samir,' Erica soothes. 'It's a terrible thing that's happened, but it's not your fault. Everything's going to be okay.'

'But what are we going to do, love? You know what I'm talking about. What's going to happen to you? To us?'

Erica straightens her back and lifts her chin. 'We'll cross that bridge when we get to it. We've been through worse.'

They share a sad smile.

'Ruby's okay, isn't she?' I ask.

Erica and Samir exchange a look. 'Yes,' Erica says, meeting my gaze. 'Baby Ruby is just fine.'

'Whoa. What?' Zac says, looking between me and Erica in disbelief. 'Ruby's *alive*?'

Erica sighs sadly, wiping a tear from her eye. 'I suppose you'd better come and see.'

Samir puts an arm around Erica's shoulder, and she leans in to him. He kisses the top of her head. 'I promise I'll take care of you. Whatever happens ...'

Zac still looks baffled as Erica beckons us down the hallway. 'Where is she?' I ask.

'I think you know,' Erica says. 'Come on. I'll show you.'

We walk to the shed in silence, and Erica unlocks the door and opens it. In front of us is a small, square room that is filled with babies' things, every imaginable item from rattles to booties to toys to books. The walls are covered in duckling wallpaper. There's a single bed in one corner, a mountain of colourful cushions and a duck shaped night light emitting a soft, yellow glow.

I give a little gasp. Beside the bed, in a cot strewn with soft toy animals and covered in a pale blue blanket, lies baby Ruby, sound asleep.

Chapter 46

Liz

August, 2017
Five weeks later

I visited her grave before coming home. It's a small, granite headstone set in a little cemetery on the outskirts of Oyster Creek, overlooking the ocean. Engraved at the top are the simple words:

DELILAH JANE WATERS,
A LOVING MOTHER

Beneath that are the dates that mark the brevity of her life.

The town held a candlelight vigil in Dee's honour the night before I left. As I watched the candles flickering in the dark, I hope that wherever she is now, Dee is finally at peace.

I can't quite forgive myself for not having protected her that night, even though I had no idea what – or whom – she needed protecting from. If I'd known who my husband really was, could I have stopped all this from happening? I'll never know. But I imagine I'll always wonder.

Tanya says that, like with Christy and Bella's murder, the sole blame for Dee's death lies with Adam. But it does little to assuage the remorse, the guilt. Because no matter who's fault it is, three people are dead – four, if you count Adam – and a child has been left without a mother. It's so senseless, so heartbreaking. But the world can be that way sometimes, I suppose.

My sessions with Tanya have been helping, and I'm pleased for the small mercy that, although Dee lost her life, her name was cleared. As I knew all along, Dee hadn't done anything to her baby, and she'd never have deliberately left her motherless. In fact, she died trying to do everything in her power to protect her.

***

It's still a shock to know how wrong I've been in so many other ways. Adam's emails have proven to be a window into the secret world he kept hidden from me. There are several from his father. In one, Tim writes that Adam was not to inherit the property unless he'd settled down. From his emails, Tim seems genuinely concerned for his son – completely unlike the picture Adam painted of his father

– because apparently Adam had 'squandered the money he'd given him' and he was 'concerned for his well-being'. Tim wanted to see him 'settled and happy with someone trustworthy' before he trusted him with his business and his finances.

It was all a far cry from Adam's version of things. But at least now I know why we needed to be married so quickly, and before Tim died. To think I'd considered it romantic: a whirlwind romance. One thing Adam hadn't counted on was me outliving him and inheriting it all. I'll admit, there is some small satisfaction to be found in that.

I also found emails from his ex-business partner, Brett. From what I can deduce, it seems Beth was in fact *Brett's* girlfriend, and it was Adam who had stolen her from him. I remember Brett's frosty reception when we ran into him one night at a charity gala. No wonder. I don't think anything could surprise me anymore.

Not even what happened this morning, it seems. I force myself to take a deep breath as I stare at the window in the living room at my father's house, watching the sun set over the hills. I think of the chain of events that occurred in the lead up to this moment, running my hands over my stomach as I think of the two pink lines on the pregnancy test I took this morning that confirmed what I already instinctively knew.

I think of Dee and Ruby, of Christy and Bella, and I'm not sure what I'll do. A life is a life, but isn't it enough that there is already one innocent child with the legacy of a murderer in her bones? A child who will grow up without her mother? Whatever I choose, I'm grateful that at least the decision about what comes next is mine and mine alone to make.

My heart aches for Erica, who was never given a choice. Knowing what I know now, I understand how she could have done what she did. She hadn't intended to keep Ruby; when she went to hand her back to Dee after minding her for the night, she found the house empty and Dee wasn't answering her phone.

Erica suspected Dee of running off without telling anyone. She was angry with her, at first, thinking she'd just wanted some more time to herself and assumed Erica wouldn't mind having Ruby. But when the evening came and there was still no sign of her, she began to worry.

By the time Erica reported it, she feared she'd left it too late and knew the police would suspect her of involvement. That's why she lied about the last time she'd seen Dee and Ruby. She managed to conceal Ruby from Samir until the day Dee was found, but they hadn't decided what they were going to do about it yet.

Samir had nothing to do with Dee's death, nor were they having an affair. Samir, as an ex-cop with connections, had been trying to help her, but there was no cancelling the hit on her head until the debt was paid. The night Dee disappeared, Samir had been going over to lend her the money but found the house empty. It was late because it had taken him that long to make arrangements to get the cash so it couldn't be traced. What I saw Samir dragging that night was nothing more than a garbage bag. Adam had been right about that much, at least. Samir expressed regret that if he'd got to Dee sooner, she might still be alive.

I think we're all dealing with different levels of guilt and grief over what happened.

Samir and Erica turned themselves in and were charged accordingly. Ruby was taken in as a ward of the state and is being found a temporary home in foster care. The thought of that child being without her mother in the care of strangers shreds my heart.

But there is some hope. Dee had written an unofficial will which she gave to Samir to read in the event of her death. She leaves everything – including Ruby – to Erica and Samir. As Dee has no living family, and Rob isn't Ruby's biological father, the case is currently being considered in court and, law permitting, it may actually happen.

Some days are better than others. Sometimes I almost feel normal. I'll be at lunch with a friend, and we'll laugh about something that happened back when we were at university, or about something one of their kids said on the way to school the other day. But other days I'm weighed down with the enormity of it all, by the sadness, the fear. The realisation that comes to me now and again – that I lived under the same roof as someone like Adam, oblivious to what he was and the danger I was in – and it steals my breath.

I'm not back at work yet. In all honesty I'm not sure I can return to that sort of role again. I've been thinking of other jobs I might try; something physical would be good, something that keeps me active so my mind doesn't have the chance to wander. I'm not sure what that might look like, but I've been doing some research and I suppose I'll find something, eventually.

I've also been thinking of moving back to the country to be nearer to Dad. He's getting on a bit now, and he's been so good to me; not just after all that's happened but being the sole parent to me growing up. It's clear now, more than ever, how hard it must have been for him; the sacrifices he must have made. Something's shifted since I've come home, after everything, and I feel closer to him somehow. We share something in common now; we were both married to people who turned out to be strangers.

The sun has set now, the end of another day. The lights across the field blink on and I get a little shiver, as I often do at this time of day.

I turn away from the window and close the blinds, listening to the sound of my father tinkering away in the kitchen. I run a hand over my stomach and take a deep, cleansing breath. Tomorrow is another day. A chance to start again. And I know what I need to do.

Acknowledgements

I find this part difficult, as there are so many incredible people who contribute to the production of a novel. But there are some who it would be simply criminal not to mention.

Firstly, as ever, I am extremely grateful to my wonderful agent Lorella Belli whose energy, tenacity and enthusiasm for this business are second to none. I feel so lucky to be working with you.

Secondly, my talented editor Hannah Todd. Across the Water would be nowhere near the novel it is today without your hard work, insight and patience. When you received this manuscript it was in a rather sorry state, but you saw its potential and helped me turn a rough draft in to a novel I can feel proud of. Thank you for that.

A big thank you to Katie Loughnane; although we didn't work together on this book you have been the most wonderful champion of my work. You were the one to snatch up Across the Water and you did all the hard work in the lead up to edits. Thank you.

Huge thanks to the brilliant copyeditors Lydia Mason

and Emily Ruston for your work on this novel, and to Ellie Game for the stunning cover design; I couldn't have hoped for better! And, of course, a heartfelt thank you for the rest of the team at One More Chapter for your hard work and dedication; it's been a pleasure working with you all.

Lastly, I want to thank my family, in particular my mum, who has always been my biggest supporter, and my husband Vidar, who is always by my side. Thanks to my in-laws for your support, my dearest friends and fellow author friends – you know who you are!

And lastly, here's to you, readers! Without you, I wouldn't be able to do what I do. It really is a privilege and I am deeply grateful to every one of you who has read, bought, borrowed, shared or reviewed one of my books. Thank you.